KT-474-096

BOOTLEG

Alex Shearer lives with his family in Somerset. He has written more than a dozen books for both adults and children, as well as many successful television series, films, and stage and radio plays. He has had over thirty different jobs, and has never given up trying to play the guitar.

Bootleg was made into a successful three-part BBC TV drama that was shown in 2002.

Books by Alex Shearer available from Macmillan

The Great Blue Yonder
The Stolen
The Speed of the Dark

BOOTLEG

Alex Shearer

MACMILLAN CHILDREN'S BOOKS

First published 2003 by Macmillan Children's Books
a division of Macmillan Publishers Limited
20 New Wharf Road, London N1 9RR
Basingstoke and Oxford
www.panmacmillan.com

Associated companies throughout the world

ISBN 0 330 41562 X

Copyright © Alex Shearer 2003

The right of Alex Shearer to be identified as the
author of this work has been asserted by him in accordance
with the Copyright, Designs and Patents Act 1988.

All rights reserved. No part of this publication may be
reproduced, stored in or introduced into a retrieval system, or
transmitted, in any form, or by any means (electronic, mechanical,
photocopying, recording or otherwise) without the prior written
permission of the publisher. Any person who does any unauthorized
act in relation to this publication may be liable to criminal
prosecution and civil claims for damages.

1 3 5 7 9 8 6 4 2

A CIP catalogue record for this book is available from
the British Library.

Phototypeset by Intype London Ltd
Printed and bound in Great Britain by Mackays of Chatham plc, Kent

This book is sold subject to the condition that it shall not,
by way of trade or otherwise, be lent, re-sold, hired out,
or otherwise circulated without the publisher's prior consent
in any form of binding or cover other than that in which
it is published and without a similar condition including this
condition being imposed on the subsequent purchaser.

To Nick
(who rarely eats the stuff)

Good For You

A man in a uniform stood pasting a notice to the boarded-up window of a derelict shop. The two schoolboys watched him closely. The man paused for a second to admire his handiwork, then glanced at them, with a look of contempt.

'That's it for you lot then!' he said, and he sounded more than pleased about it. 'No more chocolate for you once five o'clock gets here. So enjoy your sweets while you can – if you've still got any. Because you won't be getting any more. That'll teach you.'

He picked up his brush and the bag of posters.

'Crunchy apples to you, comrades,' he said. (This was now the official greeting of the Good For You Party. A simple 'Cheerio' was not acceptable.)

'Juicy oranges to you, citizen,' the boys dutifully responded.

'Have a banana!' the man answered, then he walked swiftly on, to put the last of his posters up on a nearby bus shelter. Not that the posters were really necessary. The only people who didn't know about the deadline were either dead or living on another planet.

The boys looked at the notice. It bubbled up here and there where air was trapped under the glue.

ALL CHOCOLATE WILL BE ILLEGAL AS FROM 5 P.M. TODAY.

CHOCOLATE WILL NOT THEREAFTER BE
SOLD TO ANYONE, EXCEPT ON
PRODUCTION OF THE APPROPRIATE
MEDICAL CERTIFICATE.
THE SALE OF SWEETS OR
CHOCOLATE IS OTHERWISE BANNED
AND IS A CRIMINAL OFFENCE,
PUNISHABLE BY A £5,000 FINE AND/OR
POSSIBLE IMPRISONMENT.
THIS IS A GOVERNMENT ORDER.

ISSUED BY

THE GOOD FOR YOU PARTY,

YOUR ELECTED REPRESENTATIVES.
(THE PARTY FOR BETTER HEALTH AND TEETH
AND FOR THE ELIMINATION OF OBESITY
AND DISEASE DUE TO POOR DIET.)

The two boys stood and read the sign through. Having done so once, they did so again.

'So that's it, then,' Smudger Moore said, 'we've had it. I've got one toffee left, and one last chocolate bar, and when that's gone, it's all over. How about you?'

Huntly searched through his pockets. He came up with a half-sucked sherbet lemon, a piece of liquorice and a chew. He held them out.

'That's all,' he said. 'A lifetime's sweets and that's all that's left to show for it. Once I've eaten that, I'm sweetless.'

'It's a sad day,' Smudger said. 'I never thought it would happen. Not in a month of Sundays, Mondays or any other days. Come on, let's find somewhere quiet to eat it all.'

They went on down to the old cemetery, an apt and fitting place, for both Huntly and Smudger felt as if they were going to a funeral. And, once there, they buried their chocolate in their stomachs.

They ate their last sweets together, sitting solemnly on an old tombstone, munching away with loud, rasping sucks and long, slow chews. They made the sweets last as long as they could. Then they took the wrappers and licked them clean. Instead of throwing the papers into the nearest bin, they folded them up as if they were ten-pound notes. They smoothed them tidily into small, regular shapes, and put them in their pockets.

'No more, then,' Smudger said. 'You only get it now when you're ill enough to die. And even then you've got to have a note from the doctor.'

'I bet they're all round at my mum's surgery right now,' Huntly said, for his mother was a GP at the local health centre, 'telling her that they're on their last legs and trying to get a chocolate certificate.'

Which was exactly right.

Dr Carol Hunter was sitting at her desk, facing one of her regular patients. Mrs Spivey was a rather portly woman, and the expression on her round face was one of acute anxiety.

'I've got to have that certificate, Doctor,' Mrs Spivey said, her voice managing to sound both pleading and threatening. 'I've got to have that medical certificate to let me get chocolate after the five o'clock deadline, or I don't know what I'm going to do. I'm a registered chocoholic, you know. If I don't get my chocolate, I'll get withdrawal symptoms. I'll probably start tearing my hair out.' Her eyes narrowed. 'I might even start tearing other people's hair out.'

Huntly's mother tried to give a sympathetic smile.

'I'm sorry, Mrs Spivey, but as from five o'clock chocolate will only be available for the terminally ill, unable to absorb any other nourishment. And to the best of my knowledge, apart from your ingrowing toenail, you're not ill at all.'

Mrs Spivey's eyes narrowed down to pin-pricks.

'If I don't get my chocolate, Doctor,' she said, 'I could get to be very ill. And very short tempered. And possibly even violent!'

But Carol Hunter wasn't a woman to be easily intimidated.

'I'm sorry, Mrs Spivey,' she said, 'but there's nothing I can do about that. I'm afraid that living without chocolate is something we'll all have to get used to. Peppermint?'

She proffered a tube of sugar-free mints. Mrs Spivey took one.

'Thanks,' she said. 'I suppose it'll help tide me over. But it's no real substitute. There's no real substitute for chocolate at all.'

The boys moved away from the tombstones and headed back to the road.

'I don't know what I'm going to do,' Smudger groaned. 'No sweets, no chocolate. I feel like I've swallowed a lump of stone, like something inside me up and died.'

'Your sweet tooth probably,' Huntly said. 'It's passed on.'

'Probably,' Smudger agreed. He sighed a long sigh. 'Oh well. Just got to struggle on somehow and do the best we can. At least we've *tasted* chocolate. That's something. But little kids now, who'd normally just be coming up for their first chocolate bar, won't get one. They'll never know anything about a square of milky chocolate melting on your tongue. They're the ones I feel sorry for.'

'But then they won't know what they're missing either,' Huntly pointed out. 'But we do. So it's worse for us. We'll be missing it for years. We'll probably need to have therapy – chocolate therapy for chocolate withdrawal. We might even crack up under the strain.'

The streets were quiet and miserable with drizzle, and there were long faces everywhere. But not all of them were long. If the opposite of long is short, which it plainly is, then there were short faces too. Short, beaming faces, grinning from ear to ear, pleased to see that the Prohibition of Sweets and Chocolate Act was finally becoming law.

Frankie Crawley was one of these, as was Myrtle Perkins, both classmates of Smudger and Huntly, but unlike those two friends, staunch members of The Young Pioneers.

The Young Pioneers were the junior branch of the Good For You Party. Their members swanked and swaggered about, dressed in their nicely starched uniforms, singing Young Pioneering songs, or looking out for good deeds to do.

The Young Pioneers were notorious for their good deeds. They regularly helped old ladies across the road, whether they wanted to go or not. Things had got to the point where many old ladies would hide in shop doorways when they heard the Pioneers coming, afraid they would be helped across the road against their will, and not be able to get back again through the traffic.

Twice a week after school and every Saturday morning, the Young Pioneers met for drill in the park. They would march in time across the football pitches, with a complete disregard for whoever might be playing on them. If there was a game in process, it just had to pause, like traffic at a red light, until the Pioneers had crossed.

Frankie Crawley and Myrtle Perkins would be at the front of the troop, singing as they led the others along, the Pioneers echoing their chants behind them.

'I don't want no chocolate bar!' Frankie would call.

'We don't want no chocolate bar!' the Pioneers would reply, their arms swinging, their knees rising up like pistons as they marched along.

'Or keep my false teeth in a jar!'

'Or keep my false teeth in a jar!'

'Sugar and sweets are bad for me!'

'Sugar and sweets are bad for me!'

'Rather have some celery!'

'Rather have some celery!'

'We don't want no fizzy drinks!'

'We don't want no fizzy drinks!'

'Pour that cola down the sink!'

'Pour that cola down the sink!'

'If we see somebody sin,'

'If we see somebody sin,'

'Take their names and turn them in.'

'Take their names and turn them in.'

'My party it is wise and true,'

'My party is the Good For You!'

They were at it even now. Smudger and Huntly could hear the Pioneers' voices, singing in the distance as they tramped up and down the field, watched by children with footballs at their feet, waiting for them to go away.

A car drove by. Huntly noticed that it had a sticker in its back window. It read DON'T BLAME ME, I DIDN'T VOTE FOR THEM. The two boys knew just what that meant. It meant that at the last election, the driver of the car had voted for the Eat, Drink and Do What You Like Party, and not for the Good For You Party. But he was in the minority. Too many had voted for the Good For You Party, thinking that all they intended to do was tidy up the world a little and make it a better place to live in.

Others, like Smudger's dad, hadn't bothered to vote at all.

'They're all as bad as each other,' he had said.

But maybe they weren't.

Smudger had heard his parents arguing about it, after the elections were over and the Good For You Party had got in.

'It's people like you who're to blame, Ron,' Smudger's mum had said. 'By not voting for someone else you let them get in. Remember that saying – "All it needs for evil to flourish is for good men to do nothing"? Well, nothing is exactly what you did.'

Smudger's dad hadn't said much to that, but he'd looked a bit grumpy and had gone around the bakery muttering and banging bread tins about.

He got even more grumpy when the letter came from the Good For You Party, telling him that come the deadline he wouldn't be able to use sugar in his baking any more. It also stated that wholemeal flour should be used whenever possible, as white flour lacked fibre and roughage. He wasn't very happy about it.

'When you ban sugar,' Smudger's dad complained, 'the art of the confectioner just dies. How can I make a proper wedding cake when I can't use any white flour or any sugar? When I haven't even got the basic materials? What am I supposed to do for the happy couple now?

Bake them a bread roll? Make them a cake out of mashed potatoes, with a layer of mince for filling and a cowpat on the top?'

He'd banged more bread tins around, then he'd looked at all his baking cups, awards and certificates with a kind of sadness in his eyes – the sadness of someone who is no longer allowed to do the things he loves and which he is best at.

The boys walked on. Shops were being emptied of their goods as the deadline drew nearer. Men and women in uniforms were carrying out boxes of cocoa and cartons of chocolate puddings and loading them into vans. They would be taken away for destruction.

'The thing is,' Huntly said, 'I don't see why they had to ban it. I know too many sweets are bad for your teeth. But just a few sweets every once in a while, or the odd chocolate bar, what's wrong with that? You don't need to go banning anything.'

'That's right,' Smudger agreed. 'And you can always brush your teeth after, if you're that bothered.'

'Exactly,' Huntly said. 'Or maybe have a piece of sugar-free chewing gum. That's what some people do.'

'Used to do,' Smudger reminded him. 'Not any more.'

For chewing gum had been outlawed as well.

'Besides,' Smudger went on, 'what's going to happen to dentists if they've got no teeth to work on?'

'Be out of a job,' Huntly said.

'Yeah. They'll forget how to do fillings. And then when you need one, you won't be able to get it. They'll have to get a bricklayer in to do the work, or a plasterer. They'll have to stick a great big trowel in your mouth. Or you'll have to do your fillings yourself. With a piece of plasticine and some superglue.'

The boys came to the corner where their paths usually separated.

'Well, I can tell you this, Smudger,' Huntly said, 'I don't know what I'm going to spend my pocket money on now if there's no chocolate. I suppose I could save up to buy a CD or something, but it's not the same. I mean, all right, you can listen to a CD. But you can't eat it. Whereas a thing like chocolate, you can listen to it *and* eat it – if you know what I mean. The noise you make eating chocolate is half the pleasure, all the chewing and slurping and the rest.'

'Yeah,' Smudger nodded. 'And going to Mrs Bubby's shop after school, and seeing what she's got in there. Then making your selection and opening it up. And the sound the wrapper makes as you tear it off. And the crinkly noise of the silver paper as you peel it back.'

'It's like music,' Huntly said, his stomach starting to rumble.

'It *is* music,' Smudger said. 'Chocolate is music for the ears, the eyes and especially the taste buds.'

The two boys looked at each other. For a second it seemed as if they might give way to their feelings.

'It's no use,' Huntly said sadly, 'we've just got to forget it. Chocolate's finished and we'd better just accept it. Thinking about it's too painful. It makes the whole thing worse.'

'Maybe,' Smudger said bitterly. 'But if I could get my hands on whoever thought of this – if I could just have two minutes with them in a darkened room – I'd soon show them who—'

A man walked past them. He had a saintly kind of expression on his face. He looked like one of those people who likes to tell other people what is good for them. In his jacket he sported a small lapel badge. On it were the initials G.F.Y.P. and under the letters, the logo of the Good For You Party.

'There's good boys,' the man said, in a patronizing tone. 'Not getting into any trouble now, are we? Have we done our Good Deed for the day?'

Huntly and Smudger nodded. But they hadn't done any good deeds. In fact they weren't that sure what good deeds were. Smudger had heard his dad say that a lot of good deeds were nothing but interference and ramming your opinions down other people's throats.

'Good,' the man with the badge said. 'And have we also kept our Politeness Pledge?'

'Yes, sir,' Huntly and Smudger chorused as politely as possible. The man beamed at them with approval and went on his way.

The Politeness Pledge was another of the Good For You Party's ideas. All children over the age of five were expected (in reality, obliged) to take the Good For You Politeness Promise and to guarantee to do a minimum of one good deed per day. They vowed that they would give their seats up to expectant mothers and not use their mobile phones to send text messages while in class.

Smudger had kept his fingers crossed behind his back as he had signed his pledges, and Huntly later confided that he had done the same.

'It's not that I'm against politeness as such,' Smudger had said, 'but I can't go making promises that I might not be able to keep. And much as I try always to be polite, I should think I'm bound to be rude sometimes, even if only by accident.'

And you couldn't really say fairer than that.

The boys were about to go their different ways. Smudger opened his mouth to say, 'See you tomorrow,' when something else took his attention. Something was coming down the road, the like of which he had never seen before.

Chocolate Detected

Huntly stared. It was familiar, and yet not familiar. It reminded him of something – but what?

A large, heavy vehicle was coming along the street. It moved slowly, like one of those big machines with spinning brushes that clean the gutters. Only it wasn't.

The windows of the vehicle were blacked out with dark, mirrored glass. Whoever was inside could see out, but you couldn't see in. All you could make out were dark shapes and shadows – the figures of the driver and passengers. They seemed menacing and sinister.

'Look,' Smudger said. 'At the roof.'

On top of the vehicle was a large, curved dish, in the shape of a satellite receiver. It was mounted on a turret, which enabled it to revolve in continuous circles. As the vehicle came down the street, the dish went slowly round, like a huge prying eye on a stalk, on the lookout for something. It seemed to peer right into your very thoughts. You knew you hadn't done anything wrong, and yet its presence somehow made you feel guilty.

Huntly finally knew what it reminded him of. It was something he had seen years ago, driving past his front window.

'Mum, come and look!' he had called. 'It's an army truck or something.'

She had gone to the window and laughed.

'Relax, Huntly, it's all right. We're safe. We've got one.'

'Got a what?'

'A TV licence. That's a TV detector van. It's a van to check that you've bought a television licence,' his mum explained. 'That thing on the top can tell whether there's a TV on in your house. If the detector tells them there is, but their computer list tells them that you haven't got a licence—'

'Yes?'

'You're in trouble. They stop the van, knock on your door, and they can come into your house.'

'They can come into your house? Just like that? Just to check on your TV licence?'

'They can even break the door down for all I know.'

'Break the door down! Wow! And what if it turns out that they've made a mistake? And you have got a licence after all?'

'Well, they have to apologize and fix your door and go away again, I suppose.'

'And if it turns out you haven't got a licence?'

Huntly's mum had looked pretty serious at that.

'If you don't have a licence, they can take you to court and you can be fined a lot of money. They could even send you to prison – not that I think they would.'

'Send you to prison! Wow! Just for not having a TV licence! Well, don't you worry, Mum, because I'll come and visit you.'

'Hopefully it won't come to that, Huntly,' she smiled, 'because I'm very careful to get a TV licence every year.'

'If they do send you to prison,' Huntly had said, 'can you watch TV there?'

'In prison? I suppose so.'

'And have prisons got TV licences?'

'I suppose they must do.'

'Or otherwise, all the people in prison would be arrested for not having a TV licence, and they'd all end up in, well, prison, I suppose.'

The TV detector van had turned the corner then, and vanished into the next street. But *this* was different. This vehicle was like the TV van but with certain modifications. It moved along like a big shiny bug, a huge beetle looking for something to get its pincers into. The dish on the roof was pointing directly towards them now and the van was nearly level. It suddenly stopped. Lights began to flash. A siren exploded into a loud wail. The doors of the van were thrown open and men in uniform jumped out, carrying riot sticks and wearing padded body armour and protective helmets with shatter-proof visors.

'Freeze!' A voice yelled through a loudspeaker. 'Stay exactly where you are. Do not attempt to run or you will be stopped. Back up against the wall. Then turn to face it. Stand against it with your hands up and your feet apart. Do it now!'

As he backed away, Huntly got a better look at the van and realized it was one of the new law-enforcement patrols. This was how the Good For You Party intended to keep order on the streets and to ensure that their regulations were obeyed.

Written on the side of the vehicle, spelled out in reflective yellow letters, were the words: CHOCOLATE DETECTOR VAN NUMBER 19. Under the dish on the roof was a small dot-matrix display flashing the words 'CHOCOLATE DETECTED . . . CHOCOLATE DETECTED' over and over again.

Huntly and Smudger looked at each other, their expressions a mixture of confusion and fear. They put their hands up, as instructed, and faced the blank wall. The bricks were only inches away. You could see the imperfections in them, the little cracks and tiny holes, and the flaking cement.

'OK,' a deep voice from behind said. 'Now, move nice and slow, you understand? I want you to empty out your pockets. And I want you to do it now.'

The boys were careful not to make any sudden movement. Each of them expected at any moment to feel the sharp sting of a Shriek Gun. They'd heard that it was supposed to be like touching an electrical cattle wire – or a live Portuguese man-of-war jellyfish – only about a hundred times worse.

They turned out their pockets.

'Drop the stuff on the ground.'

They did. One of the Troopers squatted down to go through their belongings, prodding at the items with the muzzle of his gun. His uniform, under his body armour, was a dark, drab brown. His eyes, behind the visor of his riot helmet, were concealed in shadow. On his sleeve was a badge. It was neat and official looking, in the shape of a shield. Inside the shield were some words, picked out in gold thread.

LAW ENFORCEMENT, the words read, CHOCOLATE SQUAD. And on the man's other shoulder was an insignia bearing his rank and number. CHIEF INSPECTOR, it said. NUMBER 171.

'Party Troopers,' Huntly whispered. 'Chocolate Police—'

The Trooper looked up. He pushed back the visor of his riot helmet. His face was hard and unsympathetic, his eyes were a strange metallic grey, almost silver, the colour of fish scales, the colour of steel.

There was another flash of silver too, coming from his hand. He held something between his fingers.

'Well?' he growled. 'And which one of you does this belong to?'

The two boys stared, transfixed. The Inspector was holding up a piece of silver foil. It was Smudger's old chocolate wrapper. And there, in amongst the folds of silver, was a tiny crumb of chocolate.

'Well?' the Inspector said. 'Well? I'm waiting.'

Smudger swallowed. His mouth was dry as cork, his throat was sawdust.

'It's mine,' he croaked. 'Belongs to me.'

Huntly tried to give him a reassuring 'Don't worry, Smudge, we're in this together, I'll stick with you' kind of look. But the only message his eyes conveyed right then was, 'Help, I'm scared.'

The Inspector unravelled the foil.

'This is a chocolate wrapper, isn't it?' he said. He knew full well it was. He just wanted Smudger to admit it.

'Y-yes,' Smudger stammered – despite all his best efforts to control the tremor in his voice. 'I s-suppose it is.'

The Inspector turned to the other Troopers.

'He supposes it is,' he sneered. 'He supposes it is.'

The Troopers laughed mirthlessly, no doubt wanting to please their senior officer by seeming to be amused by his jokes.

The Inspector turned back to Smudger.

'So if this is the wrapper – where's the chocolate?'

Smudger's eyes darted around.

'I suppose I—'

'You suppose what?'

'I suppose I . . . I must have . . . eaten it.'

The Inspector turned to his men again. 'He supposes,' he said, with mock incredulity, 'that he must have eaten it. Well fancy that! He supposes he's eaten the chocolate. It's only about the most serious crime a child of his age could commit! But is he bothered about that? No. Not in the slightest! He just supposes!'

'Yes, but—' Smudger began.

'Quiet!' the Inspector snarled.

Smudger felt suddenly afraid that he was going to cry. He could feel his lower lip trembling. He was more afraid of crying than he was of the Chocolate Inspector. He didn't want to cry in front of him. The man was a bully. Smudger didn't want to give him the satisfaction.

But now the Inspector had turned his attention to Huntly.

He was holding up the empty wrapper from Huntly's last penny chew.

'It's a chew wrapper,' Huntly explained, as calmly and politely as he could.

'A chew wrapper. A sticky, disgusting, tooth-rotting chew wrapper,' the Inspector said, holding the offending article up towards a small crowd of onlookers that had gathered to watch from a discreet distance. It was only a scrap of paper. It was hard to understand what all the fuss was about.

'Open your mouths,' he barked. 'Both of you!'

Puzzled, perplexed and apprehensive, they did as they were told.

'Wider!' the Inspector demanded. 'Mirror!'

A small dentist's mirror was passed to him. He put it inside Smudger's mouth and looked all around for signs of fillings and decay. Then he removed the mirror, cleaned it on an antiseptic wipe handed to him by one of his subordinates, and inspected Huntly's mouth in the same way.

'Right,' he said. 'No visible signs of tooth decay. No need to call in the police dentist – this time.'

He gave a sadistic smile.

'I don't suppose you've heard of the police dentist, have you?' he said. 'He's a very good dentist. Only he doesn't have much anaesthetic. And he has to do his drilling without it. You know, deep down into the nerve.'

Smudger shuddered; he had an aversion to dentists. But Huntly didn't, and he wasn't going to take any more of this.

'We haven't done anything wrong,' he said. 'The deadline's not until five o'clock.'

'The deadline's when I say it is,' the Inspector informed him. 'You two listen to me. You've been caught in possession of illegal substances. You have been found with wrappers in your pockets bearing traces of chocolate and sugar-based substances. Do you know what you could get for this?'

'No, we—'

'You could be sent away – for re-education!'

'But we were only finishing off what we had, sir,' Huntly managed to blurt out.

'We didn't buy any new stuff,' Smudger agreed. 'We were just getting rid of it. We didn't think it would be wrong to finish off what we had. We didn't know it would be wrong to keep the wrappers.'

'We only wanted them for souvenirs.'

The Inspector glared at them through his steel-grey eyes, his gaze cold and unfeeling. He seemed like the kind of man for whom chocolate had no appeal. He didn't look like a man with a sweet tooth, but a man with a sour and a bitter one, a man whose sole pleasure in life was to stop the pleasures of others.

'All right,' he said. 'I can see by looking at you, that you're pretty small fry and you're not what I'm after. It's illegal chocolate dealers and sweet hoarders, they're the ones I'm out to get. Black marketeers, bootleggers, call them what you will, dealers in illicit and underground sweets. Because sure as bugs crawl out of woodwork, they'll be popping up sooner or later. And I'll be ready to squash them! So I'll let you both off with a caution – this time. But I warn you that if I ever find you with so much as one crumb of chocolate, with one sugar-coated almond or toffee-covered raisin in your pockets, we'll lock you up and throw away the key. Got it?'

'Yes, sir,' Huntly nodded. 'Got it.'

'And you?' the Inspector snarled at Smudger. 'Has it penetrated your skull as well?'

'I heard,' Smudger muttered. 'I've got it.'

'OK,' the Inspector said. 'Be on your way. And don't let me see you again.'

He and his men got back into the Chocolate Detector Van and drove on down the street. The dish on the roof resumed its slow revolution, just as before.

Huntly and Smudger watched them go.

'So that's the Chocolate Police,' Huntly said.

'Yes,' Smudger nodded. 'Lovely bunch of individuals, aren't they? Well, they can stay out of my way from now on.'

But that wasn't quite how things worked out.

Mrs Bubby

After the shock of the incident, Smudger decided to walk a little further with Huntly on his way home. As they crossed the shopping precinct, they saw more vans and lorries belonging to the Chocolate Disposal Squad parked outside the shops and supermarkets. A small army of men and women, dressed in the distinctive dark-brown uniforms of the Good For You Party (Sweets and Chocolate Enforcement Section) were carrying boxes with familiar names marked on their sides out into the armoured vans.

'There go the Mars bars,' Smudger sighed. 'That detector van'll be going wild now.'

'Cadbury's Flakes too,' Huntly nodded.

'Here come the Rolos. I loved them.'

'And that looks like a stack of toffee. Or is it fudge?'

'And look at this, Smudge,' Huntly said, as a woman Trooper staggered from Tesco, her knees buckling under the weight of the boxes she carried. 'They're even making off with the drinking chocolate.'

'And the instant puddings!' Smudger cried. 'And the treacle, and the Golden Syrup . . .' His voice trailed to nothingness. 'Even the syrup. I liked a drop of syrup. I know some people say it's too sticky, but for me that was half the attraction. I never thought they'd take the syrup as well. What kind of a world are we living in?'

The procession of Troopers going to and fro reminded Smudger of the leafcutter ants he had once seen in a display at the Science and Nature Exhibition. The ants had toiled on and on, one following the other, each dragging a piece of leaf back to the nest. It was exactly what the Troopers looked like in their dark-brown uniforms, mindlessly labouring away, doing their duty, without ever questioning it, or pausing for thought.

The boys moved on from the precinct and came to Bubby's the Newsagent. Outside, a ferocious argument was taking place between Mrs Bubby and a Trooper, who was carrying away her stock.

'How am I supposed to live?' Mrs Bubby demanded. 'If I've got no stock! Give me that box back!'

But the Trooper put it into his van.

'What am I supposed to sell?' Mrs Bubby said. 'Is this what Good For You means? Depriving people of their livelihoods? Selling sweets and chocolate to children on their way to and from school is how I live. If I can't sell sweets and chocolate, what can I sell?'

The Trooper held out a box labelled Healthy Snacks.

'You sell these, madam,' he said. 'And to feed the mind as well as the body, we also have the new *Good For You* comic, to replace the *Beano* and the *Dandy*, with that Denis the Dodger or whatever his name is – disreputable characters like that have no place in the society of today.'

He put a bundle of comics down on top of the box.

'We're not against fun, madam, we just like it to be good, clean, healthy fun.'

'The sort nobody enjoys, you mean?' Mrs Bubby snapped, as the Trooper hurled a few more packages of sweets into the back of the van and shut the doors.

'Right,' he called to the driver. 'Move on to the next.'

Smudger and Huntly went to help Mrs Bubby as she struggled to lift the box of Healthy Snacks. She looked up and smiled, both pleased and relieved to see them.

'Oh, my best customers,' she said. 'Come inside, boys, and see what they've done. They've stripped the place. There's hardly anything left.'

Inside the little shop the shelves were mostly empty. The counters were barren and bare. It was as if a swarm of locusts had flown in, devoured everything sugary in sight, and then swooped out again, to rampage somewhere else.

'Oh, boys!' she sighed. 'I've got nothing to sell you. Even when times were hard I could always count on you two to come in and spend your pocket money. When everyone else was going on diets and worrying about their figures, I could always rely on you. The fearless consumption of snacks between meals, that was how I always thought of you two. But whatever am I to do now? They've gone and killed my business stone dead. Come on, into the stockroom, if you would. Put those boxes down in there.'

She took a tissue out from her sleeve and blew her nose on it.

'Don't be upset, Mrs Bubby,' Smudger told her. 'We've

just got to believe that things will change. That one day everything will return to normal. The Good For You Party can't run the country forever – can they?'

But there was a note of doubt in his voice, as though he feared that perhaps the Good For You Party *would* run the country forever. Forever and a day. And another day, after that.

'Look on the bright side, Mrs B,' he said, 'you'll still have these Healthy For You Snacks to sell.' He dropped the box on to the floor. 'They might be all right.'

Huntly and Smudger looked around. The stockroom was full of metal shelves, piled high with tins and packets, with obscure cans of this, strange boxes of that and jars of exotic fruits and pickles.

Mrs Bubby screwed up her tissue and, despite her advancing age and arthritis, threw it expertly into the bin.

'Yes,' she said, 'the new snacks and treats. The Good For You Chocolate Bar Substitutes and the Healthy Biscuit Alternatives. Better give them the benefit of the doubt, I suppose. Come on, let's open them up.'

She took a knife and ran it along the top of one of the boxes. Huntly read the label.

'"Official Government Snacks,"' he said. '"Passed and authorized for public consumption by the Good For You Party. Six dozen assorted healthy, sugar-free, salt-free and chocolate-free snacks. Always ask for Good For You Chocolate Substitute. A Good For You product." Shall we try them?'

Mrs Bubby unwrapped a bar of Chocco-Sub and bit into it. Her face remained expressionless.

'What's it like?' Smudger asked.

'I'd rather you boys told me what you thought,' Mrs Bubby said. 'I'd appreciate another opinion.'

She took out two more bars of Good For You Official Chocolate Substitute and watched as the boys peeled back the wrappers.

'Doesn't look too bad,' Smudger said.

'Yes,' Mrs Bubby agreed. 'That was what I thought.'

'And it does *look* like chocolate.'

'Yes,' Huntly agreed, his spirits rising. 'It does.'

'And,' Smudger held the Chocco-Sub Bar to his nose and sniffed, 'it actually smells like chocolate too.'

Mrs Bubby gave him a look of sorrow and pity. 'Why don't you have a little taste?' she said.

'A little taste!' Smudger said. 'This smells so good I'm going to have a big, enormous taste! Right now!'

The boys bit into their Good For You Chocco-Sub Bars. The taste of the chocolate-smelling, chocolate-looking, chocolate-free, fat-free, sugar-free chocolate substitute hit their taste buds.

'Oh—' Smudger grunted.

'Oh—' Huntly said.

'Yes,' Mrs Bubby agreed, 'just what I—'

'Eeeeeech!' Smudger yelled, looking frantically around for something to spit into.

'That is revolting!' Huntly moaned. 'That is so bad. That is so awful. That is just like . . . eeeeech!'

'Yes,' Mrs Bubby nodded calmly. 'I'm glad I wasn't imagining it. The toilet's through there.'

Smudger made a dash for it, Huntly at his heels.

'There's a couple of spare toothbrushes,' she called. 'And a tube of minty toothpaste.'

The sound of frantic toothbrushing came from the small washroom. After a few minutes, the boys reappeared.

'Well,' Mrs Bubby asked. 'Do you think you'll be spending your pocket money on buying any Good For You Chocolate Substitute Bars?'

'No,' Smudger had to say, 'I think I'd rather spend it on arsenic.'

'My feelings exactly,' Mrs Bubby agreed.

She held out a copy of the new *Good For You* comic.

'What do you think of this?'

'"The Healthy and Uplifting Adventures of Thomas and Tina Goodfellow, Young Pioneers,"' Huntly read. '"Today Thomas and Tina visit the dental hygienist to learn all about flossing."'

He groaned.

'I don't think we'll be wanting this either, Mrs Bubby,' he said. 'Not really our kind of thing. I mean, if they strangled someone with the dental floss, maybe, but—'

'I don't blame you,' Mrs Bubby said. 'Thanks all the same, boys. You've been such good customers of mine, but I don't suppose I'll be seeing so much of you now.'

'We'll still be in to see how you are,' Huntly promised.

'Thanks,' Mrs Bubby said. 'I'll see you around, then.'

The bell above the door tinkled behind them as the boys left the shop, and then they were gone. Mrs Bubby settled on her stool behind the counter and prepared herself for a long, long wait for the next customer.

Squashed

S mudger and Huntly went their separate ways home. Chocolate Disposal Squads were out in force, moving from house to house to demand that anything sweet left over and not consumed had to be handed in. But some people refused to come to the door. Families sat in their kitchens, scoffing the last of their sweets and chocolate. The lids were off the biscuit tins, and suddenly parents weren't saying, 'Just the one, mind,' and, 'Don't overdo it, you'll be sick.' It was, 'Tuck in and eat all you can! It's the last chance you'll ever get.' People everywhere were making complete pigs of themselves.

In Smudger's street a Trooper was at the door of a neighbour's house, banging on the knocker. Smudger stopped to watch as he bellowed into the letter box. 'It's no use pretending. We know you're in there! And the deadline's up! Come out and surrender all your chocolate! Or we'll have to break this door down!'

The man turned to a second Trooper and nodded to him to be ready.

'I'm going to count to ten!' the first Trooper shouted. 'If this door isn't open by then, we'll use force. One,' he began. 'Two. Three, four, five, six, seven, eight, nine—'

There was a sound from within, and whoever was inside posted a small chocolate bar out into the world. The Trooper picked it up, unconvinced.

He peered through the letter box, where two frightened eyes looked at him.

'What about the biscuits?' he demanded.

'Biscuits?' a trembling voice said. 'What makes you think I've got biscuits?'

Smudger walked on.

The route Huntly had taken led him past a public Sweets and Chocolate Surrender Point. Here virtuous citizens were willingly handing over their supplies of chocolate and sweets to a woman Trooper who was disposing of them in a Squash Box. The whirr and grind of its wheels could be heard as it ground and mashed whatever was fed into it into a pulp, which it then promptly ejected into an attached bin liner.

A queue had formed. It was amazing how many supporters the Party had, how willing so many people were to forego life's simple pleasures, to exchange them for the warm inner glow of abstemiousness and moral superiority. But not all were Party supporters. Many were simply law-abiding citizens, who did what they were supposed to, and didn't want any trouble.

A smug-looking woman handed over a packet of Hob Nobs for squashing.

'Take them!' she announced, with nauseating self-satisfaction. 'Throw them away! I renounce them. Biscuits – goodbye and good riddance! Save us from tooth decay and diabetes and all the ills that too much sugar can bring upon a person. Save us from temptation by taking it all away.'

'Thank you, ma'am,' the Trooper said. 'That's the attitude. That's the spirit. Next!'

Huntly watched, with grim fascination, as a young family shuffled forwards. The two children, a boy and a girl, looked nervous and apprehensive.

How could anyone do this? he asked himself. How could anybody give away the last of their chocolate? Voluntarily? Without any struggle or any kind of a fight at all. And yet it was happening, right before his eyes.

'Good day, sir, madam,' the Trooper said. 'Crunchy apples to you.'

'Good afternoon, officer.' The children's father smiled. 'And juicy oranges to you. We've brought some chocolate to hand in. Just a small chocolate cake. And a packet of digestives.'

The objects went into the Squash Box. There was the whirring of teeth, the grinding of cogs, and the waste plopped out into the bin liner.

'The children have some things too,' their mother said. 'OK now, Sam, Jenny – remember what we told you. Give the nice Trooper your sweetie bags,' she said softly. 'As we explained.'

Jenny held up the bag she was clutching.

'It's my chocolate,' she said. 'That Granny gave me. But . . . I don't want it now. 'Cause it's bad.' She took a deep breath and handed the bag over. Her brother went on holding his bag of chocolate, as tightly as he could.

'Go on, Sam,' his mother urged. 'Remember what to say.'

'Please take my chocolate away, as – I'm – I'm better off without it,' the boy stammered, abruptly thrusting the bag into the Trooper's hand. 'Take it,' he repeated, with an angry sob. 'And give it a squash.'

The Trooper squeezed the boy on the shoulder.

'Well done, son,' she murmured. She turned to the parents. 'They're a credit to you.'

But as she fed their chocolate into the Squash Box, Sam began to wail.

'My chocolate! My chocolate! I want my chocolate!'

His sister put her arms around him and said, 'Sam, don't cry. Got to be brave.'

Their mother blushed, embarrassed.

'I'm sorry,' she apologized. It's just they don't really understand. They're too young.'

'Don't worry, madam. They'll learn,' the Trooper said. 'It takes a while for the little ones to learn the truth of what's good for them. There's bound to be a few tears before bedtime along the way. We have to be cruel to be kind.'

Huntly had seen enough. He turned away and walked on.

If this was the Good For You Party in action, then what was good about it? he thought.

And the odd thing was that the majority of people in the country hadn't actually voted for them.

'I don't understand it, Mum,' Huntly said, when he got home. 'How can people win the election and become the government when most people didn't want them?'

She thought a moment.

'Apathy, Huntly!' she announced, after a pause. (Even she called him by his nickname Huntly, though the first name on his birth certificate was Richard.)

Huntly didn't quite know what apathy was.

'It means bone idleness,' she told him. 'It means too many people just couldn't be bothered to go down to the polling station and vote. They thought "Everyone else will vote against them, so I needn't bother". Only everyone else thought the same. You see?'

'Sort of,' Huntly said, not sure that he really did. 'And what's that called then, Mum?'

'Democracy,' she told him. 'And like it or not, the Good For You Party are now in power. They're the government for the next five years and they can out-vote the opposition. So if they say chocolate's bad for you, then it's bad for you. And if they say no more sugar, then it's no more sugar. And that's the law. And no sit-down demonstrations or protest marches are going to change that.'

'But, Mum,' Huntly had said, 'I can't see that there's anything *wrong* with a bit of chocolate.'

'Neither can I,' she agreed. 'All I know is that there's a lot of people in this world who think they know what's right for others, and they love nothing better than to tell them what to do and what not to do and how to live their lives. People with hard and fast opinions, who know their way is the right one and there's no doubt about it.'

*

In Smudger's road the Chocolate Squads had got as far as the Mackenzies' house, just a few yards down from where he lived. They were moving along the street like a conquering army. They'd be knocking on Smudger's front door soon. Not that it mattered, because his family had nothing left to surrender – they had already eaten it all.

Or had they?

Suddenly Smudger remembered something. The big Toblerone! Uncle Mike had brought it back with him as a present from the airport shop when he went on his skiing holiday. It was enormous. The biggest Toblerone Smudger had ever seen.

'This is for everyone,' Uncle Mike had said. 'So make sure you share it properly.'

But Smudger's mum had taken the gigantic Toblerone and had put it up out of reach on the top of the cupboard, where you couldn't even see it. 'Out of sight out of mind,' she had said. 'You've got quite enough chocolate lined up for the moment.'

For the next few days, that Toblerone had not been out of his mind. When he was alone in the kitchen he would sometimes stand on a chair and see if he could get it, and think about eating it. But after a week or two, incredible as it now seemed, he actually had forgotten about it. And so had everyone else.

And now the Chocolate Disposal Squad Troopers were moving along the road, carrying hand-held chocolate detectors. There was no way that great big, delicious, enormous, sweet, nougaty, scrumptious Toblerone would escape detection. It would be put into the Chocolate

Shredder and ground to pulp, chocolate, wrapper and all. It would all be wasted and not tasted—

Unless . . .

Smudger ran. He ran faster than he had in his life. The blood pounded through his veins. *Gotta get there. Gotta get there before they do.* He sprinted past gates, fences, hedges, lamp posts and parked cars, past the Chocolate Disposal Van—

'Hey!' one of the Troopers yelled. 'Where's the fire?'

But Smudger skidded in through his front gate and pelted along the path. The kitchen door slammed open as he burst in like a hurricane. His father, Ron, was at the table checking his bread orders for the next day. His mother was loading washing into the machine. Kylie had her painting apron on and was doing a picture of – well, probably only she knew what it was.

'Smudger!' his mum snapped. 'Take your muddy trainers off.'

Smudger stood gasping, fighting for his breath.

He pointed in the direction of the street.

'Troopers. Chocolate Squad. Coming.'

His father sighed.

'Yes. We know. They've been out there for an hour.'

Smudger gulped.

'Yes. But we – we forgot – the – the . . .' He raised his arm and pointed to the top of the food cupboard. 'The – T – T – the – Toblerone.'

Smudger's mum and dad looked at each other, horror stricken. Kylie carried on with her painting and said, 'What's a tobber roam, Huntly?'

'Not a tobber roam, a *Toblerone*. It's chocolate!'

As the word 'chocolate' came out of his mouth, there was a bang at the front door and a shrill ringing of the doorbell.

'The Troopers. They're here!' Smudger's dad was on his feet, dragging a chair over to the cupboard. He felt around on the top of it and held up the huge Toblerone, the huge, delicious Toblerone which they had all forgotten about.

'Come on. Let's eat it.'

'But they're at the door, Ron!' Smudger's mum protested.

'To hell with them, Trisha,' Smudger's dad said, his eyes glittering. 'Let's eat it.'

For a moment Smudger thought that his mum was going to say no, that it was too dangerous, that they had to open the door immediately and hand the chocolate bar over to the Troopers, that she didn't want any trouble.

But no. 'All right,' she said. 'But quick.'

Ron took the Toblerone in both hands and snapped it in two. He looked like a circus strong man bending an iron bar. He broke the pieces in half again.

'OK. A quarter each. We've all got the same.'

'Smudger's quarter is bigger than my quarter!' Kylie wailed.

'How can a quarter be bigger than a quarter if it's a quarter!' Smudger pointed out. 'Have my quarter if you want.'

They all chewed and munched as quickly as they could, and yet as slowly as they dared, to savour every mouthful.

The banging at the front door came louder than before.

The doorbell rang – once, twice, three times. Then it stopped.

On they munched, steadily, systematically. The knocking and ringing at the front door stopped. Voices were heard, and then heavy footsteps at the side of the house.

'They're coming round the back,' Smudger thought.

He had three pieces of Toblerone left.

'This is the house that kid ran into,' a Trooper's voice said. 'There's someone here all right. Put the detector on.'

Smudger stuffed another chunk of Toblerone in his mouth. His dad was ahead of him with one piece left, his mum had two, Kylie had three, no, two now. She may have been small, but she certainly knew how to eat chocolate.

A crackling noise started up outside. The chocolate detector had burst into action. It crackled like a Geiger counter detecting radiation.

'Chocolate in here all right,' a Trooper's voice said. 'Coming from the back of the house.'

Cramming in his second-to-last Toblerone chunk, Smudger scurried across the kitchen, slid the bolt into its catch, then scuttled back to the table.

'Quick,' his dad whispered. 'Quick as you can.'

Their jaws worked up and down like pistons. They chewed, swallowed, chewed some more.

'Open up!' a commanding voice bellowed; a fist hammered on the frosted glass. 'We know you've got chocolate in there! And the deadline's past! Open up!'

One piece left. Kylie's piece.

'Quickly, Kylie,' Smudger's mum whispered. 'Take it up to your room.'

Kylie took her last piece of Toblerone and sped out of the kitchen. Trisha threw the chocolate wrapper into the bin.

'Open up!' the Trooper shouted angrily. 'Your last chance! Or we smash the door.'

'OK,' Ron called. 'Just coming. What's the big panic?'

He slid back the bolt and opened the door. The Trooper turned the chocolate detector off and its crackling died away. Smudger's dad nodded.

'Afternoon, gentlemen,' he said. 'And what can we do for you?'

The Troopers marched into the kitchen, big, broad and angry. They made the room seem suddenly small and they made Huntly's dad – who was by no means little – somehow small and diminished too.

'It's time to surrender your chocolate,' the senior Trooper said. 'We know you've got some. The detector's never wrong.'

Smudger's dad stood his ground.

'We don't have any,' he said. 'You've made a mistake.'

'We don't make mistakes,' the Trooper told him.

'Well, if you can find any chocolate, you'd better take it then,' Ron said.

The Trooper muttered something to his subordinate. He turned the Chocolate Detector back on, but it remained silent. The detector could find chocolate almost anywhere – except when it was behind lead or inside human stomachs, behind a barrier of flesh and blood.

'Seems to have gone,' the Trooper had to admit. 'Maybe we did get a false reading.' Then it briefly fluttered into life as the Trooper swept it over the bin. He flipped the lid open, reached inside, and took out the Toblerone packet.

'And what,' he said, 'is this?'

Smudger's dad looked innocently at it.

'Empties,' he said.

The Troopers could see that there was nothing they could do. They were leaving the house when Kylie came down the stairs, and she gave them a huge, great brown and white grin. Her face and her teeth were covered in chocolate.

But there wasn't much they could do about that – short of taking Kylie away with them and putting her in the Disposal Van. But even the Good For You Party wasn't that bad. In fact, in many ways the Good For You Party meant well, very well, and only wanted to do things for the best. But the road to hell – as Smudger's dad was fond of saying – was paved with good intentions.

A Little Lunch

It was morning. Orange juice was already poured out into glasses on the table. Huntly's mother had an early surgery to go to. She worked long hours, as most doctors do, and when she wasn't seeing patients at the practice she was often out on call. She sat sipping her coffee and arranging her appointments for that afternoon.

They didn't speak about his dad much any more. They had done at first, every day. But now he was more in their thoughts and their memories than in their conversation.

Huntly had blamed his mother for a while and would grow ferociously, frighteningly angry with her and with the whole world.

'You're a doctor, why didn't you fix things! Why didn't you fix Dad! Why didn't you make him better!'

But now he understood that there were things in this world which not even the best doctor can cure.

So now Huntly didn't speak about him, but he thought about him all the time. And when faced with any predicament, the same question always ran through his mind.

'What would Dad do?' 'What would Dad think?' 'What would Dad have said?'

It was a touchstone. A standard by which all other things were judged.

What would Huntly's dad have thought about the Good For You Party?

Well, that was an easy one.

He wouldn't have liked them one bit.

Huntly had a bowl in front of him. He prodded its contents half-heartedly with a spoon and peered at the cereal packet.

'Good For You Breakfast Cereal! Government Approved. Guaranteed Sugar-Free, Salt-Free and Fat-Free.'

Taste-free too, Huntly thought. The cereal swam about in skimmed, fat-free milk. It was the only sort you could get.

'Sorry,' his mother said. 'It was all they had left in the shops. The chocolate-flavoured cereal had gone.'

She looked up at the wall clock and got to her feet.

'I'd better do your lunch box. What would you like?'

'Can I have anything sweet?'

Huntly's mother picked up a leaflet from the table. It was titled 'Lunch Box Guidelines For Parents'. A copy had been distributed to every household in the land, even ones without children.

'"For a sweet treat for children's lunch boxes, dried prunes are highly recommended, "' she read.

Dried prunes. Huntly's stomach sent him panic messages.

'It's all right thanks, I'll go without,' he said.

His stomach sent him its undying gratitude and promised to remember him on his birthday.

'Marmite OK?'

His mother went to the cupboard and reached inside. She found a jar she didn't expect to see in there.

'Hey! Huntly! Look what I've found!'

She triumphantly held up a honey jar, with just about enough left in it for a decent spread on one roll.

'Honey! Great!'

'You want it?'

'Course I do!' Then Huntly hesitated, uncertain. 'I won't get into trouble, will I, Mum?' he said. 'For taking honey to school? I mean, I know it's not chocolate but—'

'Come on, Huntly,' his mother said. 'It's not that bad, is it? What are they going to do? Come round and inspect your lunch box?'

Yes. He was being ridiculous.

'OK, honey roll, then. Thanks.'

And yet still Huntly felt uneasy.

What would you have done, Dad?

But the voice in his head was silent. Maybe he would have to deal with this alone. What was happening now was something his father had never experienced. Who did know – about things like the Good For You Party?

But finally the voice came, as it always did. He knew his dad wouldn't let him down.

'You be careful now, Huntly. That's all I can say. And look out for Mum too.'

'Yes, Dad,' he whispered, 'I will.'

'Sorry, Huntly, did you say something?' His mother looked up from the roll she was spreading.

'Nothing, Mum.'

She put the roll into a plastic lunch box and added some fruit, peanuts and other things. Huntly collected his homework and his games kit and picked up his bag.

They left the house together. His mother went one way, he went another. She wouldn't be able to give him a lift today. She kissed him as they parted, and though he often pretended that he was too old for that kind of thing, he was glad that she did.

Smudger was already in the playground. He waved to Huntly and started to tell him about the forgotten Toblerone until they noticed that Frankie Crawley was hovering nearby. He wasn't in his Young Pioneer outfit today, but wore school uniform, like everyone else. In the lapel of his jacket, however, was a neat, golden YP membership badge. It glittered and shone, as if he had spent the morning polishing it, along with his shoes.

Huntly and Smudger moved away, out of earshot. Frankie Crawley drifted off to try and eavesdrop on somebody else. But not many people were talking. There were a lot of long, sad faces at school that morning. Those who were in the habit of treating themselves to a chocolate bar or a packet of crisps before lessons had been unable to buy them from the corner shop, while the Healthy For You Chocco-Sub Bars were proving universally unpopular.

Lessons started. But the morning dragged. All the children seemed dull, jaded and inattentive.

'Smudger,' Miss Ross said, as she returned his maths test to him, 'this isn't like you. Half of these are wrong. In fact half of most people's answers are wrong. Are you all having trouble concentrating this morning for some reason?'

'It's all down to my low blood sugar, miss,' Smudger explained. 'I've not had my chocolate today. This healthy diet, it's making me ill.'

The class laughed – all except Frankie and Myrtle Perkins. Frankie just sat, fingering the Young Pioneer pin in his lapel, trying to look vaguely superior. Miss Ross returned his maths test to him.

'Well done, Frankie. You got one hundred per cent.'

'That's because I eat properly, miss,' Frankie smirked. 'I ate a proper breakfast, as recommended in the government guidelines, with wholemeal toast and plenty of unsweetened porridge – it's best to have it cold, actually, that way it's nice and chewy – all washed down with a tasty glass of prune juice and a bowl of figs.'

Miss Ross seemed to wince.

'Yes, well, you must tell us all about it in more detail, Frankie—'

He opened his mouth to do so.

'Another time,' she added.

Lunchtime came. Those who had school dinners queued to get them. The packed lunch brigade, Huntly and Smudger among them, sat at their designated table.

Rumours of what the Good For You Party were going to do next abounded, and Dave Cheng, sitting next to Huntly, was doing his best to spread fear and panic.

'I'm telling you, Huntly,' he said. 'If they catch you with anything sugary, or any chocolate, or anything like that, they send you off to Re-education Camp. And they do nasty things to you to put you off chocolate. And after a few weeks there, you don't want chocolate any more. In fact you beg and pray for them not to give you it. It's true.'

'Oh come off it, Dave,' Huntly said. 'Go back to fantasy land.'

Before Dave could reply, the door opened and the headmaster, Mr Prewitt, entered at the head of a small procession comprising four uniformed Chocolate Troopers and someone the boys instantly recognized.

He was out of uniform, but that made no difference. You could never mistake him. His eyes were just as chilling and grey, his gaze as cold and hard as steel.

It was the Chocolate Inspector. The man who had been in uniform, behind the wheel of the Detector Van. But now he wore a smart grey suit. He looked totally different, like an executive, a politician, a respectable businessman, except for those metallic grey eyes.

The only speck of colour in him was his Good For You Party tiepin – a fleck of warm gold amongst the steely grey. He was cold as a cloud in a winter sky, cold as the clay in the cemetery.

All talking stopped. The man was frightening and instantly unlikeable. But there was no denying that he had an immense and commanding presence. It wasn't that he was especially tall or broad. It was something else, something powerful in him – the willingness to do what others would shy away from.

Mr Prewitt the headmaster cleared his throat to attract attention.

44

'Ahem.'

He was wasting his time.

'Quiet!' the Inspector commanded.

The room fell silent.

'Thank you,' Mr Prewitt said. 'Now, everybody, attention please. We'll be having a little lunch box inspection now, to see that we're all eating properly. Carry on with your lunches but be prepared to show the Inspector what you've brought if he asks to see it. Thank you. Carry on.'

'Right! Lunch boxes open and at the ready.'

The lids were placed down on the table. The Inspector walked slowly along the length of the aisles, between the tables, looking from one to the other, nodding, murmuring, sometimes looking displeased, having a word with this girl, giving advice to that boy.

He stopped by Mike Harris.

'You, boy,' he said. 'Where are your two pieces of fruit? I can only see one here.'

Mike held up an apple core.

'I already ate it, sir.'

'Are you sure they're *your* toothmarks?'

'Positive, sir.'

'Very well, carry on.'

Huntly felt a tug on his sleeve. Smudger looked panic-stricken.

'I never knew it was *two* pieces of fruit we were supposed to have,' he whispered. 'I only brought one.'

'Didn't you read the lunch-box guidelines!'

The Inspector was by Jennifer Allun.

'Where are your two pieces of fruit, young lady?'

She held up two grapes on a stalk.

'Are you trying to be funny!' the Inspector demanded. 'A grape isn't a portion! Do better tomorrow!'

The Inspector was getting nearer to Smudger with every step.

'I'll pass you my orange,' Huntly whispered. 'When he's seen it, pass it back.'

He handed his orange under the table. The Inspector stopped by Smudger.

'Where are your – just a minute, don't I know you?'

'No, sir,' Smudger denied.

'Yes, I do. The boy with the wrapper. Well, let's hope you're staying out of trouble now.'

'Yes, sir.'

'Where are your two pieces of fruit? I can only see one banana here.'

Smudger held the orange up.

'Here, sir. I was just about to peel it.'

'All right. Carry on.'

The Inspector moved along. Smudger returned the orange to Huntly, under the table. The Inspector walked round the end of the table and back along the other side. He peered at Huntly's lunch box.

'What's that?'

'My roll, sir.'

Why hadn't he eaten it while he had had the chance?

'What's in it?'

'Marmite, sir.'

'This one. This isn't Marmite.'

The Inspector took the roll and opened it.

'This is honey.'

'Is it, sir?'

The grey eyes seemed greyer and colder.

'Honey is sugar. Chocolate, sweets and everything containing sugar has been banned! Did you not know? And being in possession of it is a criminal offence. Is it not?'

'Y-yes, sir.'

'As you knew – didn't you? Or have you been living with your head down a hole?'

'N-no, sir. I suppose I did know, sir,' Huntly stammered. 'Only – I thought the ban didn't apply to honey, sir. Because, I mean, well, honey's natural, sir. Bees make it.'

The cold, grey eyes flickered briefly.

'Then maybe it's time the bees learned to make something else,' the Inspector said, with grim sarcasm. 'Maybe it's time bees learned to make something a bit more socially responsible.'

'Like chips, sir!' a voice shouted.

The room erupted with laughter.

'Who said that!'

It was obvious who had said it. Ken Dacre was grinning his head off and everyone around him was gazing at him appreciatively.

'You! Wait for me outside!'

The smile vanished from Ken's face.

'It – it – was just a joke, sir.'

'Let's see if you're still laughing in fifteen minutes. Wait out there by the door and don't move.'

Ken was so shocked, he looked as though he couldn't

get up from his seat. But he tottered to the door and went to wait outside, quaking with terror. The fear was the punishment, as he later discovered. Nothing else happened to him. Just the fear of something happening was enough. That was something the Inspector understood very well.

The Inspector turned his attention back to Huntly's roll. He squashed it in his hand.

'Good For You,' he said, pointing to the Party Membership pin in his tie. 'Bad for you!' He dropped the flattened roll back into Huntly's lunch box. 'Try and learn the difference.'

'Yes, sir,' Huntly muttered, looking at his roll and thinking what a waste of good food.

There weren't many lunch boxes left. The inspection would soon be over. But then the Inspector stopped and turned back. What now?

He paused by Dave Cheng.

'You,' the Inspector said. 'That lunch box. Let me see it again.'

Dave was truly proud of his lunch box. He had made it himself in DT. He had cut all the parts out, and slotted them all together. It was a lunch box and a half.

'A lunch box? Wood?'

'Made it myself, sir.'

The Inspector examined the lunch box slowly, turning it over.

'You seem to be very good at woodwork.' Something clicked. A panel slid back. 'Too good if anything. Let me see. Oh yes. It even has a clever little compartment. And

what's this hidden away in here? Oh look – it's a chocolate bar!'

Silence.

Everyone watched. They saw the Inspector hold up the
chocolate bar. They saw Dave Cheng, the drops of sweat
forming on his forehead, the look of abject terror on his
face. You could almost hear the excuses creaking through
his brain, all unsatisfactory. There was no excuse, and
Dave knew it.

But he had to say something.

'It must be an old chocolate bar, sir. Must have been
there for weeks. I must have forgotten about it.'

'A greedy little guts of a boy like you!' the Inspector
chortled. 'Forget about a chocolate bar! Don't be so
pathetic! Don't make me laugh. You bought this illegally,
didn't you? On the black market.'

'No, I didn't! I didn't! No!'

The Inspector turned to the uniformed Troopers.

'Take him away.'

'No!' Dave cried. 'It's a mistake. Someone planted it
there. It wasn't me.'

It was the cry of children throughout the ages. But the
Inspector didn't even pause.

'Take him away,' he repeated. 'We've tried education
and it plainly didn't work. So we'd better try this boy with
some re-education!'

The Troopers held Dave by the arms and dragged him
away.

'No,' Dave pleaded. 'I didn't mean anything. No!
Smudger, Huntly, someone – help!'

But the Troopers were trained soldiers, and Smudger and Huntly were just children. There was nothing anyone could do, and Dave was taken away.

The Inspector paused in the doorway before he left.

'You see what happens, children,' he said, 'if you disobey the law. Let that be a warning to you, should you ever be tempted to do so yourselves. Crunchy apples to you, children.'

'Juicy oranges to you, sir,' they dutifully chorused.

'Have a banana,' the Inspector said. 'And don't forget to dispose of the skin thoughtfully afterwards. Good day.'

With that, he was gone.

And that was the last that anyone saw of Dave Cheng for a very long time.

Black Market

The children finished their lunches and went out into the playground. Some of them began playing football, but without their usual enthusiasm. Huntly dropped out of the game when he noticed Smudger waving him over from a corner of the playground.

'Listen, Huntly,' Smudger said, 'I've got something to tell . . .' He looked suspiciously up and down the playground. Creepy Frankie Crawley was hovering about within earshot again, so he dragged Huntly away towards the fence which separated the playground from the road, until he was sure that no one could overhear him. 'Walls have ears, you know, sure as trees have leaves,' he said. 'Spies are everywhere now, just waiting to sneak on people and turn them in.'

'What's up, Smudger?' Huntly asked. 'What's this about?'

'OK,' Smudger said, 'you and me and a few of us here in the school, well, we're willing to take a risk, right?'

'Maybe.'

'Some of them here,' Smudger continued, 'wouldn't say boo to a goose. They wouldn't even say boo to a goose's egg. But you and me and a few of us, we've sailed a bit close to the wind now and again. It's only human. But

we still do our class work and we hand in our homework. I mean, I'm not saying I'm a goody-two-shoes. But
I'm not a baddy-two-shoes either. I'm just a medium
kind of two-shoes, I reckon. We're just willing to take a
risk, as long as we've a good chance of getting away with
it. Right?'

'And what about it?' Huntly asked.

'Well,' Smudger said, 'we've never done anything
against the law, have we?'

'No. Don't think so.'

'At least not yet.'

Huntly looked at Smudger. Was he joking? No. His
face was serious.

'Huntly,' said Smudger, 'if a law was unfair and unjust
and downright wrong – would you be willing to break it?'

Huntly looked away. He seemed to hear his father's
voice in his head, telling him that the law was the law,
and you had to obey it. But he also remembered him saying that there was such a thing as a sense of natural
justice, of common sense. And that you should listen to
your own conscience, and fight against cruelty and bully-
ing and injustice. To not necessarily do as you were told,
but what was right.

'If the law's bad,' Smudger said, 'shouldn't we fight
against it and try and put it to rights?'

'If you mean the sweets and chocolate law – yes, maybe.
Why?'

'Because, I might know where we can get some chocolate.'

'What?'

'Listen. The word on the street is that just because the Good For You Party has banned chocolate and sweets, that doesn't mean it's the end of it. Remember what that Inspector said? To Dave Cheng? About the black market?'

'Yeah.'

'Well, the rumour is that some people hoarded chocolate up, for weeks before the ban. Loads and loads of it. There's warehouses all full up with chocolate that the government knows nothing about. And these black marketeers are selling it off. And I know where we might get some.'

Huntly gawped at him. 'You know? Where we can get chocolate? Real chocolate?'

'Yup,' Smudger said.

'Who told you?'

'Dave Cheng. On the way to school.'

Huntly gave Smudger a highly critical look.

'Oh, great,' he said. 'Dave Cheng told you where to buy chocolate, and now he's been taken away for re-education.'

'He didn't get caught *buying* it. He got caught because he was stupid enough to take it to school with him in his lunch box. And anyway, *he* got caught. Not the bloke selling it. He's still out there. And he'd probably like to sell some more. And we've got pocket money burning holes in our pockets, and nothing to spend it on. I know where he is and we can go there after school.'

Huntly mulled it over. 'Let's just think about this, Smudger. It's a big risk. You know what the penalty is for illegal possession of chocolate. We don't want to end up sharing a cell with Dave Cheng.'

'Why? Does he snore?'

'Ha ha. It's dangerous – big time. Let me think.'

Huntly thought. He sat on the low wall beneath the fence and watched the pigeons out in the street, squabbling over some crumbs. And it was the birds that made his mind up.

Because that was it, wasn't it? You could be a pigeon all your life, and you could wait for breadcrumbs and for people to throw bits of their sandwiches to you. Or you could try to be another kind of bird, like a swift or a swallow. A bird of the high air, that migrated to faraway places, flew great distances and soared almost as high as the stars. A bird that was free and adventurous and lived life to the full.

Or you could live in a world of chains, waiting for hand-outs, like a bird in a cage.

'Let's do it,' he said.

Smudger raised his hand and gave Huntly a high five.

'This afternoon?'

'OK. Straight after school.'

'Got any money?'

'Some. You?'

'A bit.'

They showed each other how much money they had.

'How much will it be?' Huntly asked. 'Black-market chocolate?'

'Expensive, probably. We'll soon find out.'

The whistle went for the end of break.

'Where do we have to go to?'

'Fallowfields. The trading estate. On the corner. Between the car auctioneers and the plant hire. Be a man there at four o'clock – sharp.'

When the afternoon bell went, they packed up and left immediately, hurrying out of the school gates. They walked briskly through the precinct, and then began to run across the park and the football fields, taking the short cut to Fallowfields Trading Estate. The Young Pioneers were already out in force, starting to practise their military drill.

'Look at them,' Smudger said. 'The goon squad.'

Frankie Crawley's voice could be heard in the distance.

'*Young Pioneers are smart and clean,*' he sang,

'*Pioneers are smart and clean,*' the troops responded.

'*We brush our teeth and eat our greens.*'

'*Brush our teeth and eat our greens.*'

Their voices faded away.

Yeah, Smudger thought, they brushed their teeth all right, they ate their greens, they were smart and clean. They were just about perfect.

The Fallowfields Trading Estate was a popular place at the weekends for cycling, skateboarding and playing street football. The wide roads were mostly empty then, free of cars and lorries. There was something fascinating too about the giant mobile cranes parked in their bays; about the huge, mysterious, stainless-steel drums in the factory yards. Possibly they were grain silos in the making or storage tanks for chemicals or fuels.

The plant-hire depot was down at the end of the first turning, a hundred yards along from where the Clean For You Laundry sent clouds of steam up into the air as it boiled up Troopers' uniforms and filled them full of starch. Around the corner from it was a great yard where weekly car auctions were held.

As the boys turned into the estate, they were disappointed to find the main street empty. There was no one on the corner who could have been a black marketeer. No stretch limousine with blacked-out windows. No Mafia-style Mr Big in a dark overcoat and mirrored sunglasses. There was only a nondescript workman in blue overalls tinkering with the engine of his tatty old van. He had the bonnet up and was wiping the oil dipstick on his sleeve as the two boys approached.

Smudger and Huntly strolled on past him and loitered a few yards away, pretending to have a game of football with an empty plastic bottle, hoping the workman would soon go away. No black marketeer would stop with him there. They might think he was working undercover for the government.

After a few minutes, the man closed the bonnet of his van and sauntered over to where the boys were playing.

'Having a kickabout, lads?' he asked.

'That's it,' Smudger said. It was pretty obvious what they were doing.

'Hungry work kicking a ball about,' the man continued.

'Makes you a mite peckish as I remember from my foot-balling days.'

Huntly and Smudger exchanged a look. They stopped kicking the bottle.

'Yes,' the man went on, 'very hungry work is kicking a ball – or even a bottle – about. Makes you long for some kind of high-energy food supplement. Something full of energy to give you a bit of a *Boost*! Something with a bit of *Fruit and Nut* in it. Makes you wonder how they cope in the rest of the *Galaxy*. Makes you wonder if they play football on *Mars*. I sometimes wonder if there's life up there in the *Milky Way*. But you'd have to be quite a *Smartie* pants to know the answer to that one.'

And having delivered this odd speech, the man returned to his van and stood by the back door, leaning on the roof, and staring up at the sky.

Huntly and Smudger looked questioningly at each other.

Was this him? The black marketeer? He certainly didn't look like one. Not for a moment. He seemed quite ordinary. You'd never have thought—

But yes! That was the whole idea. You'd never have suspected for a moment.

Huntly and Smudger walked over towards the van, just as casually as the man had a few seconds earlier. At their approach he wordlessly reached out, turned a handle and opened the rear doors, so that the two boys could see inside.

'Take a look, lads,' he said. 'Shop around. Whatever you fancy.'

They looked into the van. Then they gawped, with eyes like saucers and expressions of such surprise that the man in the overalls almost laughed.

There was everything in there! Every chocolate bar you could name or think of. The van was full up with Dairy Milk, Twix, Rolos, the lot.

'Quick as you can be, lads,' the man said, his eyes nervously scanning the horizon. 'Let's not dawdle, eh?'

Smudger pointed to a Mars bar.

'How much?' he asked.

The man told him the price.

'What!' Smudger exclaimed. 'But that's five times what they used to cost in the shops!'

'That was then, son,' the man said. 'This is now. If you can get a better deal, you take it. But those are my prices. You know the risks I'm taking here? You got any idea what'll happen if I get caught? You're a kid, you'll just get re-educated. Me, they'll throw away the key. I won't get out again.'

Smudger looked more closely at the man. Despite the grubby overalls, he was clearly no ordinary mechanic. His eyes were hard and uncompromising. There would be no haggling or negotiating with a man like this.

'OK,' Smudger said, 'I'll take it. And a couple of Dairy Milks.'

He handed over his money. The man took it and gave him the chocolate bars.

'And your mate,' he asked. 'He want anything?'

'I'll take a slab of that toffee,' Huntly said.

'Treacle sort?'

'That's it. And two Crunchies.'

The cost of it cleaned Huntly out. His last coin went and, even then, according to the man in the overalls, he didn't have quite enough.

'You're five pence short,' he said. 'But I'll let you have it anyway. Generosity's my middle name.' He laughed in a throaty cackle.

'OK, boys,' he said, and now he seemed rather nervous. 'Better scarper. Tell your mates about me if they're interested. Same time, same place tomorrow. Better hurry while stocks last. Meantime, not a word to your parents, eh? Nor your teachers. Nor—'

He didn't finish the sentence. His eyes were fixed on something else. On another vehicle which had just appeared at the entrance to the trading estate.

It was a large, cumbersome, ungainly vehicle, not one capable of high speeds, but one which seemed somehow unstoppable, one which would trundle on and on; one which – no matter how fast you ran away – would catch up with you in the end.

A Chocolate Detector Van.

'Troopers!' the man yelled. 'Scarper, kids! Get out of here! Run for your lives!'

Huntly and Smudger took to their heels. They sprinted away from the road and off up into the rough waste ground at the undeveloped part of the site.

They should have thought of it. It was so obvious. Dave Cheng would have spilled the beans by now. He would have been interrogated and told the lot. It was near suicide to have come here. But it was too late, too late.

Behind them the man in the overalls slammed the rear doors of his van shut and ran for the driver's seat. He got in and fired the engine. At first it didn't start. He fired it again.

The Detector Van was gathering speed. The sun glinted on its windscreen. The dish on its roof was slowly revolving, its alarm was *bleep, bleep, bleeping*. Crime and contraband had been detected.

Inside a contingent of Troopers pulled their helmet visors down over their faces, adjusted their body armour and unclipped their batons and Shriek Guns from their belts.

Huntly and Smudger reached the bottom of a grassy embankment which formed a kind of barricade between the trading estate and the old town. Once, a railway line had run along the top of it, but the track had been torn up and a tarmac cycle track put in its place. They ran on and up, through the nettles and brambles. Thorns ripped their skin, but they felt nothing as they sprinted on.

The Troopers were almost upon the man now. The Detector Van was only a few yards away. Desperately, the bootlegger fired the engine up once more and it finally burst into life. His foot hit the accelerator, he released the hand brake and the van tore away.

Huntly and Smudger heard the sound of squealing tyres. They turned to see the van leaving black tyre streaks on the roadway and the smoke of burning rubber.

'He's all right,' Smudger said. 'He's faster than the Troopers. He'll get away.'

But as the van skidded round the corner, it had to slam on its brakes to avoid a cyclist who had appeared from one of the factory driveways. The sudden stop made the improperly secured rear doors burst open and the contents of the van flew out into the road.

'Look!' Huntly gasped. 'The chocolate!'

It spilled out into the path of the oncoming Detector Van. All that lovely contraband. The black-market chocolate and toffee and sweets, scattered all over the road as the van raced away.

The great thick wheels of the Chocolate Detector Van ground on. They rolled over the chocolate bars, squashing and flattening them, reducing them to pulp.

The driver of the Detector Van stopped and reversed. The Troopers had obviously given up hope of catching the black marketeer, but at least they could destroy his business. Back and forth it went, squashing every last bar of chocolate until all that remained was an inedible, repulsive slush of confectionery and wrappers – a meal which would appeal to nobody but a vulture or a carrion crow. And even then not a fussy one.

This act of wanton destruction seemed to bring home to Huntly and Smudger just what was really happening. The might of those grinding wheels was like the strength and power of the government. This was what could happen to you if you stood up against the Good For You Party. You too could be squashed and flattened under its wheels and left for pulp in the road.

'Come on, Smudge, let's get out of sight. Still got your chocolate?'

Smudger felt in his pocket, afraid he might have lost it as he ran. But it was still there.

'Got it,' he said.

'Good,' Huntly said. 'I know somewhere safe.'

They scrambled down the other side of the embankment and Huntly led the way to the old railway tunnel. It was long and unlit, with a darkness at its core which would dissolve to faint light, once your eyes had become accustomed to it. It was eerie and you could frighten yourself with your own imaginings in there. But today Huntly was beyond scaring himself. He'd been scared enough already. He felt he needed something to restore him. Something sweet.

The two boys sat down on some old railway sleepers and divided the Mars bar and toffee between them.

'Think the Troopers'll come after us?' Smudger said.

Huntly shook his head. 'No. Not now. They'll go after him, if anyone.'

'They'll have his number, I suppose,' Smudger said.

'Guess so. But they'll probably be false plates.'

'Yeah. Good toffee this.'

'Mmm. Good chocolate too.'

They sat and chewed and savoured the tastes of sweetness. Water dripped in places from the roof of the tunnel, soaking down from the earth above. Smudger pointed to a small kind of growth on the ceiling of the tunnel.

'Look,' he said. 'Stalactite starting up there.'

'Yeah,' Huntly said. 'I see it.'

'Still be there in a hundred years,' Smudger mused.

'Be bigger, longer.'

'A bit,' Smudger nodded. 'Takes years and years for stalactites to grow. It's the salts and minerals in the water. Every drop leaves a little bit behind and it builds up over the centuries.'

'I wonder what the world'll be like then,' Huntly said. 'There'll be children who'll never even have seen a chocolate bar, let alone know what one tastes like.'

'We're the last,' Smudger said sadly. 'The last ones who'll ever know what real chocolate was.'

'We ought to leave a message,' Huntly said. 'For the people to come.'

'Yes,' Smudger said, chewing thoughtfully. 'You're right. Let's do it now.'

They each picked up a sharp, pointed stone from the floor of the tunnel. They had once been used as ballast for the old railway tracks. They went over to where the wall curved up and stood wondering what to write.

Others had been there before them. Names and hearts and who loved who and who hated who and who was a what, were etched into the tunnel wall, along with dates and ages, some from long ago. The wall was coated with the ancient soot of old steam trains.

Smudger raised the stone in his hand and began to write into the soot.

Smudger and Huntly were here, he wrote, *in times of trouble*.

Huntly paused then scratched carefully into the soot and the wall itself.

We were soldiers in the great chocolate wars and fought so

*that children could be free. Think of us. And if one day choc-
olate should return, eat a bar in our memory.*

'That OK?' he asked Smudger.

'That'll do it,' Smudger said.

They admired their handiwork.

'You know,' said Huntly, 'some kid in the future might
stand right here and see what we've written and say,
"Chocolate? What's *that*?"'

It would be the greatest horror of all, that chocolate
should be completely forgotten.

Maybe they should leave a bit of chocolate too. Huntly
suggested it, Smudger agreed. It was a sacrifice, but one
worth making. They wrapped one of the black-market
chocolate bars up in a plastic bag and hid it behind a loose
brick in the tunnel wall.

'Well then,' Smudger said. 'That's it now. We won't get
any more chocolate anywhere. I don't suppose that man
with the van will be back in a hurry. And I don't know of
any other black marketeers. Chocolate really is finished
for us now. This really is the end.'

They headed out of the tunnel, to go home – and start
their homework.

Chocco-Sub

'What can I do for you, Young Pioneer?'

The bakery was full of heat and moisture and the warm smell of fresh bread. Smudger's dad, Ron Moore, was standing dressed in his baker's whites, wiping his hands on his apron. Usually Smudger's mum, Trisha, helped him out with the shop, attending to the customers while he got on with the baking. But this afternoon she had taken Kylie to her swimming lesson, and Ron was on his own.

'I'd like to order a cake.'

Ron looked at the girl. He was sure he knew her. She was in Smudger's class, wasn't she? Mable something. No, Myrtle. Myrtle Perfect, that was it. No – Perkins. Yes. Myrtle Perkins. She was big friends with that other little creep, the twerp. What was his name? Crawley. Frankie Crawley. Known to his friends – of whom there were few, if any – as Frankie. Known to everyone else as 'Creepy' Crawley.

Ron had seen the pin in her lapel: YP. It figured. She was in the junior division of the Party. A right little goody-two-shoes this one then.

'A cake, Young Pioneer?' Ron said. 'Well, that presents a bit of a problem.'

'We want to order a cake for our division of the Young Pioneers – to celebrate our first twelve months of glorious service.'

Ron took a pamphlet out from under the counter. It was titled 'Guidelines For Bakers.'

'I'm afraid, Young Pioneer,' he explained, 'that I don't have much to make cakes with. I'll just consult the list of permitted ingredients here. Yes. Right. You can have Birthday Carrot Cake, Birthday Fruit and Nut – which may contain nuts – or the Sugar-Free, Fat-Free Sponge. And that's the selection. Take your pick.'

'We'll order the sponge, please,' Myrtle said. 'With layers of filling and icing on top.'

Ron gave her a withering look.

'Layered and iced with *what*, exactly?' he asked. 'Cement? I don't have any icing sugar, remember. It's been banned.' 'Thanks to your lot!' Ron almost added, but wisely refrained from doing so.

Myrtle reached into her school bag, and took out a large plastic tub with a handle on it.

'We'd like it filled and iced with this please, Citizen Baker. The delicious, healthy alternative to sugar icing. One litre of mouth-watering, Good For You Chocco-Sub Icing.'

Ron looked wryly at the tub.

'It's an honour to be chosen, Citizen, to make a cake for the Young Pioneers. When do you need it by?'

'The end of the week will be fine.'

Myrtle headed for the door.

'Crunchy apples to you, Citizen Baker.'

'Juicy oranges to *you*, Young Pioneer.'

'Have a banana.'

And she was gone.

Ron looked with disgust at the Chocco-Sub. He prised back the lid and peered at the goo.

'Smells disgusting,' he said. 'Looks disgusting.' He put a finger into the murky mixture and tasted it. 'And it flipping well tastes disgusting too. So no surprises there.'

Frankie Crawley sat patiently waiting to be noticed. The interview room was stark and bare. A bored Chocolate Trooper stood by the door, but he was really there more for decoration than protection, a symbol of status.

The Chocolate Police Headquarters was all but impregnable. To even get past the front door was a major achievement, never mind penetrating the warren of rooms and corridors, floors and basements which contained the offices of administration, and more ominously, of interrogation. Dave Cheng was probably in there somewhere – getting his views on life altered and his attitudes to illegal chocolate straightened out.

The Headquarters of the Chocolate Police wasn't a place you wanted to break into. It was a place you wanted to get out of, as soon as possible. Unless you were Frankie Crawley, with important and pertinent matters to discuss. Unless you were an informer.

A dog fetches a ball; an informer brings information. And they both sit looking at their masters with the same kind of expression on their faces, hoping for approval and possibly some reward.

The man with the cold grey eyes looked up from the file he had been reading.

'Well, Young Pioneer? What do you have?'

Frankie's small pink tongue came out of his mouth to moisten his dry lips. It looked like a mouse peeking out of a hole in a skirting board.

'Suspects,' he said. 'Two boys in my class. I think they've been buying black-market chocolate.'

'Hmm. Do you now?'

'They've been acting suspiciously for a long time. And frankly, they've never had the right attitude, ever, not towards the Party or its ideals. Not from the very start.'

'Is that a fact, Young Pioneer?'

The Inspector exchanged a look with the Trooper by the door. It was hard to know what to make of it. Was it a look of mockery?

Frankie ploughed on.

'I think they should go on the list of suspects to be kept under surveillance,' he said. 'They're always sniggering and sneering whenever they see the Young Pioneers out on manoeuvres. And they never do their good deeds as far as I know, and they won't sing the Party song during assembly. I know, because I stand close to them. They just move their lips but no words come out. Or if they do sing, it's not what they're supposed to. Instead of singing "The Good For You Party is the party for me," they sing "The Good For You Party can stick its head down the lavatory."'

A faint flicker crossed the Inspector's face.

'And then this morning, while they were playing

football during break, I went back into class and looked through their belongings. I found these.'

Frankie took out two chocolate-bar wrappers and placed them down on the desk. The Inspector prodded them with a pencil.

'They might have kept these since before the deadline.'

'They might,' Frankie agreed, 'but I don't think so. I found one of these in Hunter's desk and the other in a pocket of Moore's sports bag. That was this morning. I also searched their belongings yesterday. And there were no wrappers there then. So if they didn't have the chocolate on Tuesday, but they did on Wednesday, where did they get it from?'

The Inspector turned to the Trooper.

'That would tie in, wouldn't it?' he asked.

'Yes, sir,' the Trooper nodded. 'Black marketeer, on the trading estate. He managed to get away but two boys were seen running from the scene. They must have been buying chocolate from him.'

The Inspector turned back to Frankie.

'Very well, Young Pioneer,' he nodded. 'Good work. Thank you for this information.'

'Will I get points, sir?' Frankie asked.

'Oh, lots of them,' the Inspector laconically replied. 'More points than a Pioneer would know what to do with.'

There it was, that tone of sarcasm again.

'Are you going to arrest them, sir?' Frankie asked, sounding almost hopeful. 'Put them into custody and interrogate them?'

'I don't think so, Young Pioneer. Not yet. I don't think they'll have anything useful to give us. We'll see what they do. See what happens. Maybe they'll stop it at that and see the error of their ways. Or maybe . . . Well, we'll see. We'll watch, and wait.'

'Very well, sir. I'll keep them under surveillance.'

'You do that.'

Frankie saw that it was time for him to go. He got to his feet.

'Oh, by the way, sir,' he said, pausing in the doorway. 'It's the Young Pioneers' birthday celebrations on Friday night. Will we have the honour of your company, sir?'

The Inspector didn't even bother to look in his diary.

'Sorry, Young Pioneer. I would love to be there, but unfortunately I have a prior appointment. I'll send my good wishes.'

Frankie frowned. He had assured his fellow Pioneers that as a personal friend of his the Inspector would be sure to be there, to cut the first slice of cake.

'We're having a cake baked specially, sir, for the occasion,' he persisted. 'A healthy, Good For You Sponge with Chocco-Sub.'

'Sounds delicious. I hope you all enjoy it,' the Inspector said.

He reopened the file on his desk and took out some papers. The interview was over.

Frankie was escorted to the nearest exit. He set off for the Young Pioneers' hut. He should have felt pleased with himself. He knew he had done good service for the Party and it would one day be recognized and rewarded. But he felt vaguely as if he had been somehow short changed. Frankie felt – unappreciated.

'What's that, Dad?' Smudger asked.

'What have you been up to?' Ron Moore responded – though he had often told Smudger that it was bad manners to answer a question with another question. But that was parents. They made rules for children which didn't seem to apply to themselves.

'You making a cake?'

'Full marks for observation.'

'Come on, Dad. Who's it for? Is it for us?'

Smudger loved the bakery. It always smelled nice in there. Even on the coldest, most wintery day it was warm and hopeful. There was something about the smell of rising dough and baking bread that made you feel better about today and more optimistic for tomorrow.

'What is it? It's a fat-free, sugar-free, taste-free sponge if you want to know. To be covered with delicious Chocco-Sub icing for the Young Pioneers' tea party on Friday night. If you don't like the expression Young Pioneers, Mad Hatters would probably do just as well.'

'Why are you baking it now if they don't want it till Friday?'

'Cakes taste better when they've been left a day or two. Besides, I've got the time to do it now. Friday, I might be busy.'

The bell rang out in the shop.

'Customer, Smudger. I'll go and get it. Keep an eye on that oven.'

Ron Moore went out to serve. A second, then a third customer came in. Customers were like buses. You didn't get one for ages, then they all turned up at once.

Smudger glanced around the bakery.

'Birthday cake, eh?' he thought. 'For the Young Pioneers. I'll have to see about that.'

He looked up to the shelf on the wall opposite the oven. There was a cabinet with a red cross on the front and the words First Aid stencilled on it in unmistakable red letters.

A bakery could be a hazardous place. Smudger's dad occasionally got minor cuts and burns. Sometimes he was too busy to be careful.

Smudger opened the door of the first-aid cabinet. It was well equipped with sprays and bandages, ointments, creams and plasters. You name it, it was there.

But not what he was looking for.

Smudger moved a few tins and aerosols aside.

Where was it now? He was sure he'd seen it. No one ever used it, but it was there, he was positive. He had asked his dad about it once.

'What's syrup of figs, Dad? Is that something you use in baking?'

'Certainly not! It's something you use when you have trouble going to the toilet. And even then you take only a tiny spoonful. Or you won't just be going to the toilet the once, you'll be spending your holidays in there.'

Syrup of figs – where was it?

Ah, there it was. Hidden behind a roll of crêpe bandage. A small, dark-brown bottle, with a black screw top.

Quickly, Smudger took the bottle over to the work-bench where the large carton of Chocco-Sub waited, to be used as icing and filling for the Young Pioneers' cake.

Smudger prised the lid from the Chocco-Sub, unscrewed the top from the syrup of figs bottle and emptied its entire contents into the mixture. That should make the celebrations go with a bang all right.

He grabbed a wooden spoon and stirred until the Chocco-Sub and the syrup of figs were a smooth, creamy paste. He washed the spoon, filled the syrup of figs bottle with water from the tap, replaced the cap and returned the bottle to the first-aid cabinet.

Just in time.

'What are you up to?!'

His dad was back.

'Up to, Dad? Me?'

'What are you doing in the first-aid cupboard?'

'Nothing, Dad. Just looking for a plaster.'

'Have you been mucking about, Smudger? I've told you a hundred times how dangerous it is in here.'

'No, Dad. I haven't touched anything. It's just a little paper cut. On my finger. From school. You can hardly see it. Just stings a bit, that's all.'

For the sake of appearances Smudger put a small Elasto-plast on the invisible paper cut. His dad seemed satisfied.

'Right then. I'd better take this cake out of the oven, let it cool down and start icing it.'

'Yes, Dad.'

'Wouldn't want the Young Pioneers going without their cake.'

'No, Dad, definitely not, Dad, no.'

'Don't want to disappoint the Young Pioneers, do we?'

'No, Dad, certainly not.'

'Why are you agreeing with everything I say, Smudger? Are you sure you're not up to something?'

'Me, Dad? Oh no, Dad.'

'Then go home and do your homework.'

'Yes, Dad. Right away.'

Smudger left. His dad took the cake out of the oven and set it on a tray to cool.

He's up to something, that boy, Ron Moore thought to himself. But he soon forgot about it and put it out of his mind. When the cake was cool, he got ready to ice it. He opened the tub of Chocco-Sub. He tried a taste. It was even more disgusting than ever.

Still. Not his business. Give the customers what they want. That way they can't complain. If they want Chocco-Sub, let 'em have Chocco-Sub.

Ron reached for a long, smooth palette knife, and began to ice the cake.

Huntly and Smudger went looking for the man again, down at the trading estate. They knew that it was dangerous, but they went just the same, drawn like iron to a magnet, by strong but invisible forces – in their case, the attraction was the desire for something sweet.

They knew in their hearts the bootlegger wouldn't be there, but several times they walked home from school, taking the long detour around by the trading estate just the same. But all that remained of the incident were the streaks of tyre rubber on the road. And here and there traces of flattened chocolate, as if steam-rollered into the tarmac.

'He can't be the only one selling black-market chocolate,' Smudger said. 'There must be others who kept a bit back.'

But how could they find them? And how could they afford their outrageous prices when the cost of a black-market chocolate bar was bound to go up and up. Each time one was eaten, there was one less left to sell. Two schoolboys with only a few pounds in their pockets had no hope of competing with adult customers, with real money to spend.

They felt that all that remained for them were memories. And one day soon even they would fade. They would have to resign themselves to a drab, empty, sugarless life. It was the end of chocolate as they had known it.

They were right.

And they were wrong.

It was Friday afternoon – Golden Time – and you could do what you liked, as long as you did it quietly. Miss Ross sat at the front of the class marking books as everyone got on with what they wanted to do – reading, drawing, writing, thinking, daydreaming and imagining what it would be like to be let loose in a sweet shop.

Frankie Crawley and Myrtle Perkins sat thinking of the Young Pioneers' celebrations arranged for that evening at the grandly titled Young Pioneers Headquarters (formerly the scout hut).

It was Smudger's turn at the computer. He sat thinking about the cake he had sabotaged with syrup of figs. He wondered if it would have the desired effect. He was a little worried that his dad might get into trouble. But no. They'd all just blame the Chocco-Sub. It was a new and unknown quantity after all.

He already knew that searching the Internet for anything to do with chocolate was useless. Either the system crashed or a message came up reading: 'Website unavailable.'

For all he knew, the government monitoring agencies tried to send you a cookie too, the instant you logged on with your illicit query – a nice little parcel of information which would write itself to your hard drive and tell everyone where you had been browsing. Then they would track down your IP address. Next thing, courtesy of your Internet Provider, they'd be hammering at the door.

Instead he found an old encyclopedia disk in amongst the software box and inserted it into the DVD slot. He spooled through the index, highlighted the word 'chocolate' and double-clicked to see what would come up. An entry appeared on the screen.

Chocolate – a preparation made from the fruit of the cacao tree, which is used both as a flavouring and as an ingredient of beverages and in various kinds of confectionery. Chocolate was brought to Europe by the Spaniards who learned to use it from the Aztecs at the time of the invasion by the Spanish in 1519. It was introduced into England in about 1657.

Smudger grimaced. It was all very interesting, but it didn't tell him what he wanted to know.

He moved the cursor to *Related Topics* and clicked on *Chocolate, Manufacture of*. The screen refreshed, a picture and some text appeared. That was all very interesting too, but it still wasn't what he needed.

He gave up on chocolate and returned to the main index. He clicked on 'Find' and into the find box typed the word 'Prohibition'. He hoped that he had spelled it correctly. Then he doubled-clicked the mouse button again.

The computer whirred. After a second, some more text appeared on the screen.

Prohibition, it read, *a legal ban in the manufacture and sale of intoxicating liquor in America, at a time when drink was regarded as a social evil. The Prohibition era began at midnight on January 16th, 1920. But Prohibition always represented more of an ideal than a reality. Opportunities for disregarding the law through smuggling, distilling, fermenting and brewing alcohol were many. It generated a wave of criminal activity and gave rise to the so called 'Bootlegger', one who sold or manufactured liquor illegally. Following a major shift in public opinion, the Prohibition laws were repealed in 1933.*

Smudger looked thoughtfully at the screen. He used the cursor to highlight the word 'Bootleg', double clicked on the left-hand mouse button and waited to see what would come up.

The screen refreshed once more and a brief paragraph appeared.

Bootlegging, it said. *A term applied to the practice of illegally transporting or selling intoxicating liquors. Such liquor is* known as 'bootleg' and the seller of it as a 'bootlegger'. The term probably came into use during the America Civil War when illegal liquor peddlers hid bottled whisky in the legs of their cowhide boots.

Interesting, Smudger thought. Very interesting. You could learn a lot from an encyclopedia. It could give you ideas, a thing like that.

Miss Ross came over to see what he was doing. She said that she was sorry but he wasn't really supposed to use the old CD encyclopedia. She had forgotten but it should have been removed from the box and handed in.

She told him that anything he wanted to know could be found on the Good For You Party Educational Website, which, as it said, 'Gave children everywhere the correct version of the truth.'

Smudger went over the words in his mind.

The correct version of the truth.

But surely there could only be one version of the truth – the truth itself? How could there be more than one? All other versions would be half-truths and lies. If the Good For You Party could only claim to be a *version* of the truth, then surely it wasn't the truth at all?

'What were you trying to find in that encyclopedia?' Huntly asked, as he and Smudger made their way home that Friday night. A feeling of freedom was in the air. A sense of the weekend ahead.

Smudger made sure they couldn't be overheard.

'I was trying to find a recipe,' he said.

'For what?'

'What do you think? For chocolate, of course. What else?'

'Did you find one?'

'No. But I found out about bootleggers.'

'Who-leggers?'

Smudger explained what he had learned.

'They also had these clubs and places,' he explained. 'Called Speakeasies, where you could go to relax and drink beer and whisky – and no questions asked. Yeah, it's a pity we don't have a recipe. We could make a little bit of chocolate for ourselves. That way we'd know it was safe and good quality too.'

'Maybe,' Huntly said. But aren't you forgetting something – we've got nothing to make it with. So even if we had a recipe, what use would it be? We've no sugar, no cocoa, nothing. We couldn't even make a start.'

'No, I guess not,' Smudger sighed.

'Anyway,' Huntly continued, 'we're just kids. How could we be bootleggers? You need to be, I don't know, organized – some kind of criminal mastermind or something.'

'I don't suppose there's any way we could get the ingredients, is there?' Smudger pondered.

'Where from, Smudger? Be reasonable. You can't just go and pick up a few bags of sugar and some tins of cocoa butter or whatever it is you need. It's contraband now. We'd never get stuff like that. It's all been confiscated and destroyed.'

'Isn't there *anywhere* we could get hold of the makings?'

'No,' Huntly said. 'Believe me. Just don't even think

about it, Smudger. Put it out of your mind. You don't want to end up like Dave Cheng, do you? In re-education somewhere, having your brains washed, with someone pushing brain-floss through both your ears. There's not a hope. Not an ice cream's hope in a furnace of us getting hold of any sugar or anything like that.'

Smudger looked despondent. He went to take a kick at a stone on the pavement. But he never got that far. He froze in his tracks.

'What's up, Smudge?' Huntly stared at him. 'You look like you've had a fit.'

'Oh it's not a fit,' Smudger grinned. 'It's something a whole lot better than that. I've had an idea.'

'What idea? Where are we going?'

'To see an old friend,' Smudger said. 'That's where. Come on.'

A Bag of Sugar, a Piece of Cake

I t was a beautiful cake. But that was Ron Moore for you. He couldn't make a bad one. Even when it was only a sugar-free, fat-free sponge, the artist and the craftsman in him took over, and he had to do the best he could.

Myrtle carried it proudly into the Young Pioneers' meeting room and laid it down upon the table.

Ron had baked the cake in the shape of a Young Pioneers' badge, and had used some of the Chocco-Sub icing and some cake mixture to make two little Pioneers – one boy, one girl – and he had placed them together on the top of the cake, where they stood upright and proud. And next to them, Ron had piped the words 'Happy Birthday, Young Pioneers'.

The cake was so impressive that when Myrtle brought it in she received a spontaneous round of applause. She almost felt as if she had baked it herself and that the credit and appreciation were her own. In fact, if that was what any of the Pioneers wished to think, she was prepared to let them.

'Hey, Myrtle, the cake looks cool.'

'Pretty good, Myrtle. You did all right there.'

Frankie Crawley looked on, feeling a mite jealous. He

was the one who usually got the high marks and the distinctions and all the praise.

'It only goes to show,' Myrtle said, 'that we don't need disgusting sugar and revolting chocolate and suchlike to enjoy ourselves. Here we have health, taste and goodness all rolled together – or rather baked together – into one. And it's all thanks to delicious Chocco-Sub. So fill your glasses up to the brim, and let's all sing the Young Pioneers' song.'

The Pioneers filled their glasses with prune juice and loudly sang the Young Pioneers' Anthem, culminating in a verse specially written for the occasion.

'We're one year old today,
One year old today.
We are the happy Pioneers
Our cheers are ringing in your ears
Our good deeds are our souvenirs
Hurray, hurray, hurray!'

They drank down their prune juice. Some Pioneers were so excited by the occasion that they dashed their paper cups into the fireplace. They all watched hungrily as Myrtle took a knife and cut the cake up into slices and laid them on plates. No one was allowed to start eating until everyone had a plate with a slice of cake upon it.

'Tuck in then, you Pioneers!' Myrtle instructed. 'Let's show the world that we know how to enjoy ourselves – in the good, clean, healthy way!'

And to lead them in their quest to show the world how to enjoy itself in the good, clean, healthy way, Myrtle bit into her cake.

There was something wrong. Myrtle couldn't really say she liked the taste. It wasn't what she had expected. But Chocco-Sub was approved by the Party, after all. You could hardly say you disliked it.

'Mmm!' Myrtle said. 'Delicious – don't you think, Young Pioneers?'

There were lukewarm murmurs of agreement.

'It's very filling.'

'Very filling. Don't think I could manage a second helping.'

'I don't even know if I'll be able to finish this one.'

Frankie's brow furrowed. He glared at the Young Pioneer who had said that.

'I, for one, think that it would be extremely poor manners for us not to finish our slices. In fact, I vote for second helpings all round! Anyone who doesn't want second helpings isn't a true Pioneer and a genuine Party member.'

The cake was cut again, and as luck would have it, there was just enough left for second helpings for everyone.

Maybe the cake didn't taste quite so awful the second time round. Perhaps your taste buds got used to it – or had possibly even been permanently killed off by the first helping.

Myrtle got her second slice down and took a gulp of prune juice.

'All right,' Frankie Crawley announced, 'if we've finished our cake and prune juice, perhaps we can all sit down now for a fun question-and-answer session on general knowledge of the Young Pioneer Rule Book.'

And then the rumbling started. It seemed to be coming from someone's stomach – Myrtle's. Then Frankie realized it was coming from his stomach, and then from everybody else's stomach too.

And then the stampede started.

It began politely enough.

'Excuse me a moment, if you would,' Myrtle chirped. 'I must just visit the . . . the little girls' room. Excuse me.'

She left at a dignified pace, which soon turned into a rapid trot, which turned into a frantic dash. The rest of the Young Pioneers were right behind her, the survival instinct having taken over all other considerations.

They bolted down the corridor, like a herd of zebras fleeing from a hungry lion. There was a bottleneck as they hurled themselves at the toilet doors and tried to get in three, four, or even five at a time.

'Get out of my way!'

'I'm in here!'

'Let go of that door!'

'You can't climb over the door! This one's being used!'

'Oh, help!'

'Oh, my stomach!'

'Oh, my new trousers!'

'Oh, what's my mum going to say!'

'Oh, no!'

'Oh, what a racket!'

'Oh, what a stink, you mean!'

'There's no loo roll left in here! Quick, someone lend me a newspaper!'

It is probably best now to draw what is often described

as a veil over the proceedings. There are certain things in life about which it is neither polite nor necessary to go into too much detail. Some things are better left to the imagination. So let those who would imagine the worst, imagine it. And let those who would prefer not to linger on the subject move on to other things.

Nobody ever suspected that the Chocco-Sub had been adulterated by Smudger Moore with syrup of figs or anything else. It was simply assumed that this was the effect which Chocco-Sub had on people, and that it was best taken, in future, only rarely, and in very, very small doses.

Mrs Bubby was pleased to see them. She was pleased to see anyone. She liked people in general and children in particular and she'd hadn't been seeing too much of either since the ban had come into force. Her shop was more than a business to her. It was her social life, gossip column, and her news and information centre. It was what kept her going.

But she didn't have much to sell now, except for newspapers and comics and some Healthy For You Tasty Snacks, along with milk and some other essentials. Her shop was busy for a while first thing in the morning, with people on their way to work. But once the rush to buy a morning paper was over, she could go for hours without seeing a soul. She would sit behind the counter, slowly reading her way through the papers and the glossy magazines. She always turned the pages carefully so as not to crease them. That way she could return the magazine to its shelf and sell it as unread.

Time moved slowly for her until early afternoon when the first batch of the local newspaper would arrive. A trickle of people would come in to buy copies, mostly for the job ads or the lonely hearts or the cars for sale.

So Mrs Bubby was agreeably surprised to hear the shop bell ringing, and see Smudger and Huntly come sauntering in.

'Hello, boys,' she said. 'I wasn't expecting to see you today. I don't think I've anything to sell you. Unless you've come in for a Healthy Snack, of course, though I shouldn't think you have.'

Smudger made a face and agreed that this wasn't the reason for their visit.

'I might try the cat with one later,' Mrs Bubby said. 'He seems to like them. Not to eat so much as to play with. What can I do for you two, then?'

There was an uncomfortable silence. Smudger and Huntly fidgeted, wanting to get straight to the point, but not quite sure how to set off in that direction.

'It's a bit sort of tricky, really, Mrs Bubby,' Huntly said finally. 'And like, me and Smudger here wouldn't want to sort of, well, get anyone into any trouble or anything like that.'

'No,' Smudger agreed. 'So say no if you want to. Don't think twice.'

'About what?' Mrs Bubby asked. 'I've not even had a chance to think once about it yet. You'd better tell me what it is.'

'Well,' Huntly continued, 'the thing is, Mrs Bubby, we came in to see you a while back – on the day of the chocolate ban – and while we were in your storeroom, me and Smudger – or rather Smudger on his own, as I never noticed it at all to be honest—'

'Noticed what?' Mrs Bubby said.

'Well, what Smudger noticed – or so he thinks – was that in your storeroom at the back you had loads of tins and bags all stacked up on the shelves.'

'Quite possibly,' Mrs Bubby said. 'It used to be a grocer's here. One of those mini-supermarkets it was, before I took over and turned it into a newsagent. There was loads of stuff left behind. I chucked out all the perishables, but I kept the rest – the tinned and bagged items. You never know when things might come in handy. The Troopers never looked in there, come to think of it, when they were clearing everything out. I don't think some of those Troopers are all that bright. A lot of them have short planks or thick bricks where their brains ought to be.'

'Well, that's just it, Mrs B,' Huntly said. 'We think that the time may have arrived for that stuff in your old storeroom to become very handy indeed. Smudger says he thinks you've got a couple of interesting items in there that could be of great use and value.'

'Oh?' she said. 'And what items are those? I don't imagine you're thinking of the tinned sardines? Or the mushy peas?'

'No. Tinned cocoa,' Smudger said. 'And bags of sugar. And some cases of what I think might have been cocoa butter.'

Mrs Bubby looked at him as though she was sure he had made a mistake. But there was only one way to find out.

So she put the Closed sign up in the front door and led the way to the stockroom.

It was just as Smudger had remembered. On the bottom shelves of the storage units were brown cardboard boxes marked *Best Quality Cocoa, 6 Doz.*

The boys dragged the boxes out so that they could count them. There were twelve cardboard boxes visible, but when these were moved it transpired that there were another twelve behind them.

Smudger asked for a pen and a piece of paper, but Mrs Bubby was confident that they could do the sum in their heads.

'Each box has got six-dozen packets in it, right. So that's six twelves or seventy-two packets in each box. There's two dozen boxes – or twenty-four boxes altogether—'

Mrs Bubby got a pen after all and did the calculation on one of the cardboard boxes.

'I make that one thousand seven hundred and twenty-eight packets of cocoa powder!'

Smudger let out a long, low whistle. He thought at first that Mrs Bubby had got her sums wrong. But they checked and double-checked, and it was right enough – seventeen hundred and twenty-eight packets of cocoa. All worth their weight in gold.

'Mrs Bubby,' Huntly said, 'have you any idea what you've got here? Have you any idea what this would fetch on the black market?'

'No,' Mrs Bubby said, 'I haven't. But I've a good idea what it would fetch me if the Chocolate Police ever found it – about ten years inside. A good long stretch. By the time I got out again I'd be so wrinkled I'd need ironing.'

'But listen, Mrs Bubby,' Smudger said, 'what I don't understand is how they never found it. OK, you say the Troopers didn't look in here – but how come they didn't find the cocoa with the detectors? Surely they'd have worked even through the wall?'

'Well,' Mrs Bubby said thoughtfully, 'I guess the rumours must be true. I've heard that the Chocolate Detectors can only work on made-up chocolate and sweets. But not on the ingredients. It's only when you start mixing them up into chocolate that it shows on the monitor when the vans come round. It's a bit like gunpowder. You don't get an explosion until you put everything together.'

Smudger and Huntly looked at each other. This was invaluable information, and, if true, it considerably reduced the risk of what they had in mind.

'How come you've got cocoa butter, Mrs Bubby?' Huntly asked, picking up a heavy tin of the stuff. The manufacturer's name seemed Spanish and the tins had come from South America.

'Came with the shop,' she said. 'I think they supplied bakers and things.'

'So how about the sugar now, Mrs Bubby?' Smudger said. 'Can we look at that and see how much there is?'

The sugar was on the next shelf up. The cartons were heavier and harder to move than the cocoa. But between them they managed to get them all down on to the floor.

'Careful, don't drop them,' Smudger said. 'We don't

want them bursting and the packets splitting open. We can't afford to lose a grain.'

The boxes contained packets of both light brown and heavy brown sugar, the kind you would use in cooking for making flapjacks or maybe chocolate cakes.

The sugar was packed in quantities of forty packets to a box.

'There's got to be eight hundred packets here at least,' Huntly said.

Smudger nodded. He made it about the same. But Mrs Bubby was looking rather concerned.

'Maybe we ought to open one of these packets up,' she said, 'and take a look at the sugar. You see, I've been troubled by mice in the stockroom here from time to time. I'd hate to think they'd been at it.'

The boys examined the boxes. There didn't seem to be any signs of them having been gnawed into by mice, but Mrs Bubby took a knife, slit one or two boxes open, and checked the packets of sugar.

'Seem OK to me,' Smudger said. 'No sign of droppings or anything.' He hesitated. 'Maybe,' he said, 'just to be on the even safer than safe side, we should – have a little taste?'

Mrs Bubby gave him a smile. 'I can't see the harm in that, Smudger.'

Smudger carefully opened one of the packets of soft, brown sugar.

'Excuse fingers,' he said, and stuck his forefinger deep into the sugar bag. He put his finger into his mouth and licked the sugar off.

'Tastes all right to me, Mrs Bubby. What do you think?'

'Let Huntly have a taste next,' Mrs Bubby said with a smile – for she could see the vaguely anxious look in Huntly's eyes, the kind of look you have when you're worried that all the good things in the bag will be gone by the time it gets round to you, and that you'll miss out on all the special offers.

So the bag of sugar was passed to Huntly and he had a taste. Then Mrs Bubby had a taste, and they all agreed that it was very fine sugar, in fact it was maybe the best they had ever tasted. Then they passed the bag around again and went on tasting it until finally there was only one dab and lick left each.

'Mmm,' Smudger said. 'Now that was good sugar.'

'I agree on that,' Huntly said. 'I had some doubts to start with. But now we've got to the end of the bag, I realize my fears were unfounded. I think we can definitely pronounce this sugar to be fit for human consumption. What do think, Mrs Bubby?'

But Mrs Bubby could only think how sticky the two boys' faces looked, and how brown their mouths and lips now were.

'I think,' she said, 'you two had better clean yourselves up. Because if you go out into the street looking like that, the first Chocolate Trooper to clap eyes on you, well, the next thing he'll clap will be you two in irons.'

Inside Huntly felt a little ashamed of himself. He had vowed never to lose control over sweets or chocolate. Loss of control meant taking foolish and unnecessary risks, which might lead to detection and arrest. You had to be one step ahead of the Troopers all the time. You couldn't afford to be discovered with your head in a sugar bag and with sticky paws, looking like Winnie the Pooh on a honey binge. You always had to stay alert, and he'd let his standards slip.

Cleaned up, they returned to the stockroom.

'So then, boys,' Mrs Bubby said. 'What now? Do you need to tell me? Or have I already got it figured out for myself?'

She probably did, but Smudger went ahead anyway.

'OK, Mrs Bubby,' he said. 'It's like this. The way we see it is that you're sitting on a little gold mine here. Well, your mine isn't so much a gold mine as a chocolate-kind-of-mine. You've got the raw materials here, the cocoa and the sugar and the cocoa butter too. But things need to be done to these ingredients to turn them into proper choc-olate, and that'll take time and work and experiments and expertise. It'll need a recipe. And that won't be easy to get. All books on chocolate are banned, and they've been taken from the libraries and ripped up and thrown on bonfires. You can't even find anything on the Internet. You do a search on "chocolate" and the whole system crashes. Unless you know how to make chocolate, Mrs Bubby?'

'No, dear,' she sighed, 'I wish I did, but I'm afraid I don't.'

'OK. Well, I reckon we can find out. Anyway, Mrs Bubby, once the chocolate is made, we're going to have to sell it. Now, you're in an ideal position to do that, obviously, though we all know that what you'll be selling is contraband, illegal goods – bootleg.'

'Bootleg?' Mrs Bubby asked.

'Like in the old days, in America, when they banned drinking.'

'Oh, yes.' Mrs Bubby nodded. 'I know.'

'So what we thought was that you could start selling the bootleg chocolate in your shop here. You could keep a bit under the counter. And when people came in for a paper or a magazine, you could give them a nod and a wink, and say something like "Is that all, madam?" or "Will there be anything else, sir? A little something for later on, perhaps?" or something like that.

'We've got the contacts, and we can give the password only to people we know and trust. Kids at school who we know are on our side – no Young Pioneers or anyone like that. So what I propose, Mrs Bubby, is that me and Huntly turn the cocoa and sugar into chocolate. You sell it and keep the money and—'

'But what do *you* get?' Mrs Bubby said. 'What's your share of this, boys? I wouldn't be expecting you to do all this for nothing.'

'All we want is to have a little chocolate for ourselves. Not a lot, we don't want to be greedy. But just a few bars of chocolate, to pay us for our time and trouble and for the risks we'll be taking.'

'I can't see any objection to that,' Mrs Bubby said. 'Sounds fair. Very fair. In fact, I'd want you to have a share of the proceeds too, or I'd feel it was exploitation.'

'Well, that's very nice of you, Mrs Bubby. And we won't

say no. But it's not the money. We want to do this to keep hope alive. To show them that we won't be beaten down and treated like nobodies.'

Mrs Bubby looked at the two boys. Her face was serious.

'You know, boys,' she said. 'You put me in mind of Mr Bubby, when he was alive. He was a bit of a rebel too, just like yourselves. He was always fighting for justice and freedom. He never stopped. He was always writing complaining letters to the council and the newspapers, or parking on double yellow lines. That's the kind of man he was. Always fighting for freedom and the rights of the ordinary person. And because you two remind me of him so much, I'm going to agree to it. "The rebel is older than the kingdom", he always used to say.'

'What does that mean, Mrs Bubby?'

'You chew it over in your mind, Smudger. Well, do we have a deal?'

They did.

Smudger and Huntly took it in turns to shake Mrs Bubby by the hand.

'We're going to be bootleggers,' Smudger said, as they stood up to go. 'But for a worthy cause. This isn't to make money. It's to show that just because you're a child, that doesn't mean you've not got rights. They can't just take our chocolate away. Not just like that. We're going to fight back.'

On that noble note of defiance and revolution, Smudger and Huntly left Mrs Bubby's shop and headed for home.

'So what's our next step?' Huntly asked as they walked along.

'The plan is we're going to be bookworms,' Smudger said. 'First thing Saturday morning, we're going to find ourselves a book. A book with a recipe in it – on how to make chocolate.'

Mr Blades

S mudger had never been really big on books. He had read his share in his time, but as the years had gone on, his interest had waned. He was more interested in facts and figures and football now, and most of the information he needed he could find in magazines, or on the Internet.

But he still retained an affection for books. They were small and portable, you didn't need to plug them in to run them, and they could be very useful. They explained how to do things. Like how to make chocolate.

Only where to find one? Plainly not at the library any more.

The following Saturday morning, after the boys had visited Mrs Bubby's shop, they hopped on a number forty-seven bus and headed into town. It wasn't the modern shopping centre they were going to, but the older, seedier and more interesting part of the city – the place where bargains could be had. It was a traffic-free area of market stalls and street traders. Part of the market was enclosed under glass – though the sides were still open to the wind and rain.

The streets in the Glass Market area were narrow and cobbled and they wound round like snakes. There were sudden turnings, mysterious doorways, surprise courtyards and hidden entrances. There were junk shops, antique shops and shops selling reject china or violin bows or collections of stamps. There were second-hand record shops and old clothes shops and places selling dried fruits and spices. There was a coffee roaster, where you could buy fresh coffee or just stand downwind of the burner to smell the delicious aroma of roasting coffee beans.

The boys hurried through the crowded alleyways. The voices of the stallholders echoed around them as they passed through the fruit market.

'All your Grannies! Get your Grannies now! Best Granny Smiths! All your Coxes. Get your grapes now. Best bananas!'

Smudger stopped and bought two apples. He handed one to Huntly who polished it on his sleeve. They walked on their way, crunching as they went.

'It's not that I'm against fruit,' Smudger said. 'No one likes a crunchy apple more than me. It's just I like chocolate as well.'

'Absolutely,' Huntly said. 'Only keep your voice down.'

They entered a quiet cobbled square lined with old Tudor buildings that housed junk shops and second-hand booksellers. Stacked on the pavements were boxes of old paperbacks, shelves of hardbacks with broken spines, and signs reading *£2 each* and *3 books for £5*.

As Huntly and Smudger stopped outside one shop and started to thumb through a pile of magazines, two uniformed figures were walking past the fruit stalls. They both had an unhealthy pallor to their cheeks and were feeling frail and fragile.

'I can't think what upset my stomach the other night, Frankie,' Myrtle Perkins lied. She knew full well what had upset her, but it would have been tantamount to heresy and treason to admit it.

'Me neither,' Frankie agreed. 'It was probably something left over from our sugar and chocolate eating days.'

'Yes,' Myrtle nodded. 'Perhaps.'

She looked at the displays on the fruit stalls and gave them her wholehearted approval.

'Lovely fruit and vegetables, Frankie,' she said. 'You start to notice these things once you've joined the Young Pioneers.'

'Yes, Myrtle,' Frankie agreed. 'Absolutely. It sort of opens your eyes to the good things in life.'

He would have said more, only he spotted two familiar figures through the archway – Huntly Hunter and Smudger Moore.

Hmm, he thought. I wonder what they're up to. Maybe I'll find out.

He turned to Myrtle.

'I'll see you back at headquarters,' he said. 'I think I might go for a little walk on my own.'

Myrtle looked at him, surprised, but also a bit relieved to be spared his company for a while. Frankie was a true and loyal Pioneer, no doubt about it, and their positions as joint troop leaders meant they spent an awful lot of time together. But it was occasionally nice to get away on your own.

'Right you are, Frankie. I'll see you this afternoon for drill then. In the park if the weather keeps fine. If not, in the hall.'

'Right, Myrtle. Bye.'

And they went their separate ways.

Huntly and Smudger were investigating a stack of paperbacks. The trader, who was sitting in a deckchair out on the pavement, peered over at them from under his straw hat.

'Help you, boys?'

'Oh, just browsing,' Smudger said.

'Anything in particular?' the man asked.

Smudger was afraid to mention the word chocolate out loud, so he just asked, 'Got anything on sort of cooking and stuff?'

The man tilted back his hat.

'Cooking? You boys interested in cooking?'

'Yeah,' Huntly nodded. 'Recipes sort of thing.'

'Main courses?' the man asked.

'Not necessarily,' Huntly told him. And just then he noticed something, a flash of silver paper in the man's top pocket.

The bookseller was a chocolate eater! Just like them. He had it there in his pocket. A bar of genuine chocolate.

'Look,' Huntly nudged Smudger. 'He's with us.'

'He won't be with us much longer,' Smudger muttered, 'if he's not more careful and goes round advertising the fact like that.'

They walked over to where the man sat. He was

red-faced, chubby-cheeked and happy looking. One of life's optimists.

Smudger spoke quietly from the side of his mouth.

'Your chocolate's showing,' he murmured.

The man looked up, a flash of panic in his eyes. He looked down into his breast pocket. There it was, the silver foil, plainly visible. He swallowed hard, reached into his side pocket, whipped out a red spotted handkerchief – just like a magician – and stuffed it into his top pocket, covering the chocolate bar and hiding it from view.

'Thanks, lads,' he murmured. 'That's one I owe you. Now tell me, what do you really want? Or maybe I can guess.'

'We're looking for a recipe book,' Smudger told him, 'like we said.'

'A special sort of recipe book,' Huntly agreed. 'With the emphasis on, well . . . puddings . . . and sort of . . . sweet things.'

'I think I might have just the thing,' the man said. He lowered his voice. 'I'll go in first. Wait a minute, then you wander up. First floor. Back office.'

The man was so portly that Smudger and Huntly had to help him get up out of the deckchair. They took an arm each and pulled and the man suddenly sprang to his feet, like a puppet from a box. He was much shorter than they had expected. He had seemed taller when he was sitting down.

'See you in minute,' he said. 'Play it cool.'

He went into his shop. The sign on the door read *Roger Blades, Second-hand and Antiquarian Bookshop*. A smaller sign below it read *All Shoplifters Will Be Prosecuted*. There was also another notice which read *Beware – Savage Dog*. But there didn't seem to be any dog in sight.

There was someone in the downstairs part of the bookshop. A boy in a Young Pioneers uniform. The bookseller hadn't seen him go in.

'Help you at all, Young Pioneer?' Mr Blades asked as he entered.

'Just browsing,' Frankie Crawley said.

'Give us a shout if you want anything,' Mr Blades told him obligingly, then he went on up the narrow, creaking stairway, wheezing and spluttering like a leaky balloon.

Frankie hid behind a bookcase as Huntly and Smudger came in and went up the narrow creaking stairs. He dawdled a moment, then he went to follow them, but the staircase creaked so much that he dared not risk it – they would be bound to hear. So he remained where he was, at the bottom of the stairwell, listening intently, alert as a gun dog.

Mr Blades was waiting in his office, the door ajar. He beckoned the boys into a tiny, windowless room, dimly lit by a sixty-watt bulb. He made sure that no one was following, and then closed the door.

Back down at the foot of the stairs, where they twisted upwards, Frankie Crawley held his breath. Once he heard the door close, he risked tiptoeing up a few steps, taking care to stand on the outside, where they would be less likely to creak. Then he stopped and listened again. But all he could hear was a faint murmur of voices.

'What you boys are looking for, bookwise,' Mr Blades said, 'is the special stash – the illegal ones that escaped all the book-burnings.' And he tapped his red, bulbous nose, as if to say 'We're all in the know, but we shan't say anything about it. Mum's the word.'

His office was full of books. Just like every other room in the shop. They seemed to be gushing out of the floor and pouring from the walls like water from a burst pipe. How he ever found anything, goodness only knew, but Mr Blades put his hand on the book he wanted in a matter of seconds. It was a tatty, dog-eared paperback with a picture of succulent chocolates on the cover. He treated it with great reverence, as if it were the Holy Grail.

'*The Art of the Chocolate Maker* by Tobias Mallow,' he read. 'The definitive guide to chocolate making by the world's greatest living exponent – now sadly deceased.'

He pulled his straw hat off for a moment as a token of respect, and then just as suddenly put it back on again, as though afraid his head might get cold.

'I can't let you take it away,' he said, 'as it's the only one I've got and others might come asking. But I'll give you pen and paper and you can copy the recipe. I have got a photocopier somewhere, but it's not been right since I fixed it.'

The book fell open at the place he wanted, as if falling open at that particular page was in its destiny.

Mr Blades handed the book to Smudger.

'That what you want?' he asked. 'A basic recipe for chocolate?'

'Yes,' Smudger nodded. 'Thanks.'

Huntly peered over Smudger's shoulder to see what was on the page.

A Collection of Recipes, it read. *For Home-Made Chocolate*.

'I'll get that pen and paper for you,' Mr Blades said.

'Thanks,' said Smudger. 'How much do we owe you?'

But Mr Blades just patted his hidden chocolate bar.

'Nothing. You're already paid me, lads,' he said. 'You may have saved me from the Troopers today. No charge. We're all square.'

He fetched pen and paper.

'Here you go. I presume you kids can still do joined-up writing these days,' he cackled wheezily to himself. 'Hold on,' he said. 'Thought I heard something.'

He opened the office door and peered out. But there was nobody to be seen. Frankie Crawley had scampered back down to the bottom of the stairs.

Smudger and Huntly left the shop as casually as they had arrived.

'Thanks for that information, Mr Blades,' Smudger called as they left. 'On the – er – the local history,' he added, for the benefit of any unseen eavesdroppers.

'Pleasure, boys,' Blades said, and went back into the shop to discover Frankie Crawley still browsing among the shelves.

'Any luck, Young Pioneer?' Blades asked. 'Need any assistance at all?'

A sly look came into Frankie's eyes.

'Do you have any books,' Frankie asked. 'On local history? Maybe you have some upstairs?'

'Local history? No, sorry,' Blades said. 'I don't really handle that sort of thing. Try Matthews on the corner. He's your local-history specialist.'

'But I just thought I heard someone thank you for some information on that very subject?' Frankie said.

Blades gave a smile.

'Oh that,' he said. 'Yes. I was just telling a couple of visitors all about the old days – personal reminiscences, you know. The great days of the Glass Market here. How it used to be back when I first opened my bookshop. All about the characters I've known and – in fact, why don't you come into the back office, Young Pioneer, and I'll tell you all about it.'

'No, no. That's all right,' Frankie said quickly.

'It's no trouble,' Blades insisted. 'I can talk for hours about the old days.'

'I'm sure you can,' Frankie said. 'But I have a rather urgent appointment. Thank you, anyway.'

And he hurried away.

Blades watched him go, wondering who had out-bluffed whom. Had he fooled Frankie, or had Frankie fooled him? Only time would tell. That was how it was in the book and the bootleg businesses – you never knew how things would turn out. You just had to live for the moment.

With that thought in mind, Blades retired to his office. He closed and locked the door behind him. He opened up a book with hollowed-out pages, and extracted a bar of chocolate.

Cooking from the Books

Huntly and Smudger returned home in high spirits. At first they kept a sharp eye out for Chocolate Troopers. Every now and then they would stand in a doorway for a second, or look for passing reflections in a shop window, just in case they were being followed. But they saw no one who might be potential informers or undercover members of the Chocolate Police, and with increasing confidence they relaxed as they neared the bus stop.

Perhaps, in their excitement, they became careless, and didn't bother to look behind them any more. Even if they had, they would have seen no more than a faint shadow, a blur of motion, darting from corner to corner, from door to door.

The two boys were so elated with their success in obtaining the recipes that they had forgotten all the traps and snares which lay around them. And maybe, in thinking that they had so easily avoided them, they had actually walked into one and had triggered it. And now the jaws of some immense mantrap were slowly, very slowly, but relentlessly, beginning to close in around them.

They had sealed their own fate. As time would tell.

*

The afternoon was growing late as they got off the bus, but there was still time to call in on Mrs Bubby and to tell her about the recipe. Smudger left it with her for safe keeping and she hid it in an old tin in the stockroom. They agreed that they would meet again the following morning – a Sunday – and that the chocolate-making experiments would begin in earnest.

When they came back the next morning, they tapped on the door of Mrs Bubby's shop with the secret knock that they had pre-arranged. Mrs Bubby let them in.

She bolted the door once they were inside, and led the way to the back room where she had laid out several pots and pans in readiness.

Mrs Bubby's kitchen was accessed through the stockroom. It was small and cramped with an old-fashioned gas cooker in it, the kind which stood on bowed, cast-iron legs.

'It may not be much, but it'll do,' Mrs Bubby said. 'You'll have to make the chocolate up in small batches. I don't have the facilities for large-scale production. There's pans and pots here and wooden spoons. There's baking trays too you can use for pouring the chocolate into, and if you like, to help it set, you can put the trays into my fridge. It's a proper, full-sized commercial fridge, this one. No more than a few years old. I may not be up to the minute with everything, but I'm not completely behind the times.'

'Thanks, Mrs Bubby,' Smudger said. 'This all looks fine. One thing – would you have any milk we could use? And maybe a bit of butter?'

'I'm ahead of you.' Mrs Bubby smiled. 'I read the recipe through last night and realized milk would be needed. So don't worry. I've got plenty. A good fifteen or twenty pints here in the cooler. I'll just have to tell anyone who comes and asks for some that I've sold out.'

'Great,' Huntly said. He was reading through the recipe. 'Now, Mrs Bubby, do you have a thermometer?'

Mrs Bubby did. But unfortunately it wasn't a proper cake or sugar thermometer. It was a medical one, the kind you stick beneath your tongue or under your armpit, to find out whether you are ill enough to stay off school. It wasn't what Smudger wanted, but it would have to do.

'You've got to get your chocolate mixture to exactly the right temperature,' he told Huntly, 'or it won't set. Too hot, you ruin it; too cool, same thing. You have to get it within just a few degrees. There's not much leeway at all. OK. Let's get cooking.'

'One thing, boys,' Mrs Bubby said, 'before you start. I'm worried about the smell.'

Huntly frowned. 'Oh, yes. I hadn't thought of that.'

'Chocolate's got a smell all of its own,' Mrs Bubby pointed out. 'We ought to do something to disguise it. I'll take the toaster here into the shop and every now and again I'll stick a slice of bread in and burn it. And if anyone comes into the shop and says "What's that smell?" I can just say "It's me, burning my breakfast."'

'But you can't be burning your breakfast all day long. What if the same person comes back in the afternoon and the toast is still burning?'

'I'll tell them I'm burning my lunch,' Mrs Bubby said.

'There's no reason you can't have toast for lunch. They'll probably think I'm having beans on it. Maybe I can burn some of those as well.'

Mrs Bubby took the toaster and left them to it. She opened up the shop and laid out the Sunday papers. Before long, Huntly and Smudger heard the bell tinkle at the entry of a customer, who chatted with Mrs Bubby as she paid for her newspaper, then said, 'Smells like you've had toast burning, Mrs Bubby.'

Mrs Bubby sniffed the air. 'Oh, you can still smell it, can you? It was my breakfast. I'll have to see to that.'

But when the lady had gone, she didn't bother seeing to anything. She just spread out a paper on the counter and peered at the headline, which read *Good For You Party Rides High In Opinion Polls. Highest Ratings Ever. Most Popular Party For Fifty Years!*

Mrs Bubby snorted in disgust.

'I doubt it,' she mumbled. 'They've fiddled the figures, same as they fiddle everything else.'

In the stockroom the chocolate-making was under way

'Drop more milk,' Smudger said. 'Touch more butter. Spoonful more sugar. Pinch more cocoa.'

Huntly dropped them in. Smudger stirred the mixture with a wooden spoon, then dipped his finger in and took a taste.

'Is that finger clean?' Huntly asked.

'Course!' Smudger said. 'Anyway, that's how you do it. Top chefs are always sticking their fingers into their cooking and having a taste. Everyone knows that. I've seen it

on the telly. They even come round to your table sometimes and stick their fingers in your dinner.'

He put his finger back into the mixture and tasted it
once more. Huntly followed suit.

'What do you think?'

'All right,' Huntly said. 'Not great. But all right.'

'Pass the thermometer.' Smudger inserted it into the
mixture to get a reading. 'Bit hotter yet,' he said, and
turned up the gas. 'Keep stirring,' he told Huntly, 'while I
get a tray ready.'

He took a shallow flapjack tray and placed it on the
kitchen table.

'It's reached the right temperature,' Huntly told him. 'I
think. It's hard to know with this thermometer.'

'Let's try it, then,' Smudger said. He scooped up a
spoonful of the steaming mixture from the big pan and let
it trickle into a bowl which he had filled with cold water.
The mixture hit the water with a plop. The chocolate
scattered into small, ball-bearing shapes. Smudger fished
one of them out and put it into his mouth.

'Well?'

'OK . . . ish.'

'Pour it out then.'

They did. Carefully holding the hot pan with oven
gloves, Huntly poured the mixture into the tray. They
then scraped the pan and took it in turns to lick the
spoon; after that they took everything to the sink and
washed it while the tray of chocolate cooled.

Once it had cooled a little, they put it into the fridge,
then did a little more washing up. Then they waited.

That was the difficult part, waiting for the chocolate to set.

It was hard not to open the fridge door every few minutes to see how the chocolate was doing. Every ten minutes or so Mrs Bubby would come into the back room to check that the two boys were all right. She would have liked to have offered them some lemonade, but proper lemonade with sugar and bubbles in it had gone the way of chocolates and sweets.

'Bubbles are bad for you,' a Good For You Party spokeswoman had explained to the nation, one evening on the TV news. 'Fizzy drinks contain phosphoric acid in high concentration and excessive intake can cause dental erosion – where the teeth are literally dissolved away. (Not to mention the anti-social effects of excessive flatulence.) The government has therefore decided to act swiftly to curb this menace. Fizzy drinks will therefore be illegal from midnight tomorrow. If you have any cans or bottles in your fridge, pour them down the sink immediately.'

All Mrs Bubby had to offer the boys was tap water, milk, Healthy For You Fruiti Squash or prune juice. The only trouble with Healthy Fruiti Squash was that even the smallest drop of it was enough to ruin a glass of perfectly good water, so the boys chose milk instead.

When they opened the fridge again they were disappointed to see that the chocolate was still semi-liquid. It wasn't like real chocolate at all. It had a texture more like soft fudge. It tasted all right – not bad at all. But it wasn't chocolate.

'I don't understand it,' Huntly said, dismayed. 'We made the mixture like it said, folded it in like it said, heated it up like it said, held it at the crucial temperature, let it cool a little, did the water test and everything.'

Mrs Bubby and the two boys stared at the tray, as though willing the chocolate to congeal. But the mixture just lay there and refused to cooperate.

Although none of them said anything, they were all concerned. Their supplies of sugar and cocoa were limited and they could not really afford to waste them in failed experiments.

'We'll have to try again,' Smudger said. 'Smaller quantities this time though, so if it goes wrong again, we don't waste so much.'

'What do we do with this?' Huntly said, looking dejectedly at the tray of soft chocolate.

Smudger caught Mrs Bubby's eye.

'Eat it?' he suggested.

'Don't see what else we can do,' she said. 'It'll be a waste to throw it away. And it's nearly lunchtime. I'll get us a bit of bread to have it with.'

Mrs Bubby took a knife and smeared the chocolate paste thickly over the slices of bread.

'Hey, this is all right!' Huntly exclaimed. 'We weren't far off it, really. We've just made chocolate spread instead of solid chocolate.'

'Pass the knife,' Smudger told him, 'while I smear another inch or two on my bread here. We'll need to keep our strength up if we're going to do more cooking. And chocolate's a high-energy food.'

'Certainly is,' Huntly mumbled, cramming in another slice.

They stopped talking and concentrated on the matter in hand. Soon they sat back and contemplated the empty tray.

'Now that,' said Huntly, 'is what I call lunch.'

'Me too,' Smudger agreed. Then he added thoughtfully. 'I wonder what's for tea,' he said.

But that was Smudger for you. Always looking to the future. At least he was most of the time.

At one-thirty Mrs Bubby closed the shop. She wasn't one of those 'open all hours' shopkeepers.

'There's only me, and I need a break, and Sunday's the one afternoon I like to call my own. I do what I want to then – just as I please.'

'And what do you like to do on a Sunday afternoon, Mrs Bubby?' Huntly asked.

'Sleep,' she told him.

She left the two boys in the kitchen while she went to her living room for forty winks on the sofa, with her cat curled up next to her.

The forty winks turned to fifty winks and the fifty winks to sixty. Her heavy, rhythmic breathing and her faint, rather delicate snores barely penetrated though to the kitchen where the clattering of pans, the stirring of mixtures and the banging of wooden spoons went on throughout the afternoon.

Smudger and Huntly tried a second batch of chocolate, then a third. The second was as runny as the first had been, the third runnier still. But they were loath to pour good chocolate down the sink, just because it was the wrong consistency. Like the dedicated individuals they were – ever willing to sacrifice themselves in the cause of duty and the furtherance of freedom – they ate it.

'Look, Huntly,' Smudger said finally, 'I reckon it's not having a decent thermometer that's the problem. We just can't read the temperature accurately on this one. We need a proper sugar thermometer or we're never going to do it.'

'Yeah, maybe,' Huntly said. 'But where do we get one of those from? I don't think you can ever buy anything like that any more.'

Smudger looked up from the pots and pans.

'What have I been doing!' he said. 'I'm an idiot! I'll get us a sugar thermometer. I'll be back in ten minutes.'

'Where are you going?' Huntly asked, as Smudger sped out of the back door.

'The bakery, of course.'

Of course. They should have thought of it at the very start.

Smudger rode round to his dad's bakery on his old bike. He would have liked a nice new mountain bike, with proper suspension and all the attachments, but he couldn't afford it, and it was a long time until Christmas or until his next birthday.

As he thought it would be, the bakery was open. His dad often popped in on Sunday afternoon to check that everything was ready for the following week.

Now, how to get the thermometer without his dad noticing?

Smudger let himself into the shop. He reached up and grabbed the bell to stop it ringing as he entered. His dad was out in the back yard, cleaning the van.

Smudger tiptoed into the bakery proper and headed for the drawers where his father kept the icing nozzles and palette knives. He was silently opening one when—

'Smudger!'

He practically jumped out of his skin and back into it.

'Kylie!' he said. She was sitting under a table, making sausages out of an old piece of dough. 'What are *you* doing here?'

'Mum's gone to visit Irene,' she said. 'Dad's looking after me. And he's after you. He wants to know where you've been and what you've been up to.'

'I haven't been anywhere and I haven't been doing anything.'

There was a sound from out in the yard. His dad was coming back inside. Smudger pulled another drawer open. There it was – the sugar thermometer. He grabbed it and put it in his pocket.

'What's that?'

'Nothing, Kylie.'

'Where you taking it?'

'Nowhere.'

'What are you going to do with it when you get there?'

'I don't know.'

'You don't know much then, do you?'

'No. Now listen, Kylie, if Dad asks, you haven't seen me

114

and I don't exist. I'm doing something really special. And if you can keep a secret, then I'll bring you something back home. Something really nice.'

Kylie looked at him doubtfully.

'Like what?'

'Chocolate,' Smudger whispered.

Then he legged it out of the shop.

Ron came in and closed the back door behind him. He went to wash his hands at the sink.

'I don't suppose you'd have any idea where Smudger's got to have you, Kylie?' he asked.

'I haven't seen him and he doesn't exist,' Kylie told him.

As the boys suspected, having the sugar thermometer made the crucial difference. Finally they could get the mixture to the absolutely precise temperature and keep it there for the given time. They could see as they poured the warm mixture out into the cooling tray that it was starting to congeal immediately. It didn't even have to go into the fridge. The boys just sat and watched, fanning the chocolate gently with empty sugar bags.

'I reckon we've done it,' Huntly said quietly. 'I'm not one to leap before he looks or who counts his horses before they've hatched, but look at that.'

The mixture went on changing, becoming hard and smooth.

'You make a note of the proportions?' Smudger asked.

Huntly pushed a piece of paper across the table.

'There. They were right all along. It was all in the temperature, like we thought.'

'You make a note of the cooking time too?'

'Yeah,' Huntly said. 'All the facts.'

'Good,' Smudger said. 'Then we're in business.'

His eyes lit up with sudden inspiration. He went into the stockroom and returned with a packet of raisins and a box of hazelnuts.

'What's that for?' Huntly asked.

'For the next batch,' Smudger said. 'What do you reckon? How about some fruit and nut!'

Huntly's face lit up with a smile.

'You're on, Smudge. Let's get to it.'

The Right Mixture

By the time Mrs Bubby woke from her nap, there were three trays of chocolate in the kitchen – plain, fruit and nut, and plain again – and they had cooled sufficiently to be cut into squares and wrapped.

After first expressing her admiration (and accepting a little taste of each) she fetched a sharp knife, a roll of cooking foil and her kitchen scales.

'OK. I'll cut, you two weigh and wrap,' she said. 'We'll try to get as near as we can to 125 gram bars, as that's what people are used to. We'll wrap the plain chocolate in cooking foil with the shiny side out. And we'll wrap the fruit and nut with the shiny side in. That way we can tell at a glance which is which.'

The chocolate was soon cut and wrapped and stacked neatly into small cardboard boxes – of which Mrs Bubby had plenty.

'One hundred and twenty bars, Mrs Bubby,' Smudger said. 'A nice even number. Eighty plain, forty fruit and nut. Oh and . . .' he looked down at the table where three (shiny side out) chocolate bars lay '. . . three left over.'

'Well, now that is untidy,' Mrs Bubby said. 'And I do so hate an odd number. What could we do with them?'

'Give them to charity?' Huntly suggested.

'Not a bad idea,' Mrs Bubby agreed. 'But maybe a bit too risky these days. You know what? I think we should have one each.'

And they did.

'I'm going to take mine home,' Smudger said, 'and share it with my sister.'

'I'll save a bit for my mum,' Huntly said. 'I reckon she might be missing her chocolate by now. I'll say a friend gave it to me.'

'OK, boys,' Mrs Bubby said. 'I'm sure your families are trustworthy and won't say a word to anyone – not deliberately. But be careful about little brothers and sisters. Sometimes they don't really know the meaning of secrets and couldn't disguise the truth even if they wanted to.'

'I'll be careful. Don't worry,' Smudger assured her. But he remembered his promise to Kylie too, and he knew that if he went home empty-handed there would be trouble. He slipped the bar into his pocket.

'I've got to take it,' he explained. 'It's the price of silence – it's how we have to pay for the sugar thermometer.'

'OK,' Mrs Bubby said. 'Fair enough. But listen – If we're all bootleggers now, we've got to be very cautious. There's got to be a password, like you said. So that if you send anyone to the shop for chocolate, I've got to be able to know they came from you and can be trusted.'

'Yes,' Huntly said thoughtfully. 'We'd better have something that's not suspicious. Anyone we send along will first have to say that they've come for "a little something to keep them going".'

'And what do I say?'

'You say, "What sort of something do you have in mind?"'

'And they say?'

'They say, "Something to hit the spot". And once they've said that, you'll know they're all right. OK?'

'Sounds fair enough to me.'

'Smudger?'

'Sounds fine.'

'OK. And if they don't say it, Mrs Bubby, you pretend you don't know what they're on about. Because if they don't know the password, then they'll either be informers or plain-clothes Chocolate Police.'

'Right,' Mrs Bubby said. 'That's easy to remember. And if they don't get it right, I'll pretend I'm just a sweet, innocent, nice old lady, who's a bit out of touch and doesn't really know what's going on.'

'Good luck then,' Smudger said. 'We'll call in during the week to see how things are.'

'And to pick up your chocolate bars,' Mrs Bubby reminded them. 'And your share of the dosh. A deal's a deal after all, and I always keep my side of a bargain.'

The two boys left the shop, their silver-wrapped chocolate bars (shiny side out) securely hidden in the pockets of their coats. They made their separate ways home by the back lanes, staying off the main roads, out of sight of the Detector Vans and the occasional Chocolate Patrol which still continued to roam the streets, even on a Sunday.

In the distance they could hear the Young Pioneers practising their drill.

'*Young Pioneers will lead the way*,' Frankie sang.

'*Young Pioneers will lead the way*,' the troops responded.

'*Join the Pioneers today*.'

'*Join the Pioneers today*.'

Smudger didn't exactly hear the sound of people flocking to join them. Maybe news had got about what kind of birthday cakes the Young Pioneers had, and the sort of effect they had on you.

When Smudger got home, Kylie was painting in the kitchen. He slipped her a small piece of shiny-side-out.

'Bit of chocolate for you, Kylie,' he whispered.

Her eyes sparkled with delight.

'Cor, thanks, Smudger. Where'd you get this?'

'Never you mind. And don't you go telling anyone about it. Just eat it on the quiet. Not a word to Dad. Mum's the word, OK? Only not a word to Mum either.'

Kylie looked rather perplexed. 'I get it,' she said. Though whether she did or not was anyone's guess. But she understood enough to disappear and to eat her chocolate where she wouldn't be seen.

Smudger had been going to give his mum and dad some chocolate too. But he knew that they would only worry about where it had come from and whether there might be trouble. So best not to mention it to them at all.

As the old saying goes – 'Ask no questions, hear no lies'. If Smudger didn't give them the opportunity to ask questions, then he wouldn't have to lie to them, which he didn't want to do.

Ron Moore came into the kitchen and found Smudger at last.

'There you are! Where have you been all afternoon?'

'With Huntly, Dad,' Smudger replied truthfully. 'Ring him up and ask him if you like.'

Right at that moment, Carol Hunter was asking Huntly the same kind of question.

'I was with Smudger, Mum, all afternoon. Ring him up and ask him if you like.'

So neither of them actually told any lies. They just omitted the parts of the story their parents wouldn't have liked.

It was odd how much of the truth you could avoid telling, by not even telling a lie at all. All you needed was to say nothing at all. Silence could be a very misleading thing.

I Spy With . . .

They came and went like shadows in the sunlight; they flitted past like ghosts. The first of the would-be customers never even made it into the shop. They walked up and down the street four or five times before finally deciding that no, it was all too dangerous, even despite Smudger's reassurances, his provision of the password and his guarantee of quality goods.

They peered in through the window, they saw Mrs Bubby there, and yes, it all seemed safe and fine – only what if someone was watching, a Trooper in a van, a spy in the street? So they kept going, and went on their way, wishing later that they'd had the courage to go in and buy the chocolate, but also rather relieved that they hadn't. It was easier to go without than to be brave.

Until one small girl, whose sweet tooth was more persuasive than any butterflies in her stomach, pushed open the door of Mrs Bubby's shop and made her way to the counter.

'I'd like to buy a little something to keep me going, please,' she said.

Mrs Bubby looked down at her. In truth she was as apprehensive as the girl. What if some informant had got hold of the password? What if this was the daughter of a

Chocolate Trooper, who had sent her in, all smiles and innocence, to see if the old lady had anything special to sell under the counter? What if it was all a trap? What if the Detector Vans reappeared? She hadn't seen one for a long time, they'd moved on to other districts. But what if they suddenly came back?

'What sort of something do you have in mind, dear?' Mrs Bubby asked. She gauged the distance between herself and the stockroom. If the Troopers burst in the front way, would she be able to get out of the back?

Probably not. At least not without a hip replacement.

The girl gazed up at her, moon-eyed; she had suddenly forgotten what Smudger had told her. What was she supposed to say? Then it came back.

'I'd like something to hit the spot, please.'

Mrs Bubby nodded and reached under the counter. She picked up two silver-wrapped chocolate bars and placed them down for the girl to see.

'Shiny side out, or shiny side in? That's plain – or fruit and nut.'

'Shiny side out, please.'

Mrs Bubby told her the price. The girl put down her money. Then they both hesitated. Mrs Bubby glanced up, half expecting to see the Troopers coming through the door. The girl looked nervously over her shoulder, waiting for some invisible hand to fall, for a voice to say, 'Right! Gotcha!'

But nothing. Just silence, peace, an ordinary transaction in an ordinary shop. The girl reached out and took her chocolate bar; Mrs Bubby picked up the coins.

'Thank you very much.'

'You're welcome. Keep it out of sight, won't you?'

'I will. And then I'm going to eat it – *all* of it – first chance I get.'

Then she was gone. And that was it. It only needed one drop of rain to start the cloudburst, and after that it rained a steady stream of customers through Mrs Bubby's door.

Soon, in their own eyes, Huntly and Smudger were fully fledged bootleggers. It was hard not to swagger and to feel a bit special. And although they may have been the youngest of the bootleggers, they weren't the only ones.

As well as natural revolutionaries such as Smudger and Huntly, motivated by a sense of injustice and high ideals, there were also one or two professional and petty criminals who saw the chocolate ban as an opportunity to get rich quick.

But these bootleggers were men and women who sold inferior merchandise. Their chocolate was often made without any real chocolate in it at all. They used whatever they could get their hands on, whatever they could pass off as the real thing. They weren't above boiling up old acorn shells, or adding a spot of fish paste to their 'chocolate' mixtures. And if any of their customers complained, there was a large bunch of knuckles to argue with, or possibly even a cosh.

As well as the bootleggers on the corners, certain backstreet cafes and snack bars had appeared, also selling chocolate and sweets. These places tended to be in cellars and basements. They would be protected by thick metal doors with small sliding panels in them. The only ways to get in were with a password or a battering ram. You would knock and the panel would slide open, and a huge, tough-looking man with a face like doorknobs would grunt and ask you want you wanted.

The rumour was that if you said that 'Lou sent me,' and if you knew the correct password, you would be admitted. Otherwise the panel would be shut in your face, and if you didn't go on your way, a couple of heavy men, also with faces like doorknobs would appear at your side, and invite you to go away pronto – before your face ended up looking like a doorknob too.

Of course sometimes the Chocolate Troopers arrived. Sometimes they had discovered the passwords through informants. Other times they had brought their battering rams with them. Then all hell and confusion would break loose as bootleggers and customers ran for the exits – not that many of them ever got that far.

Some of the street-corner bootleggers were crooked too. All you got from them was a chunk of wood wrapped up in silver foil. But you wouldn't realize that until you had paid your money and unwrapped the merchandise, by which time your supplier would have disappeared down the street.

But Smudger and Huntly were honest value-for-money men. You maybe paid them a little over the odds, but you got a decent product in return.

Sometimes they thought about Dave Cheng, and

wondered what had become of him, and whether he would ever return to the school. Other times, they forgot about him, and were confident that his fate would never be theirs.

One principal difference between Smudger and Huntly and the many other bootleggers who sold chocolate on the street corners, or from the shadows of shop doorways, was that the boys weren't doing it for money. Anything they made was, for them, more of an incidental thing.

For them it was more of a cause, a liberation struggle. They were trying to strike a blow for freedom and for the right of children everywhere to have a bite of chocolate now and again.

So Smudger and Huntly were bootleggers more in the way that Robin Hood was an outlaw – because they were on the side of the downtrodden and the underdog, because they wanted to make a stand against tyranny and oppression and injustice. 'It should be part of a new constitution,' Smudger said. 'Freedom, justice and chocolate for all.'

Smudger and Huntly's activities did not, however, go unremarked or unobserved. Someone was watching them, carefully, constantly, watching and wondering. And that someone was Frankie Crawley.

'I know they're up to something,' he told Myrtle Perkins as they sat in the Young Pioneers' recreation room one evening after drill. Copies of the *Good For You* comic (with the healthy and uplifting adventures of Tina and Thomas Goodfellow) were scattered about and the prune juice was free – you just helped yourself to as much as you wanted from the big cooler in the corner.

'Such as what?' Myrtle said. 'For instance?' She was a practical, no-nonsense sort of girl.

'Things,' Frankie said mysteriously, and he tapped his nose.

'What sort of things?'

'Whisperings,' Frankie said, 'in the playground. Mutterings about a password, things like that. And people sneaking off to Mrs Bubby's shop and coming out looking a bit too pleased with themselves. Something's going on in there and I'm going to find out what. And you can help me, Myrtle.'

'I might not want to,' Myrtle said, not liking to be taken for granted. Besides Frankie didn't outrank her in the Young Pioneers, but he constantly carried on as if he did. It got on her nerves.

'Look,' Frankie said, 'I think they're buying stuff that you need a password for. I did a bit of surveillance earlier today—'

'Snooping, you mean, do you?' Myrtle said. She liked to call things by their proper names.

Frankie blushed. 'Essential undercover security work,' he corrected her. 'And I reckon I've sussed the password out.'

'Oh?'

'It's dirt simple,' Frankie said. 'I overheard the first half of it. What you have to say first is, "I want a little something to keep me going," and then they say, "What?" or "Whatever . . ."'

'And what's the next bit after that?' Myrtle asked.

'Well, I don't know,' Frankie said. 'I wasn't able to hear the rest.'

'You were being so obvious they saw you lurking about, you mean, and shoved off before you could hear any more?'

'Not necessarily. But it doesn't matter, because I've worked it out.'

'Oh?'

'Look, Huntly's mother is a doctor, isn't she? And he seems to be in on the act.'

'So?'

'So the last part of the password is bound to be "I want a little of what the *doctor* ordered".'

'Why?'

'*Because!* Isn't it obvious?'

'Yes, but Smudger's father is a baker,' Myrtle pointed out. 'So why wouldn't it be "I want a little of what the baker ordered"?'

'That's not a proper saying, Myrtle. Nobody says that.'

'Yes they do. I just said it.'

'Look, nobody goes about saying "It's just what the baker ordered". That's rubbish. I know I'm right about this. It's so obvious, and that's what they'd go for – the obvious. You know what people like Smudger and Huntly are like – brain dead from the neck up. They don't have the imagination to think of anything else.'

'You could hardly be brain dead from the neck down,' Myrtle logically pointed out. But Frankie ignored this piece of information.

'The point is that all it needs now is for someone to go to Mrs Bubby's shop, with their money and the password at the ready, and to see what they get in return. And that person could be you, Myrtle.'

'Could it?' Myrtle demanded. 'And why don't you go in and say the password yourself, Frankie, if you're so confident about it?'

'Well, she's less likely to suspect a girl, isn't she, Myrtle. Don't you think? I know everybody's equal these days, but most grown-ups still think that girls are nicer and more honest – though I can't say it's ever been my experience.'

'It's certainly been mine!' Myrtle snapped back.

'So will you do it?'

Myrtle almost said no. But then she thought of the promotion that could lie ahead, after the successful apprehension of bootleggers. She might get promoted over and above Frankie – if she had been the one to take the risks and do the brave stuff. And then she'd be able to order him about, and make him stand to attention for hours on end and she could tell him to salute her and get him to call her 'Ma'am', and he'd have to ask for permission to go to the loo and things like that.

Which sounded pretty good to Myrtle.

'OK,' she said. 'I might be prepared to help you out, Frankie. Seeing as it's for the Party and for the honour of the Young Pioneers.'

'Spiffing, Myrtle!' Frankie said. 'Top hole!' (These were expressions he'd come across in old books about wars and fighting.) 'That will teach them that they can't thumb their noses at us. That will soon show people like Smudger Moore who's boss – and it's time someone did.'

Right at that moment, however, Frankie Crawley was the last thing on Smudger Moore's mind. What concerned him there and then was the amount of sugar and cocoa left in Mrs Bubby's stockroom. It was already half gone.

'This isn't going to last much longer, Huntly,' he said.

'We're going to have to ration it,' Huntly told him. 'One bar per person per week.'

'Even at that rate it's not going to last. Another few weeks, a month at the most, and that's it – all over. And we've only just really got started.'

'Yes,' Huntly said thoughtfully, 'unless—'

'Unless what, dear?' Mrs Bubby asked, coming in from the shop to get a bit of bread for the toaster to keep the smell of cooking chocolate at bay.

'Unless we can get another source of supply.'

'Like from where?'

'Well, where do sugar and cocoa come from?'

'South America, the Caribbean – anywhere hot.'

'Well, how about Leroy, in Mr Cleeve's class?' Huntly suggested. 'His dad's a fruit importer, isn't he? Bananas, oranges, lemons, limes – and maybe a few other things as well. Who knows? It might be worth asking.'

'All right. No harm in asking, is there?' Smudger said. He was already reaching for his coat.

'Where are you going, Smudger?'

'To ask.'

He found Leroy practising basketball shots down on the

hard court in the park. Smudger didn't waste any time and got to the point immediately.

'Sugar?' Leroy said. 'Cocoa? Come off it, Smudger, that's illegal. You know that.'

'So your dad wouldn't have any in his warehouse, then? Like some left over? From before the ban? That nobody found? As the detectors don't work on ingredients? Possibly, maybe, perhaps?'

Leroy aimed the basketball at the hoop – but missed.

'Hmm,' he said non-committally. 'Possibly, maybe, perhaps—'

'In fact,' Smudger said, warming to his theme, 'maybe you even stashed a little bit away, Leroy, that your dad doesn't know about.'

'Hmm, possibly,' Leroy admitted, taking another shot at the hoop. 'Maybe. Perhaps.'

'Only what use are ingredients, Leroy,' Smudger pointed out, 'if you don't have the inside information on how to turn them into the finished product. True?'

'Possibly,' Leroy conceded, missing the hoop yet again. 'Maybe. Perhaps.'

'But if you were to supply us with these ingredients,' Smudger said, 'not only would we give you a good price for them, we would also supply you with all the finished goods that you could eat in return.'

'Hmm. Maybe. But I have to tell you, Smudger, that even if I could get you these ingredients – and I'm not saying I can – the risk involved is horrendous. You understand me? Risk with a capital R. And if you ever get caught with them, I don't know you. And if anyone ever asks you where you got these ingredients from, you don't know me. Even if they lock you up and throw away the key, you still don't know me. Right?'

'Right, Leroy. I don't know you. I've never known you, and I never will know you.'

'Definitely?'

'I definitely and positively don't know you, Leroy. So, do we have a deal?'

Leroy considered the proposition as he took aim for the basketball hoop.

'I'll think about it.'

The ball flew from his hands and dropped cleanly through the hoop without even touching the sides. Leroy caught it before it hit the ground.

'OK, Smudger,' he said. 'I've thought about it. You've got yourself a deal. But you don't know me – you understand?'

'What's your name again?' Smudger grinned.

The lines of supply were open.

Heavies

It was Saturday morning. Across the road from Mrs Bubby's, two children with bicycles were keeping the shop under close observation while pretending to do something else.

One of the bikes was upturned, resting on its saddle and handlebars; its front wheel was off. Frankie Crawley was putting a patch on to the inner tube. It was the fourth patch he had put on in the last half hour. Considering that the tube hadn't even punctured yet, it was a somewhat unnecessary repair.

'Frankie,' Myrtle said, with undisguised impatience. 'We can't go on much longer pretending to mend the same puncture, you know.'

'We have to have reconnaissance first, Myrtle,' Frankie pointed out. 'It's the basic rule of covert operations. First you have to get the lie of the land.'

'We know how the land lies, Frankie. It's a road. With tarmac in the middle and pavements up the sides. It's not that complicated. We've both lived in this area for years. Now how much longer—'

'Shush!' Frankie said. 'Watch.'

A van pulled up outside Mrs Bubby's shop. In the passenger seat was Leroy Franks. Driving the van was his elder brother Michael, who was obviously fond of his food – and possibly, considering how big he was, other people's food as well.

Leroy took out a large holdall. He went into Mrs Bubby's shop, and when he reappeared moments later, the holdall seemed to be much lighter – empty even. As he got back into the passenger seat, there was a flash of silver, almost as if the sunlight were glinting on to silver foil. He handed something to his brother, and then the van sped away. The whole incident was over in under a minute.

'Did you see that, Myrtle? What was he doing?'

'I don't know, Frankie. But I do know that I have quite a bit of homework to finish and I can't spend all day standing here pretending to have punctures!'

'Wait,' Frankie said. 'Look, someone else is coming along. It's Emily. And Melanie. From our class.'

The two girls hesitated outside Mrs Bubby's shop. Emily nodded to Melanie to wait for her and she went in.

'What's she getting in there?' Frankie said. 'Eh? What's she up to. Shall I go in and listen?'

'No,' Myrtle said. 'You'll only blow it.'

Emily was up to exactly what Frankie suspected she was up to, but he had no means of proving it.

On entering the shop, Emily went up to the counter, smiled at Mrs Bubby and said, 'I wonder if I could buy something please, Mrs Bubby.'

'Certainly, dear,' Mrs Bubby said. 'What did you have in mind?'

'Something to – *keep me going*, perhaps.'

'And when you say *something to keep you going*, dear, what kind of *something* did you have in mind?'

Emily looked around. They were alone in the shop. It was safe.

'I'd like something to – *hit the spot* perhaps, Mrs Bubby.'

Mrs Bubby reached under the counter and took out a tray, covered in bars of silver bullion; some glistened in the light, others had a duller finish.

'And is it shiny side in, you'll be wanting, dear. Or shiny side out?'

'Shiny side in, please, Mrs Bubby,' Emily said, as she chose a bar of fruit and nut. She paid for the chocolate and quickly headed for the door.

'Thank you very much,' she called.

'You're welcome, dear,' Mrs Bubby said. She hurriedly hid the tray of chocolate back under the counter.

But she didn't think the same thing about her next two customers. As Emily left, two young men entered, both tall and well-built, the heavier of them inclining to fat, but still tough looking, and with tattoos on both his arms.

Mrs Bubby watched them as the two teenagers circled her shop, picking things up, putting them back down again, until she lost patience.

'Have you ever heard the expression "if you don't want the goods don't muck them about"?'

The thinner of the two thugs put down the car magazine he was looking at, an unpleasant smile on his face. 'As a matter of fact, lady,' he said, approaching the counter, 'Me and my friend Darren here were more wondering if there was something *we* could sell *you*. Isn't that right, Darren?'

'Yeah, Tony,' the fat one said. 'That's right.'

Mrs Bubby wished that someone else would come into the shop. She didn't feel safe with these two.

'Sell me something?' she said. 'You? The salesmen who come in here usually have suits and ties on – not grubby T-shirts and studs in their noses and big tattoos of snakes going up their arms. You don't much look like sales reps as far as I can tell.'

'Please, lady, on the contrary,' Tony leered. 'We're very commercial travellers. Highly commercial, aren't we, Darren?'

'Most commercial,' Darren agreed.

'What we sell,' Tony said, 'is security, and peace of mind. I sell the security, and Darren here collects the weekly rental.'

Mrs Bubby's mind was racing. She didn't like these two at all. Not the oily, smarmy one, not the other one with the piggy little eyes that gave pigs' eyes a bad name. How much did they know? And how did they know it? Perhaps a careless customer had accidentally given her away. Perhaps they had seen someone come out from the shop with a flash of silver in their pocket. Or more than likely they knew nothing and were just chancers, trying it on.

'I don't know what you want and I don't want to know,' Mrs Bubby said. 'So if you don't want to buy anything, why don't you both just leg it!'

Tony leaned over the counter and pressed his nose so

close to Mrs Bubby's that he was practically wearing her glasses.

'Leg it?' he said. '*Bootleg* it, is that?'

Mrs Bubby felt herself go cold. But then she was saved by the bell, as the door opened and a Chocolate Trooper entered. Darren saw him and at once began edging for the door. Tony took a moment longer to realize that a customer had entered.

'What's going on?' the Trooper demanded.

'The lady thought she had something in her eye, and I was checking it for her,' Tony said. 'Just doing my good deed for the day, you know. Like you're supposed to. Well,' he said to Mrs Bubby, 'maybe we'll see you again.'

'Not if I see you first,' Mrs Bubby said quietly.

'Crunchy apples to you, then, citizen,' Tony said, and slid out of the door after Darren.

'Go choke on your pips,' Mrs Bubby muttered. Then raising her voice, she asked, 'And what can I do for you, citizen? A nice Healthy For You Snack, maybe? Or how about a bottle of Regular As Clockwork Prune Juice?'

'I'll have the *Daily Good For You*, please,' the Trooper said, pointing to a stack of newspapers. 'Thanks.'

He paid, wished Mrs Bubby crunchy apples and she wished him juicy oranges. He then advised her to have a banana, and he left the shop.

Mrs Bubby was glad to see him go. But she was equally glad that he had arrived when he did. She didn't know how she would have dealt with Tony and Darren on her own, and she hoped that they wouldn't come back. She decided not to mention them to Smudger and Huntly.

They had enough to worry about with making all the chocolate. And there was nothing they could do anyway.

That was the trouble with stepping outside the law – even an unjust law – you lost its protection in doing so. Otherwise she could have shopped the two thugs to the Trooper. But if she had, they would certainly have immediately returned the compliment, and have shopped her as well, right there, in her shop.

Myrtle's patience was at its tether's end.

'So shall we put your theory to the test, Frankie, or shan't we?' she said. 'Before someone else goes in, and we're here all afternoon.'

'OK, Myrtle. The coast looks pretty clear. In you go. And remember – *a little of what the doctor ordered.* See what you get.'

'And you can put my wheel back on while I'm in there,' Myrtle told him. 'And do it properly.'

She marched across the road and pushed the shop door open. Frankie picked up a tyre lever and began to fit the tyre back on to the rim.

The bell rang. Mrs Bubby looked up from her crossword puzzle. The girl who entered the shop was vaguely familiar to her, but she wasn't a regular. Not the way Huntly and Smudger had been regulars, in every day for a chocolate bar or a comic. No, she was a once-a-month customer at the most, the kind who only ever came in for some stationery, or a pencil sharpener when it was too late or too inconvenient to buy these things anywhere else.

There was something about her. She wasn't in a uniform, and yet she seemed the uniform type – well-scrubbed, business-like, no messing about. Prim and proper, and highly starched. Looked as if she could have been a Young Pioneer, or failing that, an ironing board.

'Morning, dear.'

'Good morning, shopkeeper person.'

'And what can I do for you today? The *Good For You* comic? A nice Healthy Snack? A beetroot-juice flavoured lollipop?'

'Actually, yes I wouldn't mind a little something – that is something to – *keep me going.*'

(Nod, nod. Wink, wink.)

'To keep you going, eh?' Mrs Bubby repeated. Had she got this girl wrong? Maybe she was a friend of Smudger's. 'And what sort of something do you have in mind, dear?'

There was a pause. Mrs Bubby had been about to reach under the counter, but the silence stopped her.

'What sort of something, dear?' she asked again.

'Something . . . to . . . keep . . . that is . . . *a little of what the doctored ordered* – if you know what I mean.'

(Wink, wink. Nod, nod.)

It was wrong. Wrong, wrong, *wrong!* And no amount of nodding or winking made it otherwise.

Mrs Bubby gave Myrtle her best twinkly smile – the nice, harmless old lady one.

'Right. You'll be needing something a little special in that case, eh?'

Myrtle nodded, barely able to disguise her mounting excitement. She was going to catch this old biddy, red-handed. There could be a medal in this. Promotion even, up through the ranks of the Pioneers. When she was in charge, she'd order Frankie Crawley to go on five-mile marches, with a heavy kit bag on his back. Two kit bags. And a suitcase. That would show him who was who.

'I keep a few under the counter for selected customers,' Mrs Bubby was saying. 'There you are, dear. That should keep you going for a while.'

(Nod, nod. Wink, wink.)

Myrtle looked down. Whatever she expected to see, it hadn't been this. A large, yellow banana lay on the counter-top, like a big yellow grin.

'I always keep back a few best bananas for special customers,' Mrs Bubby said. 'And you seem like a special customer to me. So you take that banana away, and you enjoy it. As far as the digestion goes, a regular banana is better than syrup of figs.'

Myrtle stared at the banana. But staring at it didn't make it go away. She could hardly refuse it, having gone this far. So she paid for the banana and left the shop. As the door closed behind her, she seemed to hear the sound of laughter – a sort of sniggering noise.

Myrtle crossed the road. Frankie dropped his spanner and hissed, 'What did you get? I was right, wasn't I? They're selling bootleg chocolate or home-made sweets or something in there, aren't they?'

Myrtle took the large banana from behind her back and brandished it under Frankie's nose, as if she were thinking of sticking the banana up there – without bothering to peel it first.

140

'Not really, Frankie, no. They're selling these – bananas. Here, you have it. Take it home and stick it in your fruit bowl.' She thrust the banana into his shirt pocket. 'And in future, Frankie, don't waste my time. Home-made sweets! Huh! You've got what's called an overactive imagination. It's that or a pea-sized brain.'

'But, Myrtle, I was absolutely positive—'

'Absolutely, positively wrong. I'm also positive, Frankie, that I don't want any more to do with you or your stupid spying games. I'm off to start my homework. So cheerio!'

'But, Myrtle—'

Myrtle was gone, scooting away on her bicycle. Frankie took the banana from his pocket and frowned at it. He had been so sure that something was going on. He still *was* sure of it. His guess that the password must have been wrong, that was all. But he'd find out what it was. He wasn't finished yet.

A voice interrupted his thoughts.

'*Spare some change, young gentleman. Spare some change. Hungry and homeless. Spare some change.*'

A shabby figure was huddled in the doorway of an empty shop.

'Spare some change, young sir,' he repeated. 'Help a working actor down on his luck. Spare some change.'

The man was wrapped in a moth-eaten old blanket and sitting on a piece of cardboard. He looked as though he had just woken up. There was an empty beer can beside him. Frankie frowned.

'I'm afraid that I don't approve of sparing change, my man,' he said haughtily. 'Nobody has to be homeless now that the Good For You Party is in power. There are plenty of shelters. It simply isn't necessary and it's sheer self-indulgence, going around trying to make people sorry for you and living off their charity and tender feelings. You should get yourself admitted to one of the Good For You Homeless Hostels. Then try to make a new life for yourself as an upright and hardworking member of society. And have a wash while you're at it.'

'I don't like hostels,' the man said. 'They coop me up. And it's hardly my fault that I'm out of work. I used to make good money – doing TV commercials. You'll doubtlessly remember the Chocolate Man – in the ad for Benson's Chocolate? That was me. Yet another of my triumphs. I earned top money and was a big celebrity, back in my heyday.'

'Then shame on you for ever advertising chocolate,' Frankie said, unsympathetically. 'How many children's lives have you blighted and destroyed by advertising such dreadful products.'

'It wasn't a dreadful product,' said the homeless Chocolate Man. 'It was an *excellent* product! At least it was in those days. Everyone thought so then, and it made me a good living. But when chocolate was banned, I got put on the actors' blacklist and now I can't get work any more. Oh, the slings and arrows of outrageous fortune – how they pierce the soul.'

'I've no sympathy for you,' Frankie said. 'You brought it all on yourself by trying to persuade innocent children to buy disgusting chocolate and rot their teeth with it and end up fat and spotty.'

'Ah, out, out damn spot!' the homeless man said theatrically.

'You're only suffering now for the wicked misdeeds of your past,' Frankie continued. 'As you sow, so shall you reap.'

'Rubbish. It was bad luck, that was all. And the rest is just propaganda,' the man said. 'And you giving lectures doesn't help. So are you going to spare me some change or aren't you?'

'No,' Frankie said. 'I'm not. But if you really are hungry, I will give you this wholesome, nutritious banana. There you are, my man, there's a nice big banana for you. You eat that and a few more like it, and you'll be back on your feet in no time. Goodbye.'

Frankie left the banana in the man's woolly hat, which he had set on the ground for charitable passers-by to put coins in. He rode off on his bike, feeling that he had done a major good deed for the day.

The homeless man looked at the banana with disdain.

Is this a banana I see before me? he thought. When once I was the Chocolate Man himself and used to work with all the top names at the BBC! Now all I get is a tawdry banana. Alas, the bitter bread of banishment.

But all the same, he was genuinely hungry, and you didn't turn your nose up at a nice banana when you were hungry. On the contrary, you ate it.

Which is what he did.

Eateasy

'**W**hat do the Troopers who come into your shop think about it always smelling of burnt toast, Mrs Bubby?' Huntly said.

'They just think I'm dotty, love,' Mrs Bubby explained. 'It's a great advantage as you get older. People just think you're barmy and that you couldn't possibly be up to anything. You could be a master criminal, but if you're over sixty, no one will ever suspect. But people can be wrong about that – as they'll find out once they're past sixty themselves.'

It was Sunday morning, and for the moment all was well in the world. At least it was in Mrs Bubby's stockroom. The chocolate was cooling in the trays; the toast was scorching nicely in the toaster to disguise those give-away smells; and on the shelves lay fresh supplies of cocoa and sugar, courtesy of Leroy Franks.

And yet . . .

Discontent sat upon Smudger Moore's soul like an unscratched itch. He had a bad case of the 'if onlys'.

'If only what *now*?' Huntly said. Smudger was his best friend, and he'd have stood by him to the death. But that didn't mean that he didn't get fed up with him sometimes.

144

It was the way he was never content with anything, always wanting that little bit more.

'If only *what*?' Huntly repeated. 'Look at it, we've got a great little set up here. We've got regular chocolate, we're making steady money. Mrs Bubby is happy. I'm happy. The people who come to buy our bootleg chocolate seem pretty happy. The only person who isn't happy is—'

'It's not that I'm *un*happy, Huntly,' Smudger explained. 'It's just I feel we could be doing a bit better, that's all.'

Mrs Bubby looked up from cleaning pots and pans.

'Better? In what way?'

'It was what I read,' Smudger said. 'About Prohibition. In the old days, with the first bootleggers, they didn't just make their own beer or whatever, they also provided somewhere for people to go – a little club sort of thing, with a bit of atmosphere, where people could relax and be themselves and not have to worry. Where they could forget all about things like homework and exams and the Good For You Party. Speakeasies they were called. Well, it just seems to me that things would be a whole lot better if *we* had our own little speakeasy – an eateasy in fact! Where people could come and enjoy a whole selection of chocolate, and maybe ice cream too, and milkshakes, and well, you name it.'

Huntly and Mrs Bubby exchanged a look. This wasn't such a bad 'if only' as 'if onlys' go.

'But, Smudger, you'd need to go underground for something like that,' Mrs Bubby said. 'That kind of establishment should always be underground. With a secret exit at the back, in case there's a raid.'

'I guess so,' Smudger nodded, rather discouraged.

'Yes. Moles and nightclubs should always be underground. And I don't have a basement here . . . unless . . .' She suddenly stopped, then brightened. 'Come out the back a minute. Into the garden. There's something I want to show you.'

It wasn't immediately obvious what it was. There wasn't much to see in the back garden, except a rickety old shed, made of corrugated panels, corroded and brown with rust.

'There!' Mrs Bubby said, looking at the shed as though it were a national treasure which just happened to be on her property. 'There you are!'

'Er, where, exactly?' Smudger said. 'All I can see is a sort of rusty old, well, shed.'

'Ah yes, Smudger,' Mrs Bubby said. 'That's what so clever about it. It looks like a shed.' She led them over to it. 'It sounds like a shed.' She rapped it with her knuckles. 'It even smells like a shed.'

They went inside. It certainly did smell like a shed. It was full of muddy flowerpots and decaying shelves, hammers that didn't hit anything any more, bolts that didn't fit anything, and glues that had gone hard in their tubes.

'How many sheds, boys, have got stairs in them?'

Stairs?

Huntly looked at Smudger. What was she talking about?

'Pass me that torch.'

He handed it to her and a beam of light illuminated the

146

rear of the shed. There was indeed a staircase there – steep and severe – leading right down into . . . what?

'Follow me,' Mrs Bubby said. 'And don't go breaking your necks!'

They followed her down the steep wooden steps, holding on to a handrail. At the bottom was a door which creaked loudly as Mrs Bubby pushed it open.

'Needs a drop of lubrication that,' she said.

She led the way on into the darkness and shone her torch along the wall.

'There ought to be a switch somewhere – if it's still working. There!' she pointed the torch beam. 'Give that a flick, one of you.'

Huntly gingerly pressed the old switch down, hoping he wouldn't get an electric shock in the process.

Two fluorescent strip lights flickered uncertainly, as if unsure whether to come on or fizzle out. Then one of them stayed on, and the next one joined it.

'Wow!'

The light revealed a large room with a concrete floor and some wooden partitions. It was filled with junk and debris. In one corner was a collapsed wooden bunk bed; the top bed had fallen into the lower one and seemed to be fast asleep on it.

'What is it, Mrs Bubby?'

'Air-raid shelter,' she said. 'Second World War. Half the street would have fitted in here and there'd still be room for the milkman. They used to come down here when the air-raid siren sounded, away from the bombs.'

The boys looked around. There was rubbish over half a

century old, yellowing newspapers from another era. *Peace Declared* one headline read. *War Finally Over*. And another with the one word on its front page – *Victory!*

'Well?' Mrs Bubby said. 'What do you think? Would this make a good eateasy, or wouldn't it?'

'It's amazing,' Smudger said. 'But it does need, well, serious tidying up. Very severe tidying up. To be honest, for an air-raid shelter, it looks as if a bomb went off in it.'

'It's nothing that can't be fixed though,' Smudger said, more enthusiastically. 'With a bit of DIY. And we could get some tables and chairs in—'

'Where from?'

'We'll find them in skips and do them up. Then give the walls a lick of paint. Get a little bar over there in the corner, serving milkshakes and chocolate sundaes.'

'Get a bit of music going,' Mrs Bubby said.

'Yeah,' Smudger said. 'We could have a dance floor.'

'And over here, boys. Come and see this,' Mrs Bubby said, leading them to an alcove door hidden in the shadows. 'This is the most important thing anywhere like this can have.'

The door opened to a tunnel, which led on into darkness.

'It's another way out,' Mrs Bubby said. 'Emergency exit – one that strangers coming in the front way wouldn't know about. When trouble comes in the front door, you leg it straight out the back. So if anyone raided this little eateasy, or paid a surprise visit, you'd have a means of escape.'

'Where does the tunnel come out, Mrs Bubby?'

'About a hundred yards away. In a little alleyway. There used to be two entrances to the air-raid shelter, you see, one from the garden, one from the alley near the street. There's a manhole cover over it now to stop people falling in. You give it a shove, push it aside, and out you go. And look, there's something else here as well.'

She pulled back another door which opened to reveal a kind of big larder, large enough to walk into and to contain a few weeks' worth of supplies. At present the pantry was well stocked with cobwebs and mildew. Its door didn't look like a door at all, but more like part of the wall. If you hadn't known it was there you would never have found it.

'Storage,' she said. 'And look at the back of the door. Lead-lined against shrapnel, this one. But lead does other things. It shields out radiation. And you know what that means?'

'The chocolate detectors don't work through lead!' Huntly exclaimed. 'They'll never find our stash.'

'You could have half a ton of chocolate in here and nobody would ever know. So what do you think, boys?'

'I say let's do it!' Huntly said. 'I say let's flipping well do it! What do you say, Mrs Bubby?'

'I say let's do it, boys. And let's make a start right now!'

She picked up a broom, which was leaning against some rubble in the corner, and swept round the shelter like a small tornado, sweeping up a great cloud of dust, which had nowhere to go but to settle back on to the floor again. She carried on until the head of the broom fell off, and she threw it into a bin.

Huntly and Smudger coughed and spluttered, and looking at each other's grey hair, erupted with laughter.

'We're going to have our own eateasy, Huntly!' Smudger said. 'We're going to be proper bootleggers! Just like in the films!'

He plunged his fingers into his hair and shook the dust from it. For a second he looked like a mad holy man, surrounded by a halo.

It took longer than they expected to convert the old air-raid shelter into an eateasy. Painting, decorating, clearing the place out and finding furniture for it proved more complicated and time consuming than Smudger's enthusiasm had made it sound. They raided skips and scrapyards, and even when they found things they could use, they all had to be transported. The smaller items were easy enough to smuggle in, but the larger ones, such as chairs and tables and planks of wood to make the bar and the dance floor with, all had to be moved under cover of darkness. Sometimes Smudger could even be seen pushing an old pram down the road, but there definitely wasn't a baby in it.

Then, of course, the place had to be fitted out. Smudger was good with his hands, and so was Huntly, up to a point, though he was better with his brain. Mrs Bubby, however, proved surprisingly adept at doing it herself.

'I had no choice,' she said, 'once dear Mr Bubby passed on. It was do it myself or never have it done at all. I couldn't afford to pay tradesmen. They charge you an arm and a leg just to set foot in the place.'

Other necessary items, which couldn't be salvaged from

skips, just had to be bought, and buying them took money. And the way to make money was to keep selling bootleg chocolate.

But despite the risks they were taking, as far as Smudger and Huntly were concerned, the danger of discovery seemed remote. As the weeks went by, their confidence increased. And maybe they began to take one or two risks too many.

Each Sunday morning would find them at Mrs Bubby's shop, either working on the air-raid shelter, or making up a fresh batch of chocolate for the week ahead.

Mrs Bubby, as usual, would be burning toast to disguise the chocolate smell. And, as usual, a customer or two would come in for their Sunday papers and say, 'Burnt the toast again, Mrs Bubby?' And she would nod in feigned helplessness and reply, 'Afraid so, dear. Just can't seem to help it these days. I'm a regular butterfingers – well, a burnt-toast fingers anyway.'

The customers would leave with their papers thinking, Poor old Mrs Bubby. She's starting to lose her marbles.

Smudger and Huntly were careful not to sell too much chocolate. They didn't want to flood the local market, and besides, they now needed to stockpile supplies for the eateasy. They had decided to open it at the weekends only. It wasn't feasible to open it during the week – they had homework to do, and other commitments, and besides, their parents would have become suspicious.

Despite initially resolving not to be affected by what they were doing, both boys were subtly changed by their new-found status as bootleggers. Word got around that Huntly and Smudger were the people to know.

Smudger wore his baseball cap at a defiant angle, with the peak at the side, and an old pair of slightly scratched sunglasses – even when it was raining.

'Can't cope without m' shades,' he'd say, leaning casually against a lamppost in an attempt to look cool. 'The light just seems to dazzle my eyes.'

Huntly remained reserved, but had moments when he couldn't help but check his hair in a shop window and think to himself, There goes one cool bootlegger!

They say that power corrupts and that absolute power corrupts absolutely. And while vanity is not quite in the same category as power, and is not always a bad thing (as you might not even bother washing your face without it) it can still undermine a person's character, judgement and good sense. It makes them overestimate their abilities and no longer see themselves for who they really are.

But as Smudger said, what was the point of running high risks and leading a precarious and a dangerously uncertain life if you couldn't put on a little style?

But while a bit of swagger may be excusable in a film star or a pop singer, what a bootlegger needs is a low profile. A bootlegger shouldn't stand out from the crowd. In fact, he should seem like the most ordinary and nondescript person in it.

Smudger knew these things well. But he put them out of his mind, or simply managed to forget about them.

But one person hadn't. One person in the school had

noticed this change in his classmate. He had observed, and he had made notes, and he had passed on his findings to the appropriate authorities.

That person was Frankie Crawley.

Opening Hours

Mrs Bubby looked around the room. It was unrecognizable as the air-raid shelter it had once been.

The eateasy had taken shape slowly, piece by piece. But now the pieces all seemed to have suddenly fallen into place. The jigsaw was complete.

Smudger put down his paint brush and massaged his aching back.

'How does it look?'

Huntly took a break from his polishing. He looked around at the bar, the dance area, the hi-fi system (borrowed from Smudger's bedroom).

'It looks the business,' he grinned.

'So, are we ready for the grand opening then?' Mrs Bubby asked. 'Or aren't we?'

'How about this Saturday?' Huntly suggested.

'All right with me,' Smudger said. 'Invitations to party animals only.'

'Am I a party animal?' Mrs Bubby asked.

'The original one and only,' Smudger said.

'How about Mr Blades?' Huntly said. 'Without his chocolate recipe we wouldn't have anything to eat easy about.'

'I'll post him an invite,' Smudger said. 'And if anyone

wants to know, it's the After School and Weekend Study Club we're running here. Swots, egg heads and book-worms only. And we'd better recruit a few people we can trust to help out at the bar and things. We can't manage it all on our own.'

So they set about recruiting staff.

Emily and Melanie could be trusted – one hundred per cent. And Leroy too, of course, their supplier, he might like to be involved. But there were others too. Big Arthur, in Mr Headley's class, was elected to the job of head bar-man and choc-tail shaker.

They also recruited Titch Mulholland for security. Although small, he could break an HB pencil between two fingers, he did karate, kendo and ju-jitsu, and had a fearsome temper when roused – although most of the time he kept it under strict control.

After their weeks of work, both the boys and Mrs Bubby were determined that nothing should spoil the grand opening. Smudger told his mum that he was going round to Huntly's house that evening, and Huntly told his mother that he would be round at Smudger's. It was a risk and it wasn't right and they knew it, but they did it any-way, because sometimes that's how people are – they're prepared to take their chances for the sake of something they desperately want to do, and they're ready to bend the rules a little.

Mrs Bubby didn't have to make any excuses or explain to anybody where she was going, which she felt was a pity in some ways, as it might have been nice to have someone to tell fibs to.

Invitations went out to all trusted friends and existing customers to attend the grand opening evening of 'The After School Study Club.' There were no cards, no envelopes, no formal RSVPs. The invitations went out as quiet words and whispers, and the answers came back as a nod or a shake of the head – with plenty of nodding and not much shaking. It still had to be remembered that careless talk could cost liberty, so vigilance and discretion had to be maintained. As Mrs Bubby never hesitated to remind people: 'Watch out, watch out, there's a Trooper about. And he's got his eye on *you*!'

The only thing that could have – indeed certainly would have – marred the occasion, was the knowledge that Frankie Crawley was, at ten past seven that same Saturday night, making his weekly report to the same hard-eyed Inspector at Party Headquarters.

'They're up to something, I'm sure,' Frankie insisted, in a low, unnecessarily confidential voice. There was no one to overhear him, apart from the Trooper by the door, and it was plain whose side he was on anyway.

'So you say, Young Pioneer,' the Inspector drawled, looking at Frankie over the rim of a cup of milk-less and sugar-less China tea called Gunpowder. (He hadn't offered Frankie a cup, much to his relief.) 'You're always giving us little titbits of information, aren't you?'

'Yes,' Frankie said. 'And you know why. I don't have much choice, do I? In fact I've given you lots of leads recently. So why don't you follow them up?'

'Because the trouble with all your leads to date, Young Pioneer,' the Inspector said sarcastically, 'is that none of them have any dogs on the end. Just red herrings. We've squandered a lot of manpower following up your information, and as yet have nothing to show for it. So the next time that you cry wolf, make sure there is one.'

Frankie picked his Young Pioneers' cap up off the Inspector's desk and sulkily headed for the door.

'All right,' he said. 'I'll bring you something there can't be any doubts about. There won't be any mistake next time.'

If you had been at all susceptible to headaches, the chances were that you would have had one by now. The music was still loud, even though Huntly had insisted that it be turned down, worried that it might be heard outside. But the walls of the old air-raid shelter were thick enough to trap the sound within.

Big Arthur was behind the bar, concocting choc-tails to make your mouth water, your mind boggle, your waistband expand and your taste buds cry out with joy.

In addition to the choc-tails, there were chocolate milkshakes on offer. Mrs Bubby had used some of the milk and bootleg chocolate to concoct a few batches of her famous (so she said) home-made ice cream. She had also prepared some toffee, fudge and a variety of boiled sweets for the occasion, along with home-made sweet lemonade and ginger beer and a selection of cakes.

Nobody was going short of anything. The 'After School Study Club' was jumping, the till was ringing, and everyone was having a good time.

Mr Blades was one of the last to arrive. And he looked

very different now too. No longer the crotchety, rather eccentric bookseller in the straw hat, with chocolate poking out of his top pocket. This was another kind of figure altogether. Mr Blades came dressed in a stylish grey suit, with a diamond tiepin on his tie; his shoes were polished; his cuffs were starched, and in his right hand he carried a stick of dark, polished mahogany, on the end of which was a silver handle in the shape of an eagle's head. He greeted Huntly and Smudger like long-lost friends then made a beeline for Mrs Bubby and her ice cream – both of which he seemed to take a strong liking to.

And then there was a knock at the door at the top of the steps.

Titch went to answer it. He opened the door a few centimetres and peered out into the night.

'Yes?'

Two figures stood, waiting to enter. Not children – young men. One was tough-looking with slicked-back hair; the other was fatter and had tattoos running like lizards up his arms.

'Yes, gents?' Titch said.

The 'gents' grinned at him with sharp, shark's-tooth smiles.

'We'd like to come in,' Tony said. 'It's about some insurance.'

'Can I ask who invited you, gents?' Titch asked. He could see that even a boy good at karate and kendo and capable of breaking pencils between his fingers was no match on his own for these two.

Darren raised a large, tattooed fist. Titch could make

out the letters R-I-G-H-T, the R tattooed on Darren's thumb and the other letters on his fingers. Presumably he had L-E-F-T on his other hand.

'See this fist?' he said. 'This is my invitation. I find it gets me in everywhere. I want to talk to the boss. We've got a very reasonably priced insurance policy we want to sell.'

'Are you familiar with the concept of insurance?' Tony added, as they pushed Titch aside. 'It's basically where people pay a sum of money so as not to get their heads punched in.'

Smudger saw the two thugs entering and instantly knew something was wrong. Mrs Bubby recognized them immediately.

The room fell quiet.

'Sorry, Smudger—' Titch began.

'It's all right,' Smudger said. 'We'll take care of it. It's OK, everyone,' he announced. 'Carry on enjoying yourselves.' He turned to Melanie who was at the music controls. 'Can you put the music back on – something upbeat.'

The party-goers went on partying as though nothing had happened, while Huntly and Smudger led the two heavies over to a private corner table.

Tony sat down and looked around appraisingly. 'Nice place,' he said.

Smudger shrugged deprecatingly.

'It's just a club.'

Tony turned to Darren.

'Hear that?' he said. 'They've got a club.'

'Really?' Darren said, with mock surprise. 'Well,' and he took something out from under his leather jacket, 'we don't have a club but we do have a nice baseball bat.'

He laid it on the table, keeping hold of the handle.

Tony looked at the bat.

'Now this,' Tony said, 'is the kind of reason why people need insurance. Or accidents might happen. Fire, you see, or theft, or—'

At which Darren took the baseball bat in his hands as if it were a snooker cue and 'potted' a glass clean off the table to shatter on the floor.

'—accidental damage.'

'You nasty little toe rag.'

Darren looked up. Mrs Bubby was standing staring at him, her face flushed with anger.

'Let's just stick to the matter in hand, eh? Shall we?' Tony said. 'And save the personal abuse for later. Now, if you want to stay in business here, well, there's going to be a little price to pay. You're going to be wanting us to look after you, to make sure these kinds of things don't happen again. So what we're looking for from you is, well, how much shall we say—?'

But he never did say. Because suddenly, someone else was there at the table – a figure in a light grey suit.

'Let's say nothing, shall we?' Blades said.

The two thugs looked up, surprised. Darren glanced at the polished mahogany cane with the silver eagle's head handle, which Blades held ready in his grip. It seemed that with a twist of his hand, Mr Blades could have extracted from that cane a long, slim, brightly gleaming sword. Or maybe that was just your imagination. But would you want to risk finding out?

Darren swallowed hard. The tattoo of a mermaid which he had on his throat seemed to bobble up and down on the tide of his Adam's apple.

'Let's say nothing at all, eh?' Blades repeated. 'And then let's walk out of here and pretend we've never seen the place? How about that?'

Tony stared at him malevolently, like a cobra about to strike.

Blades smiled and turned to Huntly and Smudger. 'I hope you don't think it rude, my getting involved, boys, it's just that I know this couple of thugs. They tried to get me to "insure" my bookshop once. I believe they may have regretted it.'

Tony grabbed for the sword stick, but he was nowhere near quick enough. Blades struck a sharp blow with it across the young thug's hand. He yelped and recoiled.

'Now look, Blades—'

'No,' Blades said. 'You look. You and your illustrated friend.'

Blades pointed to the baseball bat with the tip of the cane.

'Take that out of harm's way, would you please, Mrs Bubby? I don't think we want any exhibitions of baseball skill tonight. Not in a confined and crowded space. Thank you.'

Mrs Bubby took the bat away. Darren squirmed in his chair, like a toddler who has seen his favourite toy confiscated by the teacher. Neither of them seemed inclined to risk any further action.

'Now you listen to me, Tony,' Blades said. 'You and Darren here, the pet bulldog, the both of you together amount to nothing more than small time. Small-time criminals and small-time thugs. If you got any smaller time, you wouldn't even register on the clock. This place doesn't need your protection because it's got mine, and the protection of everyone I know. Now get out of here and don't come back. And don't even think of tipping the Troopers off about this place, or someone might think to tip them off about you. Got it?'

Tony rose sullenly to his feet, smouldering like a firework which somehow knew that it wouldn't be able to explode that night. He raised a threatening finger and pointed it in Blades's direction.

'One day, Blades,' he said. 'One day . . .'

But he didn't complete the sentence. He just let the unspoken threat hang in the air.

Blades gave a thin smile.

'Yes, one day,' he said. 'Maybe one day, Tony, but not today. You'll find the door at the top of the stairs. The way you came in will take you out.'

A moment's hesitation, then they turned to go.

'Come on,' Tony said to Darren. 'Let's get out. It's just a bunch of kids anyway.'

They swaggered as best as they were able up to the top of the stairs.

'And what are you all staring at?!' Darren demanded.

'OK, everyone,' Mrs Bubby called. 'Relax. Party's over

– or rather, to put it another way, the party's just getting started.'

Melanie turned up the volume on the sound system, and soon the place was jumping again, and the crowd was three deep at the bar.

Blades sat down at the table.

'Mr Blades,' Huntly said. 'How did you get rid of them like that? We thought – well – I don't mean to be rude, but we thought—'

'That I was just a creaky old bookseller,' Blades smiled. 'With a few screws loose.'

'Well, I wouldn't have said that,' Huntly blushed.

'No, of course not,' Blades agreed. 'You're too polite. But thinking, of course, that's another matter. Anyway, you're quite correct. I am a creaky old bookseller – amongst other things. Meantime—'

Mrs Bubby rejoined them. She smiled and sat down on a vacant chair.

'I'll hang on to that baseball bat,' she said. 'I'll keep it under the bed. It might come in handy.'

'Well, it's quite a place you have here, boys,' Mr Blades said, nodding with approval. 'Quite an impressive set-up.'

'Thanks, Mr Blades,' Smudger said. 'We did our best. But to be honest none of it would have been possible without your recipe.'

'It's kind of you to say so,' Blades said. 'Only listen. I don't want to bore you with good advice, but I think you need to improve security here. You need a lookout, some kind of advanced warning system. Those two thugs should never have got in. And the other thing is to be careful not to throw your money around now you're making it. Nothing attracts attention quicker than someone with a big wad of cash.'

Huntly nodded solemnly, listening to Blades's every word. But Smudger's attention was already wandering. He had maybe listened to half of what Blades had said, but the rest had failed to hold his attention. He was looking around the club instead. After all, here he was, Smudger Moore, part owner of an eateasy, bootlegger, man of status, a man to be reckoned with, a man of parts.

And what use was status if you couldn't display it? What use was money, if you couldn't throw a little of it around?

Mrs Bubby went off to busy herself at the bar. She returned a few minutes later carrying a tray. Upon it was a choc-tail in a frosted glass and a large slice of chocolate cake with chunks of chocolate in the icing.

Mr Blades certainly couldn't complain that he wasn't being looked after.

'For you,' Mrs Bubby said. And she put the tray down in front of him.

'Good heavens,' Mr Blades said. 'This is a feast! I don't know if I'll ever manage to eat all this.'

But he did.

The Lookout

The next morning, Huntly and Smudger returned to Mrs Bubby's shop to prepare the chocolate for the following week. This arrangement soon became a ritual. Leroy ensured that regular supplies of ingredients were delivered during the week, so the raw materials were always there and waiting every Sunday.

The Chocolate Detector Vans which had once so persistently roamed the streets had been pulled out and moved on to other locations. The area had been cleansed, as far as the authorities were aware, and been declared a chocolate-free zone. There was always the danger of spot checks, however, so Mrs Bubby took to keeping the bulk of the bootleg chocolate down in the air-raid shelter, hidden behind the lead-lined door.

As far as the two boys' parents were concerned, they spent their Sunday mornings going for bike rides together. The fact that their bike rides only took them as far as Mrs Bubby's shop was something they maybe forgot to mention.

Each Sunday morning, as the two boys prepared the chocolate, Mrs Bubby would sell the *Sunday Good For You* newspaper in her shop. She had moved on from scorching toast to burning joss-sticks to keep the sweet smell of boiling sugar at bay. If anybody remarked on this new affectation, she told them that she had taken up yoga and meditation classes and that the sandalwood aromas helped her to stay calm. She explained that a woman of her age had entered the spiritual time of life.

When she closed the shop, shortly after noon, she would then attend to the accounts of the eateasy, tallying up the takings, deciding how much was owed to suppliers, how much should be set aside for contingencies and how much should be shared out amongst them as profit.

As time passed, their individual earnings mounted up to what is often described as a tidy sum. In Smudger's case it was a pretty untidy sum, as he kept his money in an old biscuit tin in his wardrobe at home. It was hidden under a great pile of toys, which he no longer played with but refused to throw away. His mother, in turn, refused to tidy the cupboard up until he did. So there was no fear of discovery and his tin of untidy money was quite safe.

Mrs Bubby also had an aversion to banks.

'What the taxman doesn't know about, the taxman doesn't want a share of,' was yet another of her many mottoes.

So she kept her money buried under the contents of her socks and underwear drawer, in the bedroom of her flat above the shop.

Only Huntly decided to entrust his share of the profits to a financial institution. He opened up a Junior Saver account at the branch of his local bank. If anybody asked any questions, he would tell them that it was money he had earned from his paper round. The fact that he didn't have a paper round was neither here nor there.

The profit on bootleg chocolate was considerable. Not that Smudger, Huntly and Mrs Bubby overcharged. Because of the nature of the bootleg business, you couldn't help but make money and grow rich. In a way, the money made itself. If only the chocolate had made itself as easily.

Soon Smudger's money was itching to spend itself, and Smudger itched along with it. And the only thing to assuage an itch like that was the scratch of a good splash out on something nice, something long-yearned for.

Mrs Bubby felt the same.

'Who needs savings at my age?' she asked herself. 'If I don't spend it now, I might never live to. And I do need a few new things to wear – spiritual time of life or not. I've hardly got a stitch to put on to be honest.'

Mrs Bubby actually had a whole wardrobe full of stitches to put on. She just didn't want to wear any of them. What she wanted was something new.

So she set off into town with her bootleg money (after hanging a sign in the shop window saying 'Closed Due To Illness') and first visited the hairdresser's for a wash, cut, tint, style and perm, and then went off round the clothes shops, in search of Italian fashions for the maturer woman.

That same afternoon, Smudger Moore took himself down to the Mud and Ruts Off Road Bike Shop where he picked out a bright-yellow, top-of-the-range mountain bike, with hydraulic suspension, titanium frame, shock absorbers and a black rear mudguard with the letters SMUDGE 1 picked out on it in fluorescent characters.

He also bought himself a pair of wrap-around sunglasses with mirrored lenses, a pair of cycling gloves with red zigzags on the back and a helmet in metallic silver.

As he cycled off he looked like a boy who has just won the lottery. When he got home, he hid the bike in the garden shed under a tarpaulin. He didn't think his parents would quite believe him if he told them that he had paid it out of his pocket money. He'd wait till it had got dirty and acquired a few dents, then say he'd got it second hand or something. Nor could he really show it to his sister, Kylie, who had a tendency to reveal confidential information at inconvenient moments, even when sworn to secrecy – although she had been pretty good so far about the chocolate. But then, if she mentioned that, as she well understood, the supply would stop.

But Smudger *had* to show his new bike to somebody. The same way that Mrs Bubby maybe felt compelled to show off her new clothes and shoes and matching accessories by getting the taxi to drop her at the corner instead of the door, and swanking the rest of the way down the street to her shop, in full view of anyone who cared to look.

So when Huntly (with his share of the loot still sensibly in the bank) arrived at Mrs Bubby's stockroom for the weekly chocolate-making on Sunday morning, he was first surprised to see Smudger's yellow mountain bike and then equally astonished to find Mrs Bubby, tottering around in high heels and wearing a silk dress in turquoise blue, which wouldn't have looked out of place at a dinner party.

He looked at them both in near despair.

'It's a lovely bike, Smudger,' Mrs Bubby was saying. 'You'll be able to ride up some steep mountains on that all right. What do you think of my perfume?'

'It smells expensive,' Smudger said.

'So it should,' said Mrs Bubby.

'What are you *doing*!' Huntly gasped, unable to believe the spectacle before him.

Smudger looked at him sheepishly.

'Hey, Huntly,' he said. 'Seen the wheels?'

'Seen the new threads?' Mrs Bubby asked. 'And the new hairdo?' she added – rather superfluously, as you could hardly miss it.

'I can see the wheels, all right,' Huntly scowled. 'And so can everyone else too, probably. And they'll start asking themselves the same interesting question, won't they? Namely how did Smudger suddenly come into the money to buy himself a top-of-the-range, state-of-the-art mountain bike with personalized mudguards!'

'Yeah but—'

'In fact, to make it easy for them, you may as well go round in a T-shirt saying, "Arrest Me I'm A Bootlegger And I Need To Be Locked Away."'

Smudger squirmed. 'All right,' he protested. 'I'll take the bike out for a ride then, off-road, and muddy it up a bit. I was meaning to anyway. No one's going to notice, Huntly, honest.'

But Huntly turned to Mrs Bubby.

'As for the new clothes and the hairstyle. I mean it's all very nice, but to be honest, I'd have expected a bit more sense from you than to go throwing your money around.'

Mrs Bubby looked as sheepish as Smudger. Possibly more so. It seemed as if at any moment she might go 'Baa!'.

'It was only a few clothes, dear,' she said meekly. 'Just to cheer myself up a bit. It's been second-hand stuff out of the charity shop half my life, and I just fancied having something new for a change, something that nobody had worn before, not even the vicar's wife.'

It was Huntly's turn to squirm uncomfortably. He felt guilty now for ticking her off. She'd had a hard life, after all, and now that Mr Bubby had gone, she was probably a bit lonely too.

'Anyway,' Mrs Bubby said, 'I'll go up and change back into the frumpy old stuff, and then I'll go into the shop to light my joss sticks while you get on with making the chocolate. Excuse me for being so old and silly.'

Neither Huntly nor Smudger quite knew what to say. They watched in silence as Mrs Bubby left the room.

'Now see what you've done,' Smudger said.

'See what I've done! I haven't done anything. It's you two who've done it.'

'You've upset her.'

'I haven't'

'You have.'

'Well, I didn't mean to.'

'Doesn't matter whether you meant to or not.'

'Well, it's not right. You know what Mr Blades said. Suddenly chucking your money round is an invitation for suspicion.'

'You worry too much, Huntly,' Smudger said. 'You see trouble everywhere. Now come on, let's get started on making this chocolate.'

But maybe Smudger was wrong. Maybe it wasn't that Huntly worried too much, but that Smudger worried too little. And had he been able to overhear the conversation between Frankie Crawley and the Party Inspector which had been taking place, he might have realized his mistake.

'A new bike,' Frankie was saying. 'Yellow. And designer clothes. And new hairstyles. And it's not just that. There's more and more people going in and out of the shop.'

The Inspector looked across the desk at Frankie. He still had to prove his usefulness, though at least he kept on trying. But that didn't mean that the Inspector had to like him.

'Increase in customers?' he said. 'Hmm. Well none of our officers has reported anything. Go on.'

Frankie drew himself up to his full importance.

'They don't always come straight back out again either. They can be in there for ages. I'm sure there's something going on,' he persisted.

'Like what?'

'I don't know. Like a speakeasy, maybe? At the back somewhere? Like bootleg?'

The Inspector didn't reply for a while. He just let the silence settle like dust.

'All right, Young Pioneer,' he said finally. 'We'll take a look and see if your suspicions are correct. This weekend.

And you can come along, to point us in the right direction.'

Frankie's face cheered up at this sign of approval and encouragement.

'Inspector,' he began, 'about my brother, you won't forget—'

'As if we could, Young Pioneer,' the Inspector forestalled him.

Frankie wanted to say more. But it was obvious that the interview was over, so he headed for the door.

Frankie just hoped that his suspicions about Mrs Bubby's *were* correct. He needed a little credit on his card, one or two feathers in his cap. It would be quite a coup for them to catch the bootleggers red-handed, with chocolate on the counter and money in the till. It was a pity in some ways that it had to be Smudger and Huntly, but in other ways it wasn't. They were his classmates, after all, and they'd even been sort of friends once, years back, in primary school. But that was a long time ago now, before the Good For You Party had come to power. It would serve them right for getting too flash. And besides, it was against the law. They shouldn't have been doing it anyway.

'What's this?'

The week's chocolate was all made and the washing up nearly over. Huntly and Smudger were full of the satisfaction of a good job well done. Even Mrs Bubby was back to her usual cheerful self.

'I've kept my new knickers on,' she confided in the

boys, when she came back down from changing and setting fire to two rounds of toast. 'Nothing visible to tell anyone I'm a bootlegger, but you feel all warm and new just the same.'

Whistling, she went back into the shop.

As Huntly put the pans away, he spotted something he hadn't noticed before – two brand-new mobile phones sitting on chargers. Suspecting Smudger of even more ostentatious extravagance, he said,

'What's this then, Smudge? What's the idea of the two phones? One for each ear?'

'Not at all, mate,' Smudger said loftily. 'As a matter of fact, I had an idea. About what Mr Blades said. I wasn't just thinking of better and faster bikes, see. I remembered what he said about getting a lookout for the eateasy so we could have a bit of advance warning, in case of trouble.

'And?'

'So I got a couple of mobiles. One for us. One for the lookout. And I know just who to give the other phone to. The perfect lookout. In fact, just the man for the job. A man no one will suspect.'

'Who is it?'

'Come on,' Smudger said, checking that the phones were fully charged. 'I'll show you.'

They left by the back door. They walked along the back alleyway and circled around to the road.

A few doors down from Mrs Bubby's was the now derelict 'Gilbert's Hand-Made Chocolate' shop, one of the first casualties of the ban. The shop was empty, its windows covered in fly-posters. A notice threatened that

Bill Stickers Will Be Prosecuted to no avail. Someone had scrawled under it *Bill Stickers Is Innocent*.

Even the Good For You Party had ignored the notice and had pasted propaganda posters on the windows. *Careless Eating Costs Lives* and *Your Country Needs You – To Eat Cabbage*.

In the doorway of the empty chocolate shop sat the former actor, a living example of how things can suddenly change and bad luck can land on anyone, like an unexpected ton of bricks, falling from a clear blue sky.

His name was Charles Moffat and he had once been a household face, familiar to millions, the man and the voice of the jingle behind Benson's Chocolate bars.

The Chocolate Man, The Chocolate Man,
He eats it everywhere he can.
The Chocolate Man, The Chocolate Man.
Buy some today!

But that was then. Right now his only slogan was: *Spare some change. Hungry and homeless. Spare some change.*

A Chocolate Trooper appeared on patrol, his Shriek Gun jammed into its holster with the safety catch firmly on, in case the Trooper accidentally shrieked himself by mistake.

He stopped and looked at the homeless man with disdain.

'Spare some change, Trooper?' Charles Moffat asked hopefully. 'Help a resting actor? A man whose agent never gets in touch any more, a man whose parts have all dried up.'

'If your parts have dried up, citizen, that's your lookout,' the Trooper said scornfully. 'And who wants wet parts anyway? And there's no necessity for sitting in a doorway making out you're homeless. You should get yourself along to a nice spick and span Good For You Hostel For The Homeless and get yourself trained in a useful skill.'

'I am trained. I'm a trained actor,' declared Charles Moffat.

'A *useful* skill,' the Trooper pointed out. 'I don't mean getting dressed up and pulling funny faces.'

'*Funny faces!*' Charles Moffat said indignantly. 'Acting has nothing to do with funny faces. It is an *art*! I once played Hamlet, you know.'

'What at?' the Trooper sneered. 'Tennis?'

'I played him in the theatre, as a matter of fact!' (He pronounced the word 'thee-ate-her'.) 'If you know what that is.'

'Of course I know what it is,' the Trooper snarled. 'It's where they do the operations in hospitals.'

He walked on and rounded the corner.

Charles Moffat rummaged in his carrier bag to see if he had anything in there to eat. He thought of the Young Pioneer, the one who had given him the banana. He half hoped that he might stop by again, and let him have another one. Or maybe that was too much to hope for. It wasn't as if they grew on trees.

When he looked up again, it was to see that the other two boys had joined him. They'd stopped and given him the odd bit of shiny-side in or shiny-side out to eat, every now and then. They'd remembered him from the television, before the chocolate ban, and had been (they said) great admirers of his work.

Only what were their names again? It did things to your memory, sleeping rough, out in the cold. Huntly was the name of one of them, he was sure of that. And the other one was called—

'Hi, Mr Moffat. It's Smudger, remember? We were wondering if you could do us a favour.'

Smudger. That was it. Charles Moffat liked a person who knew his own name. It was a big advantage in life to be sure of who you were and not to dither over it when people asked. It was always confusing to have an identity crisis.

'Favour, dear boy?' he said. 'Anything within reason. After all, the quality of mercy is not strained. And by the way, that shiny-side in you gave me the other day was like nectar to the gods.'

Perhaps there might be a little more in the offing too, he thought.

Charles Moffat noticed that Smudger was holding a rather stylish mobile phone in his hand.

'The thing is,' Smudger explained, 'that we've opened up a little eateasy round the corner.'

'Ah, eateasy?' Charles Moffat said. 'And that would be? I used to know, but the line momentarily escapes me—'

'A little club sort of thing. Like a speakeasy, only with chocolate instead of drink.'

'Yes, yes. Of course.'

'But we're worried about security and need a lookout. I

noticed that you were here a lot, and no one would suspect you, so I wondered—'

'I'm with you at once,' Charles Moffat said. 'You need say no more. It's a part I could play at a moment's notice. All I would require are the props.'

And he tapped the side of his nose with his finger, in a knowing and confidential way.

'Frankly,' he said. 'I'll be glad of the work. I'm resting at the moment. I've been resting for rather a long time. Resting isn't so good when you're not tired. But I'm sure I can do it. In fact I played a lookout once in a little film called *Death Takes A Holiday*. I don't know if you ever—'

Huntly and Smudger looked blankly at each other.

'Just give us advance warning if you see anything suspicious,' Smudger said. 'Like heavies. Or Troopers hanging about. Anything like that.'

'Fine. And how do I—?'

'This mobile here,' Smudger said. 'It's Pay As You Go and there's ten pounds of calls in credit, which should be enough. It's fully charged up too. But you'd better have the charger as well, just in case. Will you be able to keep it charged up somewhere?'

'I should be able to manage that,' Charles Moffat assured them. 'We are not without resources. I'm sure I can access an electrical socket somewhere. We actors have our methods.'

'Great,' Smudger said. 'There's the phone and the charger then. Our number's programmed in. We're next open this Saturday night. But I'll give you a ring first, just to let you know.'

'OK, boys. I can envisage no difficulties there.'

'And here's something else for you,' Smudger said. He reached inside his pocket and there was a flash of silver. 'Shiny-side out this time.'

Charles Moffat took the fruit and nut bootleg chocolate hungrily and hid it away in the folds of his many pullovers. He appeared to be wearing at least three or four of them.

'Thanks, boys,' he said. 'You can rely on me. And might one ask – loathe as one is to broach the subject – my agent usually handles this sort of thing – is there – a fee?'

'Regular bootleg?' Huntly suggested.

'That would suit perfectly,' the actor said.

'OK,' Smudger said. 'We'd better go. And I meant to say, when you were on the telly you know, you were pretty good.'

The two boys left him and went on their way.

'Was I?' Charles Moffat wondered to himself. 'Was I good?'

He glanced at his reflection in that part of the window not yet covered in graffiti and posters.

'Hmm, I wasn't bad, I suppose.'

And could be again too. In fact, now that he had a telephone, it would do no harm to make a few calls, just to remind people in the business that he still existed and was available for work.

He tapped a number into the mobile phone. It would just be a quick call. He'd ring up his old agent. But he'd keep it short and sweet. There was ten pounds worth of calls credited, wasn't there? Well, he wouldn't go using it all. Just one phone call, and that would be it.

The Raid

Mrs Bubby had baked something special for Saturday night. It was a large chocolate log. In fact, the log's dimensions were so huge it was more of a chocolate tree trunk, as cut down by a chocolate lumberjack.

'There,' she said proudly, as she carried it down into the eateasy and placed it on a small table by the bar. 'I'll let it cool and slice it later. There'll be plenty for everyone.'

'Pretty good, Mrs Bubby,' Smudger said, looking at the log admiringly. 'I don't think my dad could have done better.'

'So when are we opening?' Huntly called over from the bar, where he was helping Big Arthur make up some freshly squeezed lemonade *with* sugar.

'Usual time. Five minutes should do it,' Smudger said. 'I'll just ring the lookout.'

He took out his mobile phone and pressed the stored number to connect him to Charles Moffat.

The Chocolate Man was dozing in his doorway. Early evening was always a good time for a snooze. You could get a good forty or fifty winks in before the cold prodded you awake.

'Ah!' he said, waking. 'A telephone call. For me.' He pressed the button. 'Good evening,' he intoned. 'Mr

179

Charles Moffat Esquire's residence. This is Jenks the butler speaking. Mr Moffat is presently unavailable as he is in the jacuzzi. May I take a message and ask him to get right back to you at a more convenient time?'

'Eh?' the voice at the other end said. 'What's going on? It's Smudger here. Isn't that the Chocolate Man?'

Charles Moffat reverted to his natural voice.

'Oh, Smudger. It's you. I just thought it might have been – never mind. What can I do for you?'

'We're opening up in a minute,' Smudger said. 'Can you keep an eye out?'

'Consider it done, Smudger,' Charles Moffat said. 'The old eyeballs will be as peeled as eyeballs can be. If I see anything untoward, I'll ring you at once.'

'Thanks, Mr Moffat. I'll bring you a slice of chocolate log on my way home.'

'Scrumptious,' Charles Moffat said. He sat back on his piece of cardboard.

Chocolate log, he thought. Yum. In its own way, it was almost Shakespeare.

His eyes grew heavy. It had been a long day. A long day of, 'Spare some change. Help the homeless. Put your money where your heart is.'

But some people didn't seem to have any hearts. Or if they did, no money. He hadn't slept much the previous night either. The cold had gnawed at his bones. His eyes grew heavier, heavy with sweet thoughts of chocolate logs, with layers of whipped cream and chocolate filling, and, then they closed.

He didn't see the people passing. The children, dressed

up in their smartest clothes, making their way to – well, where else than to the nearest eateasy, where children were welcome, where chocolate was served, and where, as long as you knew the right password to get in, no questions were asked.

Soon the eateasy was jumping. Smudger was jumping along with it; Emily had dragged him off to the dance floor. Smudger was generally more the 'lean against the wall and look cool' sort, rather than the dancing type. But to his surprise, he was actually enjoying it.

He caught Huntly's eye and held his thumb up.

'See!' he seemed to say. 'Worrying about nothing. It's all turning out all right.'

Huntly grinned back at him. And as the next record started, he found himself also being dragged to the dance floor by Emily's friend Melanie. She usually sat at the front of the class and kept herself to herself. But maybe it was the music, maybe it was the chocolate, maybe it was that Huntly was a bootlegger with a one third share in an eateasy – but tonight was a time for dancing.

'*Gggggggg! Snussssh!*'

The homeless man was snoring gently. He sounded like a faraway motorbike, purring over a hill. He didn't at first hear the footsteps, the voices, the slamming of van doors, the scrape of studded boots on the paving stones, the harsh voice of the Inspector.

'OK. We search the area at the back of the shop. If we find anything, we go in. But not until I say so. I want to catch them all, and I want to catch them red-handed.'

Charles Moffat was having a dream, about these men in Troopers' uniforms, and a man with cold grey eyes, and for some reason a Young Pioneer standing amongst them – the kind of Young Pioneer who might have given you a banana once, a hundred million years ago, back in another lifetime . . .

And then he opened his eyes and saw them. Half a dozen uniformed Troopers clustered near to the doorway. They were going to raid Smudger's eateasy.

'Where is it?'

Charles fumbled in his pocket for the mobile phone. The Troopers hadn't even noticed him. He was just a non-person to them, an extra, without any lines. Maybe they thought he was just a bundle of rags.

'Just wait a moment,' the Inspector was saying. 'For the back-up.'

Charles Moffat pressed the key to dial Smudger's number and put the phone to his ear.

'You are out of credit,' an unnaturally electronic voice was saying. 'Please purchase a Pay As You Go Top Up Card, or if you are registered for credit card purchase, key in your card number now.'

Charles Moffat turned the phone off. How could it have run out of credit already? There had been ten pounds worth of calls . . .

He felt himself flush hotly, with embarrassment and shame. He'd used it up. Ringing old contacts, telephoning agents and casting directors, trying to get a bit of work for himself. And now he couldn't even warn Smudger that the Troopers were on their way.

Money! Use the call box!

He rummaged in his hat. A few pounds there in small change. He gathered up the coins, and hurried past the waiting Troopers.

'Oh, look who it is. It's old "Spare Some Change".'

'Stand aside, make room – there's a flea-bag coming.'

He ignored their insults and pressed on his way. There was an old public telephone box on the corner. With a bit of luck he'd be able—

The luck ran the other way. The telephone had been vandalized and the handset lay silent in its cradle, the lead that gave it life severed in two.

Now what?

Charles looked behind him. The first of the back-up vans had arrived. The Troopers would be on the move any minute, stealthy, swift, silent, heading for the corner. Next they would be along the lane, and then through the gate and into the back garden of Mrs Bubby's shop.

He saw salvation. In the shape of the filling station across the road. There it was, an oasis of warm gold and silver light; there were the motorists, filling their cars with petrol; there was the forecourt shop with a small, but clearly visible sign.

Pay As You Go Phone Cards. All Brands. On Sale Here.

Clutching his collection of coins, tightly rolled inside his tea-cosy hat, he raced across the road. A horn blared.

'Emergency! Emergency! Excuse me.'

He ran to the counter of the filling station, ahead of the queue.

'I need a phone card! A top up! And quick!' He

dumped the coins on the counter. 'It's all there. Count it if you don't believe me.'

She did. The cashier insisted on counting every coin. It went on, for agonizing seconds.

Hurry, hurry, hurry.

The homeless man squirmed in his boots.

Come on, come on, come on.

It was like being desperate for the toilet when there was somebody in there, who had possibly fallen asleep or decided to write a novel.

Quick, quick, be quick!

'This isn't right,' the cashier said.

What!

'You've given me twelve pence too much.'

'That's all right, keep the change. *JUST GIVE ME THE PHONE CARD!*'

He snatched the card and tore the cellophane off as he ran from the shop. He grabbed his phone, dialled the top-up number and keyed in the credit.

Now. Quickly. Smudger's phone. Select the number. Press the dial key. Listen. That's it. Ringing. Come on, Smudger. Answer the phone.

Smudger – for pity's sake answer the phone!

'Hello?'

He answered. Praise be. Light a candle and say a prayer. There was the sound of dance music behind his voice.

'Smudger! It's me! Charles Moffat. They're coming! They're on their way. Right now. Troopers. It's a raid. You'd better get out!'

'Thanks!'

That was all Smudger said, then the phone went dead.

For a long, eternal moment, Smudger just stood there, looking at the telephone in his hand, as though it had suddenly grown teeth and nipped him.

Then he strode over to the disco turntable and wrenched the jack plug from the amp. The dancers froze in sudden silence, like fish whose water has vanished.

'It's a raid! We've a couple of minutes at the most. No need to panic. Mrs Bubby, show everyone the emergency exit, if you would. Huntly, get the conversion underway to the "After Study Club". All staff, please help him. Do it now!'

They didn't need to be told twice. Everybody knew what the consequences of discovery were – interrogation, the re-education camp, aversion therapy. To be taken away like poor Dave Cheng. To number among the vanished and the disappeared, along with all the bootleggers and their customers, who had been tracked down and caught with chocolate in their hands.

Mrs Bubby pulled back the false wall panel which concealed the entrance to the tunnel.

'This way,' she said. 'Quickly and quietly. Pick up a slice of chocolate log as you go. We need to get rid of it. When you get to the end of the tunnel, up the steps, push the metal hatch up, and it'll bring you out in the lane by the corner. Last ones out close the hatch behind them. Hurry and no talking. See you next week. We'll still be here,' and she muttered to herself under her breath, 'if we're lucky.'

The customers did as she said, each picking up a slice of chocolate log, wrapped in a paper napkin, as they left the club.

Behind her, great activity was going on. But it was all accomplished smoothly and swiftly and without panic.

The bar was cleared and turned into a desk. The menu revolved to become a blackboard with several complicated-looking algebraic equations upon it. The tables were also cleared; the glasses hidden away. Books were taken out from a box behind the bar and handed around. The dance music was replaced with an orchestral classical piece, the sort considered by adults to be conducive to study.

Pencils and jotters were handed out, along with atlases, notepads, calculators and pens.

As Huntly helped with this, Smudger and Mrs Bubby swiftly moved the chocolate and locked it away behind the hidden lead-lined door, where the detectors could never find it.

'Come on. Quick now,' Huntly called. 'Positions everyone!'

The last of the customers had gone. Mrs Bubby closed the emergency-exit door and slid back the panel to disguise its existence. She looked around for any telltale signs. Nothing.

There was a thumping at the main door. The Troopers had found the shed, entered it, discovered the stairs and now . . .

'Open up in there! Open up! This is the authorities!'

Smudger and the others were sitting at tables with books and papers, pens and calculators, and all the paraphernalia of the good student.

'OK, Mrs Bubby,' he said. 'Let them in.'

Mrs Bubby walked calmly to the door. From the noise it sounded as if somebody outside was laying siege to it with a battering ram. Either that or a very large Trooper's boot, on the end of a very large Trooper-sized foot.

Mrs Bubby slid back the bolt and opened the door just as the Trooper who had been attempting to kick it down launched another salvo. Having nothing to kick but empty air, he hurtled into the room and crashed into the wall. Half a dozen Troopers were right behind him, some carrying Chocolate Detectors, others armed with Shriek Guns. Following them in was the Inspector, the man with eyes like stainless steel, and behind him was a rather nervous Frankie Crawley.

'Good evening,' Mrs Bubby said. 'Were you looking for me? The shop's closed now, I'm afraid. Could you come back tomorrow? I'll be open from seven thirty onwards.'

'Out of the way!' the Inspector snapped.

Mrs Bubby stood aside to let him in. He stopped and looked around the room. If what he saw came as a surprise to him, he didn't show it. His eyes remained as cold and as expressionless as ever.

There were six or seven children, sitting at tables with what appeared to be school books. They had furrowed brows and the serious faces of those who did not wish to be interrupted in their studies, lest they lose their trains of thought, and never get them back on track again.

'And what exactly is this supposed to be?' the Inspector asked.

'It's the After School Study Club,' Mrs Bubby said.

'After School Study Club?' the Inspector repeated. From the tone of his voice, he might as well have been saying the words 'dog mess'.

'Yes,' Mrs Bubby nodded. 'It's a club, you see, for people who want to do studying, after school.'

'Is that a fact?' the Inspector said.

'Yes,' Mrs Bubby said. 'I just try to help the children out, you see. At home there's so many distractions for them – TV, computers, the Internet, videos, Playstations, Gameboys, oh you name it. But here, there's nothing but peace and quiet and pure concentration – or at least there was until you lot barged in.'

'Look around,' the Inspector snarled. 'Use the detectors.'

The Troopers circled around the room. Huntly looked up from his algebra equations to see that Titch was pretending to study a geography book which was upside down. Huntly elbowed him and Titch hurriedly turned the book up the right way.

Smudger noticed Frankie Crawley, trying to make himself invisible in some shadows by the door.

'Hello, Frankie,' he called. 'What are you doing here?'

'I just happened to be passing,' Frankie said unconvincingly. 'And was asked to help as an observer, in my capacity as a Young Pioneer.'

'I thought that maybe you'd come to join us for a bit of studying.'

'Since when were you ever interested in extra homework, Smudger? I thought the only sort of homework you were interested in was less homework.'

'Well, I don't want to get left behind, do I?'

A Trooper ran a Chocolate Detector over Smudger's books. There wasn't even the faintest crackle.

'What're they looking for with those detectors, Frankie?' Smudger asked with an innocent expression.

'As if you didn't know!' Frankie replied, and turned away.

The Troopers ran the detectors over every square inch of the place. There wasn't a crumb of chocolate anywhere. Or maybe there was. Mrs Bubby spotted a chunk of it under one of the tables. With a deft movement she pretended to drop a pencil, stooped to pick it up and got the cube of chocolate as well. She turned her back and put it straight into her mouth – fluff or no fluff – and swallowed it in one bite.

The Inspector turned to the most senior of the Troopers.

'Well?'

'Nothing, sir,' the Trooper said. 'Not a crumb, not a flake. Nothing.'

'Hmm . . .' Something wasn't right. The Inspector knew it. He could feel it. He looked at Emily and Melanie, who were sitting at a table studying irregular French verbs. What was wrong with them? Something. Something that didn't quite fit.

'You two!' the Inspector said. 'You girls. Why are you dressed up like that? You girls always get dressed up, do you, for a bit of extra studying?'

'Something wrong with looking smart, is there?' Emily asked indignantly

No, but you didn't need to look that smart to study irregular verbs, the Inspector thought. But he could prove nothing. And whose idea had this whole thing been? Who had provided the information which had led to this raid? And caused this public humiliation for him and for his men?

Where was that numbskull?

There he was. Desperately and unsuccessfully trying to render himself invisible to avoid the Inspector's eyes. But you couldn't avoid eyes like that. They bored into you and nailed you where you stood.

The Inspector led Frankie outside to the garden, where they would not be overheard.

'Well, Young Pioneer?' he demanded.

'W-well,' Frankie blustered. 'I don't know. I don't understand. I could have sworn—'

'Sworn?' the Inspector said. 'Could you indeed? Yes. I think I probably will.'

The squad of dejected Troopers walked away from the After School Study Club towards the patrol vans out in the street.

An outwardly humble, yet inwardly seething Frankie Crawley followed at a distance. He walked disconsolately along, his eyes to the ground, his chin to his chest. He *knew* that he was right. He *knew* something was going on. He just hadn't been able to prove it, that was all.

The doors of the patrol vans were pulled back with a clatter and the Troopers clambered on board.

Then Frankie saw it. The evidence he needed. Lying on the pavement in a paper napkin.

'Inspector, look!'

The Inspector turned.

'What is it now? I'm getting rather tired, Young Pioneer, of you and your everlasting—'

'Look. Chocolate cake!' He picked it up carefully. 'Someone must have dropped it, as they left the place. There must be another door, another way out. Someone tipped them off and they all managed to get out in time. Let's go back. They won't expect that. That After School Study Club is completely bogus. It's nothing but a front, a—'

The Inspector seemed about to agree, but then said slowly, 'No. I don't think so.'

'But we'll get them, Inspector. Red-handed.'

'No.'

'But they'll think they're safe now. They'll be sitting there laughing at us.'

The Inspector shook his head.

'There's time enough, Young Pioneer. First we'll watch them, and they'll lead us to others. We can take our time, find out who their customers are, their suppliers even. We'll watch and wait. And then when we have them in our grasp, we'll crush them.'

And the Inspector put his hands around Frankie's and

closed them round the cake. Frankie could feel it squashing and squishing up between his fingers.

'Yes. We'll crush them. It'll be a piece of cake.' The Inspector turned to go. 'Crunchy apples to you, Young Pioneer.' He sounded almost cheerful.

Frankie looked at the gooey mush of the chocolate log. He glared after the Inspector.

'And juicy oranges to you too, sir!' he muttered. He wiped the cake from his hands and dumped it into the nearest bin. Sometimes Frankie didn't feel properly appreciated. He didn't feel appreciated at all.

Back at the eateasy, Smudger was ecstatic.

'Did you see their faces, Mrs Bubby,' he said triumphantly. 'Did you see them! I think they turned green! They couldn't believe there was nothing here. How about chocolate milkshakes all round now to celebrate?'

'Good idea,' Mrs Bubby agreed. 'Why not!'

She went to the hidden lead-lined door and opened it up, fetching out milk and cocoa powder and the mixer.

But Huntly didn't feel like joining in the celebrations. Their narrow escape hadn't filled him with euphoria like Smudger. It had started him chewing at his fingernails.

'None for me, thanks,' he said, as Mrs Bubby made up the milkshakes. 'I'm going home. That raid was a warning to us. We're getting too flash and too reckless and taking too many risks. Or at least some of us are,' he added, with a look in Smudger's direction.

'Don't go yet, Huntly,' Melanie said. 'It'll spoil the party.'

'Sorry, I have to,' Huntly said. 'Or—'

He had been about to tell the truth and say, 'Or my mum will be wondering.' But that suddenly felt like a rather childish and embarrassing thing to say in the present circumstances, when Huntly was supposed to be a bootlegger, and a pretty tough one at that. But he didn't feel tough, he just felt worried. He'd had enough for one night and he wanted to go home.

'Stay for a bit,' Melanie insisted.

'Ah, let him go if he wants to,' Smudger said. He and Huntly rarely fell out, but tonight Smudger felt irritated by Huntly's excessive caution. As irritated as Huntly was by Smudger's increasing recklessness.

'I'll see you all on Monday,' Huntly said. 'Bye.'

The metal door clanged shut behind him. Smudger drew the bolt.

Mrs Bubby poured out the milkshakes into tall, frosted glasses.

'Well, cheers then, everyone,' Smudger said, raising his glass. 'I reckon we've made it. We're the best bootleggers with the best chocolate and the best eateasy in the world. We're top of the world, Mrs B. And the only way is up. To the universe and beyond!'

They all laughed and raised their chocolate milkshakes to their lips.

'To us!' Mrs Bubby said. 'To us and to the future!'

They all echoed her words, and they drank the milkshakes down, giving a toast to themselves and to the future.

With not the faintest knowledge of what it would bring.

Chocolate Forever

A while after his visit to the eateasy, Mr Blades invited Mrs Bubby, along with Huntly and Smudger, to attend a meeting at his bookshop.

It was described as an 'Early Editions Evening' and Huntly and Smudger went reluctantly and only at Mrs Bubby's insistence, because it sounded dry, tedious and dull.

It proved to be anything of the sort. Far from being attended by elderly and crotchety types, only interested in uncut pages and leather bindings, the meeting was packed with people of all sorts and ages, united in one objective, to see the Good For You Party toppled from power and chocolate put back where it belonged, on the shop counters and into the mouths of the hungry.

Blades made a rousing speech, talking of 'liberty, justice and the rights of individuals to decide for themselves what they wish to eat!' Then he handed round some bootleg, inviting everyone to dig in and munch freely. Security was tight, and every face was a known and trusted one.

'Yet what can we, a mere handful of dissidents, do against the forces of the Good For You Party,' he asked rhetorically. It was a question which had already occurred to Huntly. Yes, what *could* they do?

'More than you may imagine,' Blades went on to say. 'For all over the country, small groups like this are meeting, organizing, preparing for revolution. But change will not come of itself. There will be struggle, toil, sacrifice. Until one day we will rise up and rid ourselves of this oppression forever!'

At that, everyone waved their chocolate bars and muttered, 'Hear, hear!'

'So let us get to work,' Blades said. 'Recruit anyone you can trust, sympathetic to the cause. Any funds you can spare, please donate them. But be careful, be ready. And remember, you are not alone. And soon we hope to give you the word that the day of revolution is at hand!'

Another muffled cheer went up (nobody wanted to risk cheering too loudly in case the Troopers heard them) and then, once the chocolate had all run out, people drifted away in ones and twos, so as not to attract attention.

It was a pleasant evening, Huntly thought, and all well and good. But anyone could talk about revolution – accomplishing it was a different matter. He felt it hard to take the evening seriously, and felt that most people had only come for the free chocolate. Smudger, meanwhile, was less concerned about revolution than about spending his next share of the bootleg money – which he intended to do as soon as possible.

But then something happened to put Mr Blades and his tiny band of so-called rebels right out of the boys' thoughts.

Dave Cheng came back.

Like a distant, long-forgotten memory. He had been

gone so long it was almost as if he had moved away forever and there was no expectation of his return.

It happened one morning. A maths test was underway and Smudger, having finished it a few minutes early, was sitting, doodling on a scrap of paper. He should have been checking through his answers, but he didn't feel like it. The doodle started off as the vague outline of a heart, which soon became more and more ornate as the final minutes of the test ticked by. He surrounded it with roses and briars, then drew a cupid-like arrow going through it. He was just writing in the words 'Chocolate Forever' in his best italics when Miss Ross called out, 'OK, that's it. Time's up. Pass your papers to the front, please.'

Smudger passed his maths sheet forward to Emily, but her attention was distracted by something going on outside in the school yard. Some adults, accompanied by a boy, were walking across the yard.

'Miss,' Emily said. 'There's someone outside. It looks like Dave Cheng.'

Children left their desks and clustered around the window.

'Sit down, everyone. Don't make a fuss. Back to your places, please.'

As Miss Ross gathered up the rest of the maths papers, there was a knock at the door.

'Come in.'

Smudger looked up. It was the headmaster. Accompanied by someone else – the Chocolate Inspector, the man with the grey steel eyes. And next to them was a third figure, small, lost and peering around him in an uncomprehending way.

Dave Cheng.

Smudger glanced at Huntly, but Huntly's eyes were fixed on Dave Cheng. He was staring at him with blank horror. It was him, and yet it wasn't. What had happened? What had they done? Dave stood there meekly, his arms by his sides, looking bewildered and confused. Yet Dave had been so full of life, fun, mischief. Never short of an answer or a question. But now . . .

'Good morning, Miss Ross,' the headmaster said. 'I hope we're not disturbing you. But the Inspector here is returning one of our lost lambs to the fold, as it were. David Cheng is back from his time away. I think he's learned the error of his ways – chocolate-wise.'

Dave looked around, seeming to recognize no one. Every child in the class stared at him. It was Dave on the outside all right, but inside, there seemed to be nobody there. It was as if someone had completely removed his old personality and had forgotten to replace it.

Miss Ross went over to him. 'Hello, David. How are you?'

'Hello,' he said, his voice hollow.

'It's Miss Ross.'

'Yes, miss.'

'You remember where you sit, David?'

'Sit? No.'

Miss Ross showed him to his place.

'Over here.'

Dave sat down. Smudger and Huntly turned to him.

'Hey, Chengy.'

'Hi, Dave.'

'Excuse me?' he said, puzzled. 'Are we friends?'

'Dave, it's us – Smudger, and Huntly. You remember us?'

'Sorry,' Dave said. 'I don't recall. I'd best get on with some work now. Work is good for you, I know that. And so are Healthy Snacks. They're good for you too. But other things are bad, very bad.'

Smudger suddenly felt his eyes fill with tears. They had brainwashed Dave Cheng, broken his spirit, taken away his mind. He knew that everyone in the class was thinking the same – with the exceptions of Frankie Crawley and Myrtle perhaps – Poor Dave, he was no worse than the rest of us. All he did was to be too fond of a bit of chocolate. That could so easily have been me, he thought.

The Inspector seemed to read their thoughts.

'Observe your classmate,' he said. 'And what happens to those who flout the rules of the Good For You Party. Notice what becomes of those who deal in black-market chocolate and such contraband goods. Remember what you have seen, children. And bear it in mind, should you ever be tempted to stray a few steps from the straight and narrow path.'

The Headmaster turned to go, but the Chocolate Inspector hesitated. He looked down at something, a small scrap of paper lying on the floor. He picked it up.

It was Smudger's doodle. It had fluttered from his desk when the door opened. He hadn't noticed.

His mouth was suddenly dry. The paper had fallen a

short distance away. Nothing on it said it was his. He hadn't initialled it or written *Property of Smudger, touch this and you die!* on it, as he sometimes did on his things.

The Inspector turned the paper over. The heart with the arrow through it and '*Chocolate Forever*' stared him in the face.

'Who did this?'

There was silence. Only the mechanical things in the room made any sound – the ticking of the clock, the hum of the heating.

'I said who did this drawing? Well?'

The seconds passed. Nothing. No one.

Hickory-dickory . . .

They all knew it was Smudger. They'd all seen his drawings and doodles before. It was his unmistakable style. Huntly knew, Miss Ross knew, Emily, Melanie, everyone . . .

Nothing. A conspiracy of silence.

Only—

Myrtle Perkins raised her hand.

'Please, sir, I think I know who it was!'

The Inspector turned his steel grey eyes towards her.

'It was—'

But before Myrtle could finish, something happened to save Smudger. Something both wonderful but ghastly. First a hand slowly went up into the air. Then a voice spoke, hollow and toneless, like the voice of robot.

'Please, sir, it was probably me.'

Dave Cheng stood up to confess to his crimes.

'It was probably me, sir. I've done a lot of bad things. It

must have been me, sir, I expect. I confess, sir. I accept the punishment, sir, whatever it may be. If you like, I'll sign a confession, sir. Anything, as long as – as long as – I don't – have to go back – to that place.'

Everyone knew it wasn't Dave. Except Dave himself. Even the cold-eyed Inspector shifted a little, looking slightly embarrassed and uncomfortable.

'No, I don't think it was you,' the Inspector said. 'Not on this occasion.'

He ripped the drawing into pieces and threw it into the waste basket.

'Just let whoever did this drawing reflect on where such misbehaviour can lead. Good day to you, children. Crunchy apples!'

He and the Headmaster left the room, leaving a chill of fear behind them.

Huntly tried to catch Smudger's eye. 'You see the risks we're taking?' his glance seemed to say. 'You see why we have to be careful?'

But Smudger wasn't looking at him. He was already busy with another doodle.

Bugged

Mrs Bubby sat behind the counter, filling in the blanks in the *Daily Good For You* easy crossword. The trouble was that the easy crossword was too easy, and the cryptic crossword was too hard. What she needed was a crossword along the lines of Baby Bear's porridge – the one which Goldilocks had found so satisfactory. Not too simple, not too difficult, but just right.

Brrring!

She looked up. A delivery man was entering the shop backwards. He had managed to push the door open with his behind, for his arms were laden with boxes marked *Good For You*, *Healthy For You*, *Tasty For You* and *What You Always Wanted*.

It crossed Mrs Bubby's mind that this was advertising at its worst. The louder the labels on the boxes screamed that their contents were good, healthy, tasty and what you had always wanted, the less likely they were to be so.

Mrs Bubby watched as the man looked around for somewhere to put the boxes. She offered no suggestions and gave him no sign of welcome.

'Morning,' the man said. 'Deliveries.'

'Again?' Mrs Bubby said. 'Of what now?'

'Good For You Cookies, Healthy For You Roughage Bars, Tasty For You Muffins—'

'Oh yes,' Mrs Bubby said. 'You mean the sawdust-flavoured. I tried one once. It took me a week to swallow it.'

'And some What You Always Wanted Rich Tea Biscuits,' the man said, looking around for somewhere to dump his boxes.

'What was wrong with the old rich tea biscuits?' Mrs Bubby demanded.

'Too rich,' the delivery man said. 'Where can I put these boxes down? My back's killing me.'

'So how can all that stuff be good for you if carrying it round is doing your back in?' Mrs Bubby asked.

'Because you're supposed to eat it, not carry it. Now where can I put—?'

'Over there,' Mrs Bubby said, pointing to an un-cluttered piece of the counter.

The man dumped the boxes down, and massaged the small of his back.

'I don't know how you expect me to sell all this stuff,' Mrs Bubby said mournfully. 'I get more deliveries in here than the maternity hospital. If they got as many babies turning up there as I do boxes in here, they'd be stacking them up six to a cot.'

'Well, government quotas, isn't it?' the delivery man said, fishing in his hip pocket for the paperwork. 'Sign here,' he said.

'Before I do,' Mrs Bubby told him, 'I've got some sell-by dates you can take back.'

'Yeah, all right then, missus,' he sighed. 'I'll give you a credit note.'

'See you do,' Mrs Bubby said, and she headed for the stockroom.

The delivery man sniffed.

'Your shop smells of burnt toast and joss sticks,' he called after her. 'In fact, come to think of it, it always smells of burnt toast and joss sticks in here.'

'So?' Mrs Bubby said. 'Is it a crime to like your toast well done and to be a bit spiritual?'

'No, I suppose not,' the delivery man conceded.

'No,' Mrs Bubby said. 'Just wait there. I'll be back in a second.'

And she went out to the stockroom.

As soon as she was gone, the delivery man sprang into action. Mysteriously his back no longer troubled him. Instead of slow and weary, he became quick and nimble.

With one smooth movement, he rested a hand on the counter and leaped over it to the business side. He reached into his pocket and took out a small listening device, a tiny radio-controlled microphone, no bigger than a five-pence piece. He tore off a strip of paper from its base, exposing an adhesive surface. He looked at the shelves, chose the underside of the one which he thought would best conceal the device, yet afford the optimum sound quality, and he fixed the bug to it.

Then he vaulted back over the counter. His mission accomplished, he began to rub his back again, just in time for Mrs Bubby's return.

'Here we are,' she said. 'There's a whole load of Chewy

and Chompy For You Cereal Bars here that I couldn't even give away. I don't think Chewy and Chompy is the right description for this. You ought to call it something more truthful like "Lies On Your Stomach Like A Large Stone", or maybe something catchy like "Instant Gut Ache".'

The delivery man drew his eyebrows together, as if he was closing curtains, and tried to look grave and serious.

'I only deliver them, I don't make them,' he said defensively. 'And also, I don't think that's any way to talk about the delicious healthy products of the Good For You Party.'

'I don't think that's any way to talk about the delicious healthy products of the Good For You Party.'

The voice was clear as a bell. The Trooper at the controls in the surveillance van held the headphones out for the Inspector. He took them and put them to his ears. He listened, then nodded. There was even the outline of a smile on his lips.

The van was parked only a street away from Mrs Bubby's shop. From the outside it was a nondescript vehicle, with a few dents and spots of rust in it. In the dust and grime on its rear door, someone had written *Wash Me*, while on the other door someone else had put *Also Available In White*.

'Keep listening,' the Inspector said. 'Monitor every conversation. And when you find out what password they're using to sell the stuff, let me know.'

The Trooper nodded. The Inspector peered out of a spy lens set into the rear door of the van. Satisfied that the coast was clear, he slipped out and walked around the corner to his waiting car.

It was just a matter of time now. And then he would have them.

It didn't take long.

There was nothing of any interest throughout the day. But come the late afternoon, once school was over, a child's voice was heard. First there was the sound of the door opening, the ring of the bell, then Mrs Bubby's friendly voice saying, 'Afternoon, dear. What can I do you for? A *Good For You* comic, is it? A nice Healthy Snack?'

And then a youngster's voice speaking. 'To be honest, Mrs Bubby, I wouldn't mind a little something to, well, to "*keep me going*" perhaps.'

The eavesdropping Trooper in the surveillance van could almost hear the italics and the inverted commas, even as he listened, even as the recording tape revolved slowly, languidly, memorizing every word.

'Oh, something to keep you going, dear?' Mrs Bubby's voice was heard to say. 'And what sort of "*something*" do you have in mind?'

There they were again, those italics and inverted commas.

'Em – something – "*to hit the spot*" perhaps?'

A moment's hesitation. The Trooper frowned. He'd thought that this was it. But maybe he'd been mistaken.

But then—

'Something to "*hit the spot*", dear? Well, let me see.'

The Trooper listened intently, trying to conjure a picture from the sound. Was she was reaching for something?

From under the counter maybe? What was that crinkling sound, like cooking foil? Then her voice again.

'One of these ought to do it, I think. Which do you fancy? There's plain, or fruit and nut?'

The Trooper sat back in his chair. The van interior was cramped and stuffy and littered with old coffee cups. But he didn't mind now. Wait until the Inspector heard this. He'd be pleased, very pleased. There might even be a promotion in it.

The Trooper took a sip of cold coffee and reached to unwrap a Healthy Snack. The recording tape ran on.

Every word you say may be – could be – definitely will be – taken down and used in evidence against you.

Even when you didn't know it.

The Inspector sat behind his desk. For once he was contemplating the features of Frankie Crawley with a look of near benevolence. Frankie had never seen the Inspector in such a good mood. He looked so happy that for a moment Frankie thought that somebody must have died.

'I've a job for you, Young Pioneer,' the Inspector said.

'A job? Gosh!' Frankie said, trying to sound keen but feeling rather nervous inside. 'For me? Of course, sir. What do I have to do?'

'I want you to go shopping, Young Pioneer. At the famous Mrs Bubby's emporium. I want you to buy a little something – from under the counter.'

Frankie swallowed and cleared his throat.

'Em, yes, of course. Only the thing is, you see, sir, that,

well, I – we – have already tried that. Myrtle and I. Citizen Myrtle Perkins, that is. Young Pioneer Myrtle. And she went in and tried to ask – and well – ended up with a rather large banana. We don't have the right password, you see.'

The Inspector's eyes glimmered.

'We do now, Young Pioneer. Rest assured of that.'

'Oh?' Frankie said, interested. 'How did you manage to find it out?'

'Let's just say,' the Inspector said, 'that a little bug told me. Now, let me play you a short tape recording here. And then you'll know just what to say. We'll be listening to you when you go in. From quite near by in fact. And when the password has been said, and the chocolate is on the counter, we'll be there. And we'll have them – red-handed.'

Frankie swallowed again.

'Em, yes, sir. But doesn't that mean that for a while there, I'll be on my own – in the shop? And if they suspect that I'm – well – a sort of – well – informer – or anything – they could turn a bit, well – nasty.'

'Don't worry, Young Pioneer, we'll be there before anything can happen. We won't want them chopping you up into little pieces. It would be too much of a mess.'

Frankie did his best to smile at this joke – if it was one.

'When do you want me to go in?' he said. 'Now?'

'I'll tell you when,' the Inspector told him. 'In a day or two. When I've got the manpower ready. We're a little busy right now. There seem to be little groups of law-breakers sprouting up all over the place. But we know how to deal with these clumps of weeds. Don't you worry, Young Pioneer, we'll know where to find you – we know where to find almost everyone.'

Despite the raid of the preceding week, the eateasy was soon open again for business – though only for the select few. New customers were discouraged. Only known names and faces were admitted now. Strangers brought too much of a risk. The customers were directed to make their way around to Mrs Bubby's back garden, arriving in ones and twos. They clung to the shadows and furtively entered the shed. Then they tapped on the door and uttered a password – which was changed frequently – in order to gain admittance.

Even Huntly's rather diminished confidence had returned to him. For a time he had felt a looming presence at his shoulder, as if a hand were about to fall and a voice say 'Gotcha!'. But the days went by and they were all still at liberty. So when Smudger and Mrs Bubby proposed opening up the eateasy again at the weekend, he could see no real reason to object.

It was hard work though, running an eateasy. So much effort went into letting other people enjoy themselves. And when they all finally went home, there was the clearing up afterwards. And then, next morning, while the church bells were ringing, there was a fresh batch of chocolate to make for the following week.

It was hard work all right, being a bootlegger. It wasn't all riding round on flash new mountain bikes and getting your highlights done at the hairdresser's.

Huntly woke, yawning, on the Sunday morning. He washed, dressed, and ate a bowl of 'Crunchy For You Brekkie-Flakes'. The cardboard packet said that they were full of nutrition. But then the box probably tasted better than its contents.

Huntly's mum came into the kitchen in her dressing gown, studying a recipe book.

'Up already?' she said.

'Said I'd go for a bike ride,' Huntly told her. 'With Smudger. If that's all right.'

He hated lying to his mother, and it was on the tip of his tongue to tell her the truth. He knew that she disliked the Good For You Party as much as he did and had no respect for such unjust laws. But she wouldn't have liked him being involved in bootlegging. Too dangerous, she would have said. So it was best not to talk about it. Best to ignore it, if you possibly could, with a couple of little white lies.

After all, he *was* going for a bike ride (down to Mrs Bubby's shop to make chocolate) and he'd more than likely meet Smudger on the way. (Also on his bike.) So it was sort of true.

'OK. But don't be late back. Arnold's coming for lunch, remember?'

He looked at his mother blankly. So that was why she was reading the recipe book. Who was Arnold?

'Your cousin Arnold,' she said.

Oh, that Arnold. Huntly remembered. A long-lost and distant cousin who normally lived several hundred miles away. He was one of those cousins who are described as once removed, or twice removed – which made them sound as if they lived in furniture lorries and got taken from place to place.

'What's he like, Mum?'

'I don't really remember. It's fifteen years since I last saw him. He was running round in short trousers then, as I recollect, playing at soldiers.'

'What's he doing here?'

'I don't really know that either. But he said he'd call in for lunch and I dare say we'll find out when he arrives. Be back at twelve, eh?'

'OK, Mum. Bye.'

Huntly got his bicycle from the shed and set off for Mrs Bubby's to get the chocolate-making underway.

'Where you going, Smudger?'

Kylie was outside playing hopscotch on the pavement as Smudger wheeled his mountain bike along the path. It was no longer as pristine as when he had bought it and the yellow frame was splattered with mud.

'Places,' Smudger said, putting his helmet and his shades on.

'What places?' Kylie asked.

'Just places,' Smudger told her, wishing that little sisters weren't quite so nosy.

'What do you do at places, Smudger?'

'Nothing. I just go there.'

'What's the point in going places if you don't do anything when you get there?'

'It's a change of scenery,' Smudger said.

'You mean you just go places and then you come back?'

'Something like that.' Smudger nodded.

'Can I go places with you?' Kylie asked.

'No,' Smudger said firmly. 'You're too young. You can't go places till you're ten.'

'Who says?' Kylie demanded.

'People,' Smudger said.

'What people?'

'People – in places.'

'What places?'

'High places.'

'What high places are those?'

But Smudger had had enough.

'I'll see you, Kylie.'

And he rode off.

Kylie watched him go, wondering if he would bring her back some chocolate. He usually did. It was funny how Smudger always turned up with chocolate after he'd been places.

The places he went to must be more interesting than he made out.

Mrs Bubby's shop was open a half day on a Sunday. She had newspapers to sell, the *Sunday Good For You* amongst them, which ran to several supplements and a colour magazine – it took a lot of paper and ink to remind people how good things were supposed to be.

The early rush had now eased off, and Mrs Bubby was in the stockroom, along with Huntly and Smudger.

Chocolate mixture was melting in a pan, and out in the shop a half-ejected, half-charred piece of toast was emitting a cloud of fumes.

Mrs Bubby put her hand up to stifle a yawn.

'I'm dead on my feet,' she said. 'I feel I've been up half the night partying.'

'You have, Mrs Bubby,' Huntly reminded her. 'When I left last night you were doing the limbo.'

Mrs Bubby looked embarrassed and concentrated on stirring the mixture. Once it was ready, they poured it into trays and left it to set. Huntly started the washing up and then noticed that the time was nearly five to twelve.

'Can I leave you two to finish off?' he said. 'I've got to get home. We've got someone coming for lunch and I promised I wouldn't be late.'

'Of course you can,' Mrs Bubby said.

'Yeah, you shoot off, mate,' Smudger said. 'I'll see you at school tomorrow.'

'OK. See you both then,' Huntly said, and he took his bicycle helmet and left by the back door.

A few seconds after that, the bell rang as someone entered the shop.

'Better go,' Mrs Bubby said. 'Sounds like a customer.'

'I'll finish the washing up,' Smudger said.

Mrs Bubby went out into the shop. There was a boy standing at the counter, staring at a smouldering joss stick.

'My incense,' Mrs Bubby explained. 'It helps with stress. What can I do for you, dear?'

The boy didn't look well. There was perspiration glistening on his forehead, and he had a strange pallor, as if he were sickening for something.

'You all right, dear?' Mrs Bubby asked, concerned. 'You look a bit under the weather.'

'No, I'm fine thanks. I was just wondering if – if I could buy—'

What was it again? His mind had gone blank. It had turned into an empty sheet of paper. With not a word of writing upon it.

'Yes, dear?'

If he could buy—? What had the Inspector told him to say? Frankie's memory had suddenly turned into a great Arctic waste.

'If you could buy what, dear?'

It came back to him.

'If I could buy "*a little something*" please. A little something "*to keep me going*".'

Oh right, Mrs Bubby thought.

Yet this boy didn't look like Huntly or Smudger's usual kind of friend. A bit too creepy-looking to tell the truth. But you shouldn't judge by appearances, and as long as he got the rest of the password right.

'A little what sort of something did you have in mind, love?'

'Something to – er – keep me going – something to – to "*hit the spot*" that is.'

Well that sounded right enough. No problems there.

Mrs Bubby reached under the counter and took out a small tray of chocolate.

'So what's it to be, dear? Shiny-side out? Or shiny-side in? You take your pick. No problem.'

There was a problem. He was staring at something. Not her. Not even at the chocolate. But at something behind her. Level with her head. She turned and looked. It was odd, weird. What *was* he looking at? There was nothing to see. Just an empty shelf and—

But what was that? On the underside of the shelf. It looked like – it couldn't be. But it was. Even an elderly lady not at the cutting edge of technology could recognize a radio microphone when she saw one.

Bugged! The place was *bugged!*

Then Smudger opened the stockroom door and began to say, 'That's it, Mrs B. I'll be off now—' when he stopped and stared at the boy at the counter.

'Mrs Bubby – what's he doing here? He's a Pioneer—'

Then Mrs Bubby knew that it was already too late.

'We've been set up. Bugged! Run for it, Smudger!'

She stared at Frankie Crawley with vehement hatred, with far more viciousness than you would ever have dreamed a kindly old lady could have.

'Why you—' she said. 'I ought to—'

'Come on, Mrs Bubby! Let's go! Run!'

'Go without me,' she cried out. 'I'll hold them up. You get out the back!'

Smudger hesitated for a split second.

'You creep, Frankie.' He spat the words out. 'You creep—'

Then he could hear the heavy boots, the clamour, the splintering wood, the shattering glass—

So he ran.

But it was too late. Far, far too late. The Troopers were already in the shop. So many of them, all at once. And more, breaking in through the stockroom door. Smudger ran and ducked and weaved and squirmed. But they grabbed his arms and held him fast. And when Smudger kicked out, there was a sudden awful pain in his leg, as if he had been hit with something, or had maybe felt the voltage of a Shriek Gun. It was the worst pain he had ever experienced in his life.

The fight was over, as suddenly as it had begun. In the shop doorway stood the Inspector, his cold, grey eyes seeming strangely warm and contented for once.

'We've got them, sir,' the squad commander said. 'It's all here, on the counter. And more inside in the stock-room. They've just been making a fresh batch by the look of it. We got here just at the right time.'

'We did.' The Inspector nodded. 'Thanks to the help of our heroic young pioneer. Where is he?'

They looked around the shop. Frankie Crawley was nowhere to be seen. Then two feet, two legs and a bottom appeared, from under the counter.

'I'm here,' he said. 'I was just – checking to make sure that – that there wasn't any more chocolate – hidden away.'

'Very thoughtful of you, Young Pioneer,' the Inspector said. He turned to his men.

'Take them away for interrogation,' he ordered. 'And radio for the Disposal Squad. I want everything out of here. I want all this chocolate destroyed.'

He turned to his commander.

'You come with me, Sergeant,' he said. 'We're going to have a little look at a certain After School Study Club.'

They went through the garden, and into the old air-raid shelter.

It was a different place now. There were still signs of revelry from the night before. Glasses which had held chocolate milkshakes were piled on the bar. Plates on which cake and chocolate had been laden were stacked beside them. Mrs Bubby had intended to wash them all before she had gone to bed. But it had been too late. She would have done it in the afternoon, after the chocolate had been made.

'Well, well,' the Inspector said. '"The After School Study Club"! My, it has changed, hasn't it, Sergeant? Academic standards seem to have slipped. It doesn't look to me as though much studying has been going on here recently.'

He moved through the eateasy, opening every door and cupboard.

'Quite a bit of gluttony going on though, by the look of it. A lot of stuffing of greedy little faces, I think—'

The hidden door to the tunnel had been carelessly left ajar. The Inspector saw it as he turned around.

'So this how our friends got out the other night,' he nodded. 'Very good.'

He pulled the lead-lined door open. Behind it a fridge, which Smudger and Huntly had liberated from a scrap heap and had got working, sat humming quietly. The Inspector yanked at the handle, to reveal chocolate cakes and chocolate bars and – in the freezer compartment – tubs of chocolate ice cream.

'Well, well,' he said again. 'They have been busy.'

The two men contemplated the store of goodies.

'What do you want us to do with it, sir?' the Sergeant asked.

The Inspector gave one of his very thin smiles, the kind of smile which might have been on a diet for a year.

'Pulp it,' he ordered. 'In fact pulp the whole place.'

The Sergeant collected reinforcements, and they set to work with gusto.

Cousin Arnold

Huntly rode home in the sunshine and arrived at his gate just as the church clock rang the last stroke of midday. He left his bike propped against the side wall, and went in by the back door to the kitchen, catching the smell of cooking.

'Hi, Mum!' he called as he entered. 'I'm back!'

As he headed for the sink to wash his hands, he froze. Standing in the centre of the kitchen was a Chocolate Trooper.

A tide of thoughts flowed through his mind. The house had been raided. More honey had been found? Or chocolate discovered?

But the podgy, overfed face relaxed in a great beaming smile. The Trooper gave Huntly a pat on the shoulder and extended his hand in greeting.

'You must be Richard,' he said. 'I'm your Cousin Arnold. Pleased to meet you.'

It took a second for Huntly to get over the shock of being called by his real name. Even his mum hadn't used that for a long time. But the greater shock was that Arnold was a *Trooper*. The enemy. And he was standing right there in their house, beaming and grinning and pumping Huntly's arm up and down, as though he were some kind of slot machine, and if he went on doing it long enough, he might get some money out of him. But he didn't. Finally, he stopped, just as Huntly's mother entered, carrying a fresh tea towel.

'Ah, Huntly, you're back. And you've met Arnold, I see. Well, the food's nearly ready. If you'll wash your hands, we can sit down and eat.'

Huntly was glad to wash his hands. Cousin Arnold's grip was warm and clammy – a bit like shaking hands with a damp sponge.

They sat at the table and Arnold didn't let either Huntly or his mother get a word in edgeways. He talked non-stop about the Good For You Party and of his life and times in the Troopers.

It was remarkable the way Arnold could talk and eat and still keep breathing. Eventually he might pause to swallow a piece of pasta. But it was only a short hiatus. And then he was off again.

'Are you in the Young Pioneers, Richard?' he asked.

'Em, no, not exactly, as yet,' Huntly replied cagily, seeming to imply that he might join the Pioneers at some time in the future.

'Well, you ought to consider it. They're always on the lookout for keen young lads. I take it that you *are* a keen young lad.'

'Oh, very keen, Arnold,' Huntly said. 'None keener. I'm ever so keen, aren't I, Mum?' Huntly said.

'Famous for it.' His mother gave Huntly a look intended to silence him before he went too far.

Arnold paused to shovel more peas on to his plate from the serving dish.

'Well, it's very nice to see you, Arnold,' Carol said. 'But what exactly brings you to the area?'

Arnold's piggy little eyes looked suddenly sly. He seemed smug and pleased with himself. But wearing a uniform can have that effect on some people.

He looked around, as if to make sure that nobody else had tiptoed into the room, then dropped his voice to a confidential whisper.

'To tell the truth, we're here on standby, Carol,' he said. 'Reinforcements.'

'Oh?'

'Yes. There's going to be a big clampdown in this area, on bootleggers and such.'

Huntly froze again. His mouthful of food turned to ashes. All its taste had gone.

'Bootleggers? Around here?' his mother was saying, without the slightest notion that what Arnold had just told them impinged so directly upon their lives.

'You'd be surprised, Carol,' Arnold nodded, 'at what the most innocent-seeming people can get up to. In fact, confidentially, there were a few raids planned for this morning. Several raids, in fact, on the premises of known and suspect bootleggers and chocolate users.'

'Really?' Carol said.

'Several suspects who thought of themselves as untouchable will be behind prison bars by now,' Arnold said with satisfaction.

'You mean,' Huntly began, trying to sound

unconcerned, 'that you raided some bootleggers – this morning?'

'Well, not me personally, Richard. I'm not on duty until later. Though I might get to do some raiding tomorrow, if I'm lucky. But yes. There was quite a major raid planned for this morning. I must find out how it went. They get overconfident, you see, and think they're untouchable. And that's when we move in. Could you pass the pasta dish there, please, Carol? And perhaps a spoonful more of that delicious sauce?'

Huntly sat there in shock, feeling cold and shaky. He could barely finish eating the food in his mouth.

'Are you OK, Huntly? You look a bit pale?'

'I just – need to leave the table a moment, Mum – excuse me, Arnold—'

'Oh, don't mind me. Bit under the weather, are we? Bit of an upset tum-tum. Oh my. You carry on. Your mum and I can have a nice long chat, can't we, Carol?'

'Yes, of course,' Carol answered. 'Try not to be long though, Huntly.'

Huntly left the kitchen and went along the corridor as though making for the bathroom. But instead of going up the stairs, he walked straight on, quietly opening the front door and closing it softly behind him.

He circled the house, keeping low so that he wouldn't be seen from the windows, still hearing the murmur of cousin Arnold's voice, droning on in the kitchen.

'It's a great life in the Troopers, Carol – travel, see the world, good food, healthy exercise and a decent pension at the end of it. You could do a lot worse. You could join the medical division, if you were interested. They'd give you a very nice uniform and a new stethoscope. I could put a word in for you, if you like.'

Then Huntly was on his bike, speeding towards Mrs Bubby's shop, as fast as his legs and wheels would take him.

'One, two, three.'

Kylie hopped over the chalked-out hopscotch grid which she had drawn on the pavement outside the house.

She wondered how much longer Smudger would be. When she was ten she would definitely go places with him and find out what he did when he got there. She skipped back and started again. Smudger would soon be home from places, with the shiny-sides-in or out – she didn't mind which.

Kylie looked up at the sound of an approaching vehicle. Not so many cars came along their road on a Sunday, though it was busy the rest of the week. And this wasn't a car exactly, either. It was one of the patrol vans.

Aha! Patrol van full of Chocolate Troopers approaching!

Kylie got ready to stick out her tongue, to put her thumbs to her ears and waggle her fingers at them. Smudger had shown her how to do it. He knew lots of clever things.

The patrol van drew nearer, climbing up the hill. The grim-faced troopers were visible, expressions like stone, ignoring the small girl on the pavement, who was plainly getting ready for an outburst of cheek.

She raised her hands, put her thumbs to her ears, half stuck out her tongue, but then, as the van passed and she saw inside, her face changed.

And, instead of 'Na, na, nee, na, na!' the words that came out were, 'Smudger, Smudger—'

Then she turned and ran for the door of her house, calling, 'Mum! Dad! Smudger! They've got Smudger!' Her game of hopscotch was forgotten, and her vision was a blur, as she ran up the path as fast as she could go, the tears falling from her eyes, the sobs starting to rack her small body.

Huntly felt a wave of nausea. One glance was enough to tell him everything. Yellow and black police tape was on the windows and doors of Mrs Bubby's shop. Notices read, *No Entry. Authorized Personnel Only.* And Huntly knew without asking that Authorized Personnel did not include him.

There was no one around. He peered in through the shop window. Objects lay scattered on the floor; flashes of silver foil, squares of chocolate trampled underfoot.

Huntly felt sick and empty, his stomach in knots. He wheeled his bike around the corner to the lane, and left it hidden by some bushes where it wouldn't be stolen. He climbed over the fence and into Mrs Bubby's back garden. There was more black and yellow tape and another 'Authorized Personnel' sign at the entrance to the old air-raid shelter. Yet there seemed to be no one around here either.

Huntly stepped over the cordon, went into the shed

and down the steps into the eateasy. The door was hanging off its hinges.

He stepped down carefully. One solitary bulb illuminated the darkness – enough for Huntly to see that the other lights had been smashed. Wires dangled from the ceiling. Some sparks sputtered along a length of cable, and then went dead.

They had wrecked it – pulped it. Everything was ruined, destroyed. All their work, all their effort, all those wonderful evenings, those great times, when people had been free and happy for a while. All gone. His best friend taken, and Mrs Bubby too. Both of them maybe in prison by now, at the mercy of men with cold, grey eyes.

The panels had been crowbarred from the walls. The bar had been smashed and splintered, the tables upturned and shattered. The door of the fridge had been broken off. A trail of melting ice cream dribbled to the floor.

Then there was a sudden movement. A noise. Someone in a corner, hiding in the darkness. Huntly swivelled round, ready to fight, ready to run.

A figure emerged from the shadows.

'Only me,' a familiar voice said.

It was Charles Moffat. 'I thought there might have been a little bit of chocolate left, just a morsel or two.'

'Is there?'

'No,' he said sadly. 'They've pulped the lot. What they didn't pulp, they poured stuff over – bleach, toilet cleaner – you couldn't eat it now.'

But Huntly wasn't really concerned about the chocolate. That wasn't important any more.

'What happened? Did you see anything?'

'I was in my doorway,' Charles Moffat said. 'Just thinking about luncheon. And this smarmy-looking type went by. Looked like a Young Pioneer, only without the uniform. He went into the shop, and a few moments later the doors of this broken-down old van flew open – been parked there for days, it had, I thought it was abandoned – and these Troopers poured out of it and went for Mrs Bubby's. Next thing, Mrs Bubby and Smudger are being taken away in a patrol vehicle. Then the racket started. As if someone had gone mad with a sledge hammer – all smashing and crashing. Then that stopped and they drove off too. So I thought it might be safe to have a look. But there's not much left, as you can see.'

'What time was this?' Huntly asked. 'Twelve?'

'Just after,' Charles Moffat said. 'I heard the clock striking. At least I think I did.'

'I had to leave,' Huntly said. 'Or I would have been there too.'

Then a terrible thought came into his mind. He had left, and a few moments after his departure, the Troopers had arrived.

'They won't think it's *me*, will they?' he gasped. 'Smudger and Mrs Bubby? That *I* betrayed them – they won't think *that*, will they?'

The homeless man stared at him, as if trying to think of something comforting to say. He mumbled a few words, but Huntly's mind had already moved on. Right at that moment, even a sense of guilt was not the kind of luxury he could afford to indulge himself in. There were others in danger. 'Several raids', hadn't that been what Arnold had said? 'On the premises of known and suspect bootleggers and chocolate users'.

What about Mr Blades?

What if they were on to him too? He didn't have an eateasy in his bookshop, but he had something else, something equally as valuable and equally as damning. He had *The Art of the Chocolate Maker* by Tobias Mallow. He had the very recipe for chocolate.

In some ways more valuable than chocolate itself.

Or what if Blades was in danger for his political activities? He and his friends who opposed the government? Yes, maybe the Troopers had put him under surveillance too. Maybe he'd got careless again and his chocolate had been showing. Or, even if he was safe, at least he might know what to do, how to help Smudger and Mrs Bubby. It was someone that Huntly could turn to, someone he could trust.

'Mr Blades,' Huntly said. 'I've got to tell him.'

'Who?'

'The bookseller! They could be on their way to him too, right now.'

Just then there was a sound, a soft miaow. They both looked down to see Mrs Bubby's cat entwining itself around Huntly's legs.

'It's all right,' Charles Moffat said. 'I'll look after him.'

Huntly smiled, with relief and gratitude, and hurried on his way.

*

It took Ron and Trisha Moore a good ten minutes to calm Kylie down and to get any sense out of her.

'What do you mean they've got him, Kylie? Who's got who?'

'The Chocolate Troopers. Just now. In the van. They've got Smudger. And Mrs Bubby. In the back.'

'But how? That's not possible,' Trisha said. 'He's gone for a bike ride. He's not at Mrs Bubby's, he—'

Then she spotted something in Kylie's hands – a small piece of silver foil, which she was twisting and pulling and winding around her fingers.

'What's that, Kylie?'

'It – it's my shiny-side in.'

'What?'

'Chocolate.'

'Who gave it to you?'

'Smudger. He's always giving me chocolate. First he goes places, then he brings me some chocolate.'

Ron and Trisha stared at each other.

'Oh no,' Ron said. 'What has he done?'

Mr Blades replaced the telephone receiver and looked down into the street. He was fortunate in having friends in many places – high ones as well as low. Forewarned was forearmed, and even if it only put you one step ahead of the opposition, it was enough to let you make your escape.

He moved swiftly and calmly and without any sense of panic. He still had a minute or two yet. They weren't quite at his door. He threw a few things into a holdall and then went to pull the overalls on over his clothes. It was time for a change of identity and occupation.

The overalls were a pale, faded blue. They looked lived in and worked in. A badge on the pocket read NATIONAL WINDOW CLEANERS. He zipped them up.

He went to the window again and looked back down into the street. A second patrol van had arrived. The reinforcements were there. They were ready now. They were getting down from the van. The Inspector he recognized. And the boy with him too. The last time he'd seen him, he'd been wearing a Young Pioneers' uniform, he'd been in the bookshop, pretending to browse.

It only went to show. What came around went around; actions had consequences; and you never knew quite what they might be.

Who had informed on his activities, he did not know. Maybe that Young Pioneer had put them on to him; perhaps someone, pretending to be a customer, had bugged his shop. Maybe one of those who had attended his meetings had informed on him and turned him in. It hardly mattered now.

Blades hurried down the back stairs and went out to the bookshop yard. He went to his van and loaded a ladder on to the roof rack. He then peeled the magnetic sign from the side of the van, the one reading *Blades Bookshop – Rare and Antiquarian Editions*. He threw it into the back of the van and replaced it with another sign reading *National Window Cleaning Company*.

He threw a bucket, a scraper and a few rags into the van, then he tied a piece of cloth to the end of the ladder on the roof. He wasn't sure why he did it exactly, maybe for a sense of authenticity. Or maybe because details can make all the difference between captivity and freedom, between life and death.

He took a flat cap from his overall pocket, put it on his head, pulled it over his eyes, got into the van and drove away.

He had to drive past the front of his bookshop. The Inspector and the Troopers were there. The Young Pioneer was watching them. On the Inspector's command, one of the Troopers took the crowbar he was holding and inserted it into the door frame.

There was the crack of breaking wood. It sounded like a gunshot, echoing over the quiet of the deserted market.

As Blades drove away, the Young Pioneer turned around, hearing the engine of the van. Their eyes met. But there was no recognition on the part of the Young Pioneer. He turned away. There was another rasp of splintering wood. Then the Troopers were inside the bookshop.

But Blades was already turning the corner. They had missed him. He was free.

Ron Moore put the phone down. The news was every bit as bad as he had expected.

'Will Smudger be back for lunch, Dad?' Kylie said.

Ron was a tough man; he felt himself swallowing back tears. How could they tell her? Smudger wouldn't be back for lunch or dinner or breakfast the next morning. Who knew if Smudger would ever be back?

'Well?' Trisha asked. 'What did they say?'

'He's being held at Police Headquarters. They're charging him with bootlegging. It'll mean re-education, interrogation, aversion therapy even . . . who knows—'

'Can't we do something?' she said.

Ron flared up. 'What, Trish? What?' he said angrily. 'You tell me what to do and I'll do it. What's the answer? Eh?'

'Ron—'

He threw himself into a chair. He knew he was being unfair but he couldn't help it. He was afraid. And he couldn't tell them, because he could see they were afraid too. Kylie was looking at him hopefully, expecting that Dad would rub it better, or fix it, or make it right. But not this time.

'I'm sorry, Trish, I didn't mean to lose my temper like that. I just—'

'It's OK, Ron.'

He gathered Kylie up in his arms and passed her over to Trisha.

'You take her,' he said. 'I'll drive down to the Police Headquarters. They've got to let me see him, haven't they? I mean, they can't say no to that. I'll take my mobile. I'll ring you, as soon as there's any news.'

Trisha nodded. 'If you do manage to see Smudger, tell him that we – that we . . .'

She reached for the tissue box.

Ron put his hand on her shoulder. 'I know what to say to him, love.'

He picked up his car keys and headed for the door. He

stopped and turned. 'Someone must have shopped him,' he said. 'I'm not saying what he did was right, but someone must have turned them in.'

A thought came to his mind.

'Kylie,' he said, 'when you saw Smudger being driven away, who else was in the van?'

'Troopers. And Mrs Bubby.'

'What about Huntly? Did you see him?'

'No.'

Ron looked at Trisha. He said nothing, but he held her gaze for what seemed like a long time. Then the door closed behind him, and he was gone.

National Window Cleaners

By the time Huntly had sprint-cycled the distance between Mrs Bubby's shop and the Old Market, the Troopers had already been and gone.

The door of Mr Blades's bookshop yawned wide open. A breeze blew in, fluttering the pages of the books which lay open on the corridor floor.

There were books everywhere. It was as if every single book in the shop had been taken from its shelf and its rightful place, had been examined and then discarded. And so it had gone on, until whoever had been responsible for this vandalism had found what they had been searching for. There it was, on the top of the heap, ripped apart, its pages torn, its covers discarded. Its title was still clearly visible at the top of its pages.

The Art of the Chocolate Maker *by Tobias Mallow. 'The world's greatest living exponent – now sadly deceased.'*

Huntly smiled sadly at his memory of Mr Blades's joke. Things had seemed so different then, so new, so full of hope. But now—

Footsteps. The creak of the door. Someone behind him. He spun round, ready to run. A man there. Familiar, yet unfamiliar. A workman of some kind. Dressed in a faded blue boiler suit. And yet he seemed to know his way around, and what he was looking for. He knelt down beside Huntly and took the book from his hands.

'There it is. Damaged, but not beyond repair. Too dangerous to keep, but too precious to throw away. That's what I had to come back for.'

They knelt there, the book between them, looking like two monks at prayer. One young and thin, one old and stout, but still agile and with plenty of puff left.

'Mr Blades – they've got Smudger.'

'I know. And Mrs Bubby.'

'You know? How?'

'No time to explain here, Huntly. Come on. They could be back any moment. We need to get out of here. Chuck your bike in the back of the van. I'll give you a lift.'

'Where to?'

Mr Blades pointed to the National Window Cleaners insignia on his overalls breast pocket.

'The depot, my boy. To the depot. When the going gets tough, the tough get going to the depot.'

'National Window Cleaners, Mr Blades? But I thought you—'

'Yes, yes. That I was a bookseller. And I am. Well, I *was* until this happened. But it's always as well to have a couple of strings to your bow – that way you can fire twice as many arrows. Remember my Early Editions Evening? The rebels? The like-minded souls? Well, we're finally getting organized. Come on. Let's go.'

Not knowing if he was doing the right thing, Huntly went. If he had to trust someone, and he felt that he did, then he would trust Mr Blades. A man who would risk his liberty to come back for the sake of a book of chocolate recipes was not a man to let you down.

Mr Blades helped him to put his bike in the van, and they drove a mile or two until they came to a dead-end street. At the end of it was a yard surrounded by a fence of corrugated iron. A sign read *National Window Cleaners – Main Depot*.

Mr Blades tooted the horn twice. The gate was opened from inside and they drove in. As soon as they were in the yard, the gate was closed and bolted.

'Welcome, my boy,' Mr Blades said, 'to National Window Cleaners. The home of the revolution. Every man and woman you see here is a true chocolateer. Every single one a rebel, who has taken the oath of loyalty, to fight to the very end. I'd have asked you along to more of our meetings, but I thought you were a little too young – my mistake, I now see.'

Blades led the way from the van towards an unprepossessing warehouse.

'But why a window cleaner's, Mr Blades? I don't understand.'

'Look at it this way, Huntly. Who else has such free access to so many places? Often with only the most cursory of security checks. Sometimes even with none at all. The humble window cleaner. If it's information you're after, if it's a bit of surveillance you're doing, if it's papers you want to borrow from someone's desk, if it's a computer you want give a virus to, if it's a little bit of sabotage you have in mind – who's the one you suspect last? But who's also the one who gets in everywhere? The man with the ladder and the bucket. Come in and meet the rest of the team.'

A bank of screens ran along one wall of the warehouse. Half a dozen people were busy at work, emailing and organizing and trying to hack into the government computer systems, to extract information from them or to infect them with destructive viruses.

'Everyone!' Blades announced. 'I'd like you to meet a friend of mine – one of our younger colleagues. Young to be a bootlegger, but a bootlegger just the same. Everyone – Huntly Hunter! Huntly – the team.'

People waved and nodded. Some stared at Huntly with unabashed interest. Could he *really* be a bootlegger? At his age? Wow!

Blades turned to a man who was sitting at a computer screen.

'Chips,' he said, 'our friend here has just had a very narrow escape and a few bad shocks. Would we have a piece of chocolate for him?'

Chips nodded and went to see what he could find. He returned shortly with a small bar of bootleg chocolate – not as good as the stuff Huntly, Smudger and Mrs Bubby had made, but not bad just the same

He gave it to Huntly, who thanked him and offered the chocolate around. But Mr Blades said no and insisted that it was all for Huntly, and that they wouldn't be happy until he'd eaten every last crumb.

So he did.

When he had finished, he asked Mr Blades the

question which he had been afraid to ask since he had first heard news of the raid.

'Mr Blades – about Mrs Bubby – and Smudger . . .'

'Yes?'

'Now that they've arrested them, what will they do to them?'

Mr Blades didn't answer immediately. He took a deep breath, looked straight at him and said, 'The truth is that our friend Smudger could be in for a very rough ride. We can only hope and pray that he will survive.'

Huntly swallowed. The chocolate he had eaten suddenly made him feel ill.

'But if anyone can pull through, Smudger can,' Blades said. Only there was maybe more hope in his voice than confidence. 'Come on,' he continued, trying to lighten the atmosphere. 'Let me introduce you to everyone else and show you what else we're doing here. You and I aren't the only ones with a taste for chocolate and a distaste for the Good For You Party, Huntly. We have plans to fight back. Plans to put an end to, well, we'll see. We may need your help, when the time is right.'

'Anything, Mr Blades,' Huntly told him. 'You only have to ask.'

'Come on then. Now over here we have—'

'Mr Blades,' Huntly interrupted him.

'Yes?'

'Someone informed on us, didn't they? Smudger, Mrs Bubby's shop, somebody set us up, didn't they? Someone pretty close. Someone we know.'

Blades nodded.

'It looks that way.'

'Yes. Well, I'm going to find out who it was. I'm going to find out who betrayed Smudger and Mrs Bubby, and when I do—'

Blades looked at him solemnly.

'What then?'

Very good question. Huntly hadn't quite thought that far ahead. What would he do when he found the one who had betrayed them?

'I don't know, Mr Blades.'

Or maybe he did. Maybe he knew exactly what he would do. He just didn't want to admit it yet, not even to himself.

'Huntly, listen, people say revenge is sweet. Believe me, it isn't. It may seem so at first. But in the end, it isn't like that. Chocolate is sweet. Revenge is like acid. It eats away at everyone it comes in contact with. It corrodes your very soul. Remember that.'

'I'll try to, Mr Blades. I'll try to.'

But he didn't make any promises.

Interrogation

Police Headquarters was a cold, foreboding building. But maybe it had been built that way, a symbol of the Good For You Party's power and authority.

Heavy gates swung out as the patrol van approached, then once it was inside the yard, they closed behind it, like the jaws of a great leviathan, swallowing its prey.

Huntly and Mrs Bubby were marched from the van, separated, and taken to the holding cells.

'I'm allergic to confined spaces,' Mrs Bubby told the Trooper who led her to cell 14J in the women's block.

'You should have thought of that before you started doing things that would get you locked up in them,' the Trooper replied, unsympathetically. 'Inside,' he told her.

'There's someone else in there,' Mrs Bubby said, peering in.

'So you'll have to share, won't you. It's not the Ritz hotel here, you know.'

'Obviously,' Mrs Bubby mumbled, 'I can see that from the staff.'

The Trooper slammed the door. Mrs Bubby took stock of her surroundings. There were two narrow bunk beds in the cell, and on the lower of the two sat a nun, saying her rosary.

Mrs Bubby rubbed her eyes. She had to be hallucinating, didn't she? It was the stress. But when she opened her eyes again, the nun was still there.

'Hello,' Mrs Bubby said.

The nun smiled a beatific, slightly apologetic smile but said nothing.

'Vow of silence?' Mrs Bubby asked.

The nun nodded. She was quite young really, Mrs Bubby thought. It was difficult to tell with that lot on, but she couldn't have been much over twenty.

'Chocolate offences?' Mrs Bubby asked.

The nun nodded sadly again.

'Never mind, dear,' Mrs Bubby said. 'We all have our weaknesses.'

The nun nodded, and then went back to her rosary.

There was a chair in the cell, and next to it a small table. Mrs Bubby sat and looked at the motes of dust floating in the beam of sunlight which entered through the small window, set high in the wall.

If they were going to ask her questions, then she needed an approach, a way of not answering them – a *credible reason* for not answering them. A way in which she could not possibly be *expected* to answer them.

Only what could that be?

She sat for a while. There was no sound but the beads of the rosary moving through the nun's hands.

Then it came to her. She knew just what to do when they came to interrogate her. She was an old lady, wasn't she? And sometimes old ladies aren't supposed to be all there. And people are only too ready to believe that.

Because it fits in with their view of old ladies – it conforms to their expectations.

So if that was what they wanted, that was what she would give them.

She'd let them think that she had lost her marbles.

Smudger meantime was taken straight to the interrogation room, and left on his own for a while, under the surveillance of a video camera. They left him there to stew, to worry, to grow anxious and fearful, to imagine the worst.

But he knew that, and did his best to keep calm, optimistic and even hopeful – which in the circumstances was not easy.

After an hour or two, the Inspector came into the room, accompanied by a Trooper. He carried a green cardboard file on which Smudger could clearly see his own name – Moore. S. (The S standing for Stephen, his real name, not the 'Smudger' everybody knew him by.)

The Inspector sat down at the other side of the interview table. The chairs were bolted to the floor and could not be moved. He lay the file down, opened it and extracted a paper.

'So, it's Mr Moore. The famous bootlegger!' he said, his voice rich with sarcasm. 'Now let me see. First name "Stephen". Also known as "Smudger", I understand.'

'To my friends,' Smudger retorted.

'Ah yes. Your friends, Mr Moore. And who would they be exactly? We'd be very interested to learn a little more about them.'

Smudger adopted an expression of trying to think hard, but all to no avail.

'Well, isn't that peculiar,' he said. 'I've suddenly forgotten all their names. I must be suffering from, well, isn't that peculiar too! I can't even remember what I'm suffering from. So I must have it bad.'

The Inspector looked at him.

'Then if you've forgotten, maybe we'd better give you some time to remember. That's one thing we have plenty of. We have all the time in the world. You can stay here as long as you like, Mr Moore. In fact, until you answer my questions, you won't be going anywhere at all. So, shall we resume? Let me ask you again. These friends of yours – what are their names?'

When Huntly got home, the house seemed empty and quiet. He had half expected to hear the voices of Arnold and his mother, engaged in conversation. Or maybe it would be Arnold talking and his mother trying to appear interested, as he droned on and on, about what a wonderful life it was in the Troopers.

But Arnold, by the look of it, had gone. Maybe his mother too had gone out for—

'Huntly!'

There she was. She had been sitting in the deep armchair with the earphones on, listening to her favourite classical music. She was always trying to get Huntly interested in it too. But he wasn't that keen on opera.

'Where have you been! Fancy just going out like that! Honestly! If your cousin Arnold hadn't been as thick as half a ton of bricks he might even have suspected that—'

'I'm sorry, Mum. I can explain. It's just I had to go. I had to. What did you tell him?'

'I told him that you'd gone upstairs to lie down for a while. That you weren't feeling very well and weren't to be disturbed. Where did you go, for heaven's sake? What took you so long?'

When all else fails, there is perhaps only one thing for it – to tell the truth.

'Mum, Smudger's been taken.'

Carol Huntly sat up. She reached for the remote control and turned the stereo off.

'What do you mean?'

'For interrogation. Him, and Mrs Bubby.'

'But – but when? Why?'

'This morning. They were making chocolate. They were bootleggers.'

'*They* were? Then what has this to do with you, Huntly?'

'When I say they were – I mean *we* were – I was too.'

'Oh no. *No!*'

'I'm sorry, Mum. It was just a bit of chocolate. We didn't mean any harm.'

Carol stood up, agitated, angry, flustered. She was normally so calm and in control, the way a doctor should be. Huntly had never seen her like this.

'*Harm?* Didn't mean any *harm*! They've both been *arrested*, Huntly. How much harm do you need? Why you might have been arrested too!'

'I would have been,' Huntly nodded. 'If I hadn't had to come back because of Arnold.'

'I knew you were up to something.' Carol paced around the room. 'I knew!' She said. 'I knew something was going on. I felt it all along—'

'It was just a bit of chocolate, Mum,' Huntly said again. He felt bad enough already and her reaction was making him feel even worse.

His mother stopped pacing and flashed an angry look at him.

Huntly sat at the table. He rested his head in his hands.

'I'm sorry, Mum.'

She took pity on him, and sat down beside him, and put her arm round his shoulders.

'It wasn't you, Huntly,' she said. 'You were right. It's an unjust law. It deserves to be broken. It's not you who's wrong. It's them. Will you be OK on your own for a while?'

'I'll be OK. Sure. Where are you going?'

'I'm going to see Smudger's parents. I'll be back soon.'

'Mum . . .'

'Yes?'

'Tell them it wasn't me – who betrayed him. Say they're to tell Smudger too, if they get to see him.'

'They won't need to, Huntly,' Carol smiled. 'He knows that already. You know he does.'

'Names!' the Inspector shouted, banging the desk with his fist. Flecks of spittle were around his mouth. His self

243

control was slipping away and soon it wouldn't be the desk which felt the impact of the blows.

'Names, boy! We need names! Give me names! Of customers! Suppliers! Friends! Associates! I want names!'

Smudger wished he could think of something to say, something which would placate the Inspector, if only temporarily. Something to buy him a little time.

The fist banged on the desk again, the knuckles white, the flesh red with the impact.

'And if I don't get names—'

Before he could complete the sentence, there was a brief tap on the door, and then it opened and a Trooper entered.

The Inspector wheeled round angrily.

'Well? I'm busy. What do you want?'

'Em – everything all right in here, sir?' the Trooper asked hesitantly.

'Of course it's all right,' the Inspector snapped. 'Why shouldn't it be? What is it?'

'Just to inform you that the other prisoner's waiting for you, sir. They've brought her down and put her into Interview Room Two.'

The Inspector looked at Smudger, who kept his eyes averted, his face without expression.

'All right. I don't think we'll get anything useful out of this one anyway.'

'Take him to his cell, sir?'

'Yes.' A cold smile appeared on the Inspector's face. 'Then arrange transport – to Re-education Camp. Let's see how he likes it there.' He leaned over and spoke to Smudger. 'That might help cure your amnesia,' he said.

Smudger didn't betray his inner feelings with the slightest display of emotion. He didn't even blink.

The Inspector left the room. Smudger looked up at the Trooper.

'Re-education Camp?' he said. 'So what goes on there exactly?'

'You'll find out soon enough,' the Trooper said. 'On your feet.'

If Smudger had proved to be a tough nut to crack, then Mrs Bubby, in her own unique and individual way, proved his equal.

The Inspector discovered her in Interview Room Two, sitting at a table, hunched over, prodding with her finger at some invisible particle of dust.

'Round and round she goes,' Mrs Bubby said, with a kind of mad gaiety in her voice. 'There goes Mrs Dusty. Round and round she goes.'

The Inspector flashed a questioning look at the woman Trooper on guard.

'Been like this since we put her into the cell, sir,' the Trooper whispered. 'I think she's had a breakdown.'

'Or pretending to have had one,' the Inspector said. He sat down across the table from Mrs Bubby. She looked up and gave him a smile.

'It's Mrs Dusty!' she said, pointing at the invisible dust on the table.

'Is it now?' the Inspector said. 'Well, leaving Mrs Dusty

to one side for a moment, I wonder if you can supply us with some names, my dear? Could you do that?'

'Names?' Mrs Bubby said. 'I know lots of names. And so does Mrs Dusty. She knows lots of names too.'

'Good,' the Inspector nodded. 'And whose names does she know? The names of any bootleggers, perhaps? Suppliers of ingredients and raw materials? Clients, customers? Would she know their names, their whereabouts?'

The elderly lady across the table from him smiled her smile and went on tracing out shapes on the table with her finger – strange, complicated shapes.

'I'll ask Mrs Dusty,' she said.

'You do that,' the Inspector agreed, and he watched as the woman mouthed soundless questions to 'Mrs Dusty' and listened to the answers by holding her finger up and then inserting it into her ear. It was a bizarre and pitiful spectacle indeed. It was probably the shock of the arrest, the Inspector speculated. Such things could unhinge people of her age.

'And what does Mrs Dusty say?'

Mrs Bubby extracted her finger from her ear.

'Mrs Dusty says she knows lots of names.'

'Would Mrs Dusty like to tell us what those names are?'

The Inspector felt hopeful. Mad or not, that didn't mean she wouldn't give some useful names away, even if only by mistake.

'Well, Mrs Dusty says there's Smudger . . .'

'Yes,' the Inspector said encouragingly, 'we know about him. Who else?'

'Then there's Roger,' Mrs Bubby said solemnly.

The Inspector made a quick note of the name. Roger. Probably some bootlegger. He'd need to find out more about this.

'And his second name? Roger's second name?'

'Dodger,' Mrs Bubby said.

'Roger Dodger?'

'No, Roger *the* Dodger!'

'Roger the Dodger?'

'That's right. And then there's Pudger . . . and Gnasher . . . and Homer . . . and Kalamazoo and—'

The Inspector's patience snapped like a twig.

'Get her out of here—'

'And Snapper and Fishy, and Dongo-Pongo, and Horty McSnorty and—'

'Take her back to her cell! She's useless. Completely gaga! If she ever did have any marbles to begin with, the woman's totally lost them now!'

The Inspector stormed from the room. He had far more important things to do than to waste his time on barmy old bats like this one.

'Come on, love,' the woman Trooper said, 'I'll take you back to your cell.'

Mrs Bubby got slowly to her feet. She seemed reluctant to leave a friend of hers behind – a friend invisible to others – a little friend, who lived on the table.

'What about Mrs Dusty?' she said. 'Can she come too?'

'Of course, love,' the Trooper nodded. 'You bring Mrs Dusty as well.'

'Come along, Mrs Dusty,' Mrs Bubby said, and she carried her aloft, perched on the end of her finger.

As they marched along the corridor back towards the cell block, Mrs Bubby turned to Mrs Dusty and said quietly, 'You know, Mrs Dusty, it doesn't matter how barmy they think you are, just as long as you don't give any information away.'

Mrs Dusty nodded. You could see that she agreed with that.

Yes, Mrs Dusty and Mrs Bubby – they made a great team.

Before sending Smudger to Re-education Camp, they gave him a haircut.

As he sat in the chair, a memory came to Smudger, of long ago. The day it had first started. When he and Huntly had been stopped by the Detector Van. And the Trooper had threatened them with the Police Dentist. What was it he had said? '*He's a very good dentist, he just doesn't have much anaesthetic.*'

Well, the Good For You Party hairdresser seemed remarkably similar.

'He's a very good barber,' Smudger could almost hear the Trooper say, 'he just doesn't have much by way of style books, or scissors. All he's got is his razor and clippers. And he runs them – all over your head.'

Which is what he did. The razor buzzed. He could feel the vibrations through his skull. His teeth buzzed in sympathy. Then, finally, the noise stopped.

'There.'

For some perverse reason, the barber took a mirror and held it up behind Smudger so that he could see the reflection of the back of his head. Maybe it was pride in his work that made him do it – satisfaction in a good job well done. Maybe he took a twisted pleasure in showing people what he had done to them.

Smudger wasn't really that bothered. Short hair and a scalp like sandpaper were the least of his worries. His hair would grow back. It was what awaited him at the Re-education Camp that concerned him now.

He wondered if they'd give him a hat. It was surprisingly chilly without your hair.

After the compulsory haircut, Smudger was marched down to the shower block, where he was handed a small piece of soap and pointed in the direction of a shower cubicle.

Smudger was glad to wash. Clipped hair had gone down the back of his neck and irritated him. When he came out of the shower, his own clothes had gone, and in their place was the standard-issue prison uniform of denim shirt, dark-blue pullover and dark-blue trousers. For his feet were a pair of uncomfortable-looking boots.

He put the clothes on, then stood and waited for someone to come for him. It was an odd feeling wearing clothes which weren't yours and which you hadn't chosen. You felt depersonalized, an object, someone whose control over their own life was slipping away.

Footsteps echoed along the corridor as the Trooper returned to march him away.

'Left, right!' the Trooper barked. 'Left, right!'

Smudger walked, wondering why the Trooper found it necessary to keep saying 'Left, right' over and over. For how else would you walk? Right, right? Left, left? No, Left, right (or possibly Right, left) seemed about the only way to do it.

They marched on through the warren of corridors, until finally they turned a corner into a pool of brilliant sunlight. They were at a checkpoint.

'Prisoner 1571, Moore, S. For transportation to re-education facility!'

'OK. Sign here and take him out. Bus is waiting.'

The Trooper led him out to where a grey, unmarked bus was parked.

'On board.'

Smudger got on. A handful of other prisoners, mostly boys of about his age or older, were already on board, also awaiting transportation. But there were older people too. Some in their twenties and thirties, even forties and fifties. Bootlegging seemed an occupation open to all ages – if such, of course, had been their crime.

And then he saw Mrs Bubby, sitting watching him from a rear seat. Next to her was a nun, with a rosary in her hands, wordlessly murmuring prayers.

At least Mrs Bubby still had her hair. She looked up. She didn't seem to recognize Smudger at first. But then he saw her hand move, and she clenched her first in the universal symbol of strength and rebellion, in the willingness to fight against insuperable odds, even to the end of life itself. Smudger smiled. He clenched his own fist, and raised it slightly, so that she could see that whatever may have happened to him, his spirit had not been destroyed.

Not yet, anyway.

'You! Siddown! What are you waiting for!'

Smudger sat down. The bus started up and drove away from the compound. The electric gates whirred shut behind it. They drove through the city, all the familiar landmarks were there. He felt a sudden surge of affection for even the most ordinary things.

Soon the city gave way to the high-rise apartment blocks of the periphery, then these were supplanted by the neat rows of suburban semis, with Good For You Party flags flying in almost every garden. And then the semis were a long way back down the road, and the bus was driving past muddy fields, where potatoes sprouted in long, geometric rows.

Then the bus was climbing hilly roads, and the scenery around them was windswept and bleak, with heather and bracken and sheep which ran in panic along the crests of the hills, or which stood, puzzled, by the side of the road.

Finally, they were there. The inhospitable outlines of the Re-education Facility came into view. It was the sort of place you wouldn't send a dog to, for fear it would get depressed, and leap off the nearest cliff.

The bus waited while a barrier guard checked the driver's papers. Then it was allowed in. It came to a halt by a building marked *Re-education Facility – Arrivals*. The driver opened the door and a guard clambered on board.

'How many?' he asked.

'Seventeen male, five female – one a senior. All medium risk – except one. One high risk.'

'Which one?'

The driver pointed to Smudger.

'Him.'

The guard turned to him.

'OK. You,' he said. 'Off first. Come on, son, move it.'

Smudger got up and walked to the door. He paused at the top of the steps and looked around the encampment. The buildings, the sky, the very earth itself seemed to have been painted in a drab, utilitarian grey. All the colour had washed from the land. There was nothing but greyness, and the howl of the wind as it blew down from the hills.

There wasn't a tree in sight. He had never seen such a bleak, depressing place in his whole life.

The guard seemed to read his mind. 'Come on, boy,' he said with a sneer. 'It's "Home Sweet Home" for you for a good long while and the welcoming committee is waiting. So move it. *ON THE DOUBLE!*'

He prodded Smudger with his baton. Smudger stumbled down the steps of the bus, painfully whacking his shin bone as he did so. It hurt badly. He could feel his eyes starting to water. But he swallowed back the pain.

Never let them know they've hurt you, he thought. And that way, you might just survive.

Frankie Crawley

Huntly sat in his place in the classroom. He tried to follow what Miss Ross was saying, but he couldn't really concentrate on it at all. His mind just wandered, like an animal in a field, grazing where it would. Only it kept returning to the same place – to Smudger.

He looked around the class, at all the faces, at those busy taking notes as Miss Ross drew another diagram on the board. And there was Smudger's desk, unoccupied; his chair, empty.

Huntly tried to pay attention. He tried to screw his mind up tight, the way you compressed your hand into a fist, the way—

—Smudger had done. He could picture him. His hand in a fist, a victory salute of revolution and solidarity.

'*Freedom, Huntly! Freedom and justice – and chocolate for all!*'

Huntly knew that he should be taking notes, like all the others, like Myrtle Perkins and Frankie Crawley and Dave Cheng and—

Dave. Dave Cheng. Huntly studied him carefully. He looked OK, seemed OK. He was taking notes as diligently and attentively as all the others. And yet, behind

253

his eyes, it wasn't really Dave at all, not really, never had been, not since his return from, well, yes, that was it, from the Re-education Camp. Part of him had been crushed and destroyed during those exhausting, endless days of 'rehabilitation'.

Days which Smudger was living through right now.

And what would become of him? What would become of that essential part of Smudger which made him so uniquely himself, so full of hope and fight and enthusiasm and zest for life? Would what had happened to Dave Cheng happen to—

'Huntly.'

'Yes, miss?'

'Are you paying attention?'

'Yes, miss.'

'Then try to look as though you are.'

Miss Ross turned back to the board. She was worried about him really. He used to be such a good student. Never anything less that a B grade usually. But now . . .

Huntly made a few notes. Then his mind wandered again. Who had betrayed them? He glanced over at the face of Frankie Crawley. He had decided to have a word with him. It was just a matter of picking his moment.

It came that very afternoon, when he was dawdling on his way home through the park. The Young Pioneers were practising their drill out on the football field .

'*Chocolate will give you spots!*' Frankie Crawley bawled at the top of his voice.

'*Then your teeth will start to rot!*' the Pioneers repeated.

'*Health is what it's all about!*' Frankie chanted.

'*Go and eat a Brussels sprout!*' the Pioneers advised.

They came to a halt by the goal posts.

'Pioneers . . .' Frankie said, 'dis-missssssed!'

The squad broke up and the Pioneers went their ways in tidy groups of threes and fours. Everything was tidy about the Pioneers.

Frankie remained behind, talking to Myrtle Perkins about some matter of administration. She nodded her agreement, then briskly walked away. Frankie stood a while, smoothing the creases from his uniform, picking real and imaginary flecks of fluff from his sleeves.

Huntly got to his feet. He had been sitting on the old see-saw, the one he and Smudger had played on when they were small.

Now was his chance. Frankie was alone.

'Frankie! I want a word with you!'

Frankie looked up, nervous, eyes like a startled rabbit.

'Stay right there! I'm coming over!'

The width of two football pitches separated them. Frankie saw that it was Huntly. Whatever words he said, whatever explanation he gave to him now, would never be believed.

'Frankie! Come back here! Now!'

He ran like a hare. He had a good head start on Huntly, and the swiftness of fear on his side. But Huntly was fitter, stronger, and something else too – absolutely *determined* that Frankie was going to answer for what was happening to Smudger and Mrs Bubby.

'Frankie!'

Frankie didn't really know where he was going, but it didn't matter. Just to get away, that was the thing. His lungs were rasping, but he had to run. He looked back over his shoulder. Huntly was gaining. There was only one thing to do. If you couldn't run, you had to hide.

Only where?

He ran from the park, along the track to the scrubland. He slid in some mud, almost fell, righted himself, and ran on.

Where? Where? Where?

Then there it was – salvation. The old, disused railway tunnel. Full of the dark, of hidden crevices and nooks and crannies and pillars. A place to hide.

He ran inside. The sound of his running feet was soon swallowed by the tunnel. It was as if he had entered the mouth of a dragon and had been consumed.

Breathless, Huntly came to the end of the scrubland track and looked to see where Frankie had gone.

He heard the faint sound of shoes on gravel. Far, far away.

The tunnel. Had to be. There was nowhere else. Unless he'd vanished into the air.

Huntly walked inside, letting his eyes get accustomed to the dark. If Frankie was in here, then he was trapped. The other end of the tunnel had been sealed off by a rock-fall, years ago.

Local knowledge, Frankie. Didn't you know that?

He walked on, along the tunnel. He wasn't thinking any more of what he was going to do; he moved on, instinctively.

'Frankie!'

Cat.

And mouse.

Hide.

And seek.

Seek.

And ye shall find.

'Frankie!'

No sound. Nothing. Fear, maybe – if you could sense it. Fear in darkness, hiding behind a pillar somewhere.

On he moved. A drip, drip of water now, leaking through the roof. Splish, splash, splosh, falling almost like music into the puddles.

'Frankie! It was you, wasn't it! You turned Smudger in. And Mrs Bubby. Me too if you could have done. You informed on us. It was you, all along.'

Still nothing. Huntly stopped moving, stood stock still, listening for breathing, for movement of any kind.

Scurry, scurry, scurry. Excuse me, in a hurry.

A rat ran over his feet.

He felt disgust, but didn't react. The rat hurried away. Then there it was. Nobody could stand still forever. Just a slight movement. Someone easing the discomfort of standing in the same position for too long. The crunch of gravel. He was there. Over on the left, behind the brick pillar.

Huntly moved quietly ahead.

And there was Frankie, standing as still as he could. He even had his fingers crossed, to ward off bad luck.

'Frankie . . .'

'No, Huntly, no—'

Huntly moved forwards. Only a few paces separated them.

'No, Huntly, I can explain—'

'Oh, I'm sure you can. I bet that's something you're very good at – explaining. And betraying, And sneaking and spying. But telling the truth, not so good at that, maybe.'

One more step. Huntly was beyond thought now, beyond conscience, beyond feeling. This was the person who had betrayed his friends. There was only one thing to do. There would never be a witness. No one to see but the rats.

'No, Huntly, no!'

Yes, Frankie. Afraid so.

'Huntly, please.'

'You turned them in, didn't you, for interrogation!'

'No. It wasn't like that! They made me. I had no choice!'

Huntly hesitated. What did he mean – no choice? Everyone had a choice – didn't they?

'They've got my brother, Huntly.'

Brother? Frankie didn't even have a – wait, wait, yes he did. Much older than him. The skeleton in the Crawley family cupboard. Had left home in a bit of disgrace. Gone off to lead the wild life somewhere. Looked like the kind of chancer who could end up as—

'You're lying!'

—a black marketeer.

'I'm not!'

Or a bootlegger.

'He was one of the very first to be taken, Huntly. They've kept him in re-education ever since. They said that if I worked for them, then they'd be easy on him. They said there wouldn't be any more aversion therapy. It's true, I swear.'

Huntly hesitated, there was doubt now in his mind. Doubts and uncertainties weren't things the Good For You Party suffered from. They were sure of everything. They were filled with the rightness of their cause. Doubts and uncertainties were for those with a few shreds of their humanity still intact, for those with compassion, a dash of pity.

'But you would say that, wouldn't you, Frankie. You'd say anything.'

'It's true. Please don't hurt me. I'm sorry for what I did. What I'm telling you is true. It was my brother – what would you have done? If it had been your mum – or – or Smudger?'

Huntly didn't know. What would he have done? Faced with a choice like that? He couldn't be that sure of himself.

'I'm sorry, Huntly. I didn't know what else to do.'

Huntly felt ashamed. He could hear his mother's voice, ringing in his head: 'There's never any excuse for violence, Huntly, never.'

He didn't know if he agreed with that. But then there was his father's voice too, a long distant memory, but still strong and clear.

'Who knows, Huntly? What someone else has been through? We shouldn't be too quick to judge people. Who knows what we would have done if we had been in their shoes?'

'Come on,' he said to Frankie. 'Let's go.'

They walked in silence along the tunnel. As they walked into the light, Huntly looked at Frankie. His face was pale. His shirt was askew. Huntly must have grabbed at him in his anger.

'You look terrible, Frankie. You'd better sort yourself out before you go home.'

'You tore my shirt,' Frankie said.

They walked away from the tunnel and back across the park. They parted wordlessly at the gates. And that was all there was to it.

For now.

There has to be forgiveness, Huntly thought. Or there is never an end to the war and trouble in the world. Yes, there had to be forgiveness.

But that didn't mean you had to forget.

Re-education and Release

Time moved differently. A week in Re-education Facility 17 was the equivalent of six months anywhere else, possibly even a year. A year of abject misery.

It started early in the morning with the five o'clock rise and shine, when rising, let alone shining, was the last thing you felt like doing.

Rising and shining was immediately followed by bed-making, followed by bed-inspecting, followed in turn by Trooper Grigson ripping most of the beds apart – and by more bed-making.

Then, before there could even be any thoughts of breakfast, it was time for the ten-kilometre run – rain, snow, whatever.

Then it was time to have a nice, cold shower. Then, finally, it *was* time for breakfast. This was an all-star, rooting-tooting, Good For You breakfast, very big on the prunes, the prune juice, the cereal (with dried prunes), the high-fibre toast, and the sugar-free preserves (including prune jam).

After breakfast, it was time for indoctrination. It wasn't, of course, actually called indoctrination, it was called 'education'. The line between indoctrination and education is often a very fine one, and it was one which the Good For You Party neglected to draw.

The gist of the lessons was always the same – that the Good For You Party knew what was best. It had your interests at heart, and should be left to make all major decisions for you, including what you were to eat, drink and do with your life.

Lessons went on until after noon. Then there was lunch – big on lentils and with a wholesome dessert to follow, often prunes.

Then the murder started.

Well, it wasn't murder in the strict sense of the word. But it was murder to endure. Because after lunch came 'activities'. These activities usually involved long off-road marches, in full kit, carrying heavy backpacks. All this was intended to 'build character'.

'But I've already got a character,' Smudger would mumble to himself, as he marched over sodden gorse, or waterlogged peat, his boots letting the water in, his socks squelching.

And that was true. Smudger did have a character. But it plainly wasn't the sort of character the Good For You Party wanted him to have. They wanted him to have a different character, not the one he had grown up with, but one they intended to construct for him. One which might suit them – if not Smudger – a bit better.

Other activities included cross-country runs, visits to a military training circuit, army drill, cleaning toilets, polishing windows, repainting the barracks, cutting grass, weeding it, spreading manure, sawing logs, or simply carrying heavy objects from one end of a field to the other. And then carrying them back again. And again.

Then there was 'individual assessment'. Which meant whatever the authorities wanted it to. It could mean that you would suddenly be freed and given ten minutes to pack your belongings and be sent home. Or it could mean a session of chocolate aversion therapy – a long one, with all kinds of imaginative and subtle refinements to it.

In the evening, after dinner, there would be study and homework. There was no television, no films, few amusements of any kind. Just approved Good For You Party literature to read, and the odd copy of the *Good For You* comic.

Bedtime came early.

There was no cocoa.

Nobody came round to kiss you goodnight.

Which at least was something, considering the look of the Troopers.

And then, before you knew it, it was five in the morning again and there was rising and shining to do, followed by bed-making and bed-unmaking, and—

And so it went on.

Mrs Bubby had been moved. They had kept her in the senior's wing of the Re-education Facility for only a day or two. But her pretence at senility was so convincing it was enough to get her transferred back into the city – to the Good For You Secure Unit For Seniors (Cerebrally Challenged Ward).

Here she was expected to pass her days knitting (with special soft plastic needles with blunt ends, so that she couldn't harm herself or others) or making baskets. Other activities on offer comprised watching the television, or sitting staring at the wall. Staring at the wall was quite a popular pastime, so Mrs Bubby joined in once, to see what the appeal of it was.

She couldn't see the fun in it, however, as all she could think to herself as she sat and looked at the wall was, How am I ever going to get out of here?

And the wall seemed quite unable to answer her question. She just went on puzzling over it, occasionally looking out of the window, as if she half hoped to see a familiar face – Huntly or Smudger or Mr Blades – coming to her rescue.

And so the days passed, and the world turned, and the Good For You Party seemed to have taken over completely. Every television bulletin carried fresh news of another eateasy discovered and destroyed, of another bootlegger taken away for 're-education'.

Troops of Young Pioneers would gather in the city squares in the evening, for 'spontaneous' and 'unprompted' singing of the party songs:

> Good For You, Good For You,
> My party it is wise and true,
> We know what's best for you and you
> And you and everyone.
> No need to think, no need to think,
> Sit down and have forty winks,

We'll tell you what to eat and drink,
We know what's best for yoooooooou!

And people sang along, and applauded at the end. And nobody seemed to disagree with the sentiments expressed. For most of those of a rebellious nature were already in the re-education camps, being helped to see the error of their ways. So there was nobody left to object to anything.

Or maybe there *were* just a few people. People, for example, with interests in window cleaning. People who were biding their time, keeping a low profile, and waiting for the moment to be right.

'Mum . . .'

'Yes, Kylie?'

'When's Smudger coming home?'

'Soon, Kylie.'

'You said that last week.'

'I know.'

'And the week before. And the week before that too.'

'I know, Kylie, but Dad's gone to get him now. He'll be back very soon. Promise.'

Kylie missed Smudger. Smudger was her brother, after all. And not just that, he was nice to her most of the time. And he gave her chocolate. There hadn't been any chocolate since Smudger had gone away. Maybe now that he was coming back the chocolate would start up again. The special chocolate. Not like the chocolate you used to get, all nicely packaged and squarely cut with printed wrappers telling you what was in it and how many calories were in a hundred grams. It was more sort of chunky and home-made. It was quite delicious, and Smudger seemed to have unlimited supplies of it. But there was no need to mention that to anyone just now. Because people seemed to get upset these days, whenever you mentioned Smudger and chocolate. They started frowning a lot, and didn't like you talking about it for some reason. So it was best just to wait quietly till Dad brought Smudger home and the chocolate arrived.

Then there he was. Ron's van was pulling up in the driveway and he and Smudger were getting down from it. Trisha hardly recognized him at first, his hair had been cut so short. He looked thinner too, yet taller, stronger, more grown-up. They ran out to meet him. Kylie was first out of the door, sprinting along the path.

'Smudger! Smudger!' Then she did an emergency stop. 'Smudger! You've gone bald!'

A wry, sad smile crossed Smudger's face.

'Hello, Kylie. Yeah. I know. I had a lot of worries.'

'Will you be stuck like that?'

'No, it'll grow back. Hi, Mum.'

'Hello, Smudger. How are you, love? Are you OK?'

'Come on,' Ron said. 'Let's go inside.'

Smudger seemed to hesitate. He looked up at the window of his room. He squinted up as if he could see something there, or maybe it was just that the sun was in his eyes.

'Smudger—'

'Coming, Dad. Coming.'

They went inside and sat in the kitchen and made tea

and talked. And it was just like old times, except that Smudger seemed different somehow, more quiet, reserved, reluctant to tell them anything about what it had been like in the Re-education Facility. All he would say was that it 'wasn't too bad' and 'I got by'. And no matter how Trisha tried to prise more from him, it was all that she could get.

Kylie badgered Smudger to go out into the garden and to push her on her new swing. It was only an old car tyre tied to a branch of the tree. But she seemed proud of it and wanted to show it off.

'Later, Kylie,' Smudger said. 'Later. I'm just going up to my room for a while. Just to have a read and listen to my Walkman or something.'

Kylie looked crestfallen as Smudger went upstairs.

'I'm sure Smudger will play with you later, Kylie,' Trisha said. 'It probably all seems a bit strange to him. He'll have to get used to being back.'

Ron put on his jacket.

'I'll have to get back to the bakery. I'll be home later.' He called cheerio to Smudger on his way out. 'And it's good to have you home, son,' he added.

But there was no reply. Maybe he hadn't heard him.

'Mum . . .' Kylie said.

'You've just got to be patient, Kylie. You can't always expect people to be playing with you.'

'No. It isn't that, Mum, it's Smudger.'

'What about him?'

'He isn't Smudger any more. Not like he used to be.'

Trisha went to wash up the cups. She knew Kylie was

right. Smudger was no longer the boy he had been. It was as if a spark had died in her son. His eyes had seemed dull, his thoughts preoccupied. Something must have happened during his time in re-education, something he simply didn't want to talk about.

I wonder if would help for him to see someone – a friend that he used to know, Trisha wondered.

She thought of Huntly, and picked up the phone.

'OK, Mrs Moore. Yes, I will. I'll come straight round, And thanks. Thanks for telling me. I'll be there in half a hour.'

Huntly hung up the phone. His mother had heard him take the call. He looked up at her.

'It's Smudger. He's back. I ought to go round.'

'Yes, of course. You must.'

Huntly hesitated.

'Feels a bit awkward, really,' he said. 'I feel that I won't know what to say – I mean – what if he hasn't survived, Mum? I always said that if anyone could survive, Smudger could. But what if he didn't? What then?'

'Then he'll need a friend more than ever, won't he?'

Huntly nodded. He picked up his bike helmet and went to the door.

'I'll be back,' he said, sounding uncertain, as if he didn't really believe he would be. Then he went.

It didn't take him long to cycle to Smudger's house. He was earlier than he'd said. He cycled around the block a few times, just to give himself a chance to think. He knew why he felt so awkward and apprehensive. It was Dave Cheng. What if Smudger was the same now – blank, empty, his personality erased? He wouldn't be able to bear it. Not if Smudger had been destroyed.

But he couldn't postpone it any longer. He couldn't go cycling round the block forever. He wheeled his bike up the drive way of Smudger's house, and knocked softly on the kitchen door.

Mrs Moore let him in.

'He's upstairs, Huntly, in his room.'

'How is he, Mrs Moore?'

'Not himself, love. Hardly says a word. Maybe he'll perk up a bit when he sees you. Go on up.'

Huntly steeled himself for the worst, and went on up the stairs.

'Smudger?'

'Come in.'

And there he was. Huntly was shocked at the change in his appearance.

'Hi.'

'Hi.'

Difficult to know what to say, what to do. It all felt so awkward and clumsy, not like it used to, not like it ought to.

'Take a seat.'

'Thanks.'

Huntly sat uncomfortably on the beanbag. Smudger was at his bedroom table, looking through some school books.

'Just catching up,' he said. 'On lessons and stuff.'

'Right,' Huntly nodded.

Smudger began to write a few notes on a jotter pad.

'Just got to write something down, before I forget it.'

'Right.'

Silence. A big heavy cloud of silence, which seemed to muffle everything in the room except the scratching of the pen across the paper.

Huntly cleared his throat.

'They – they cut your hair, Smudge.'

'It'll grow.'

'I'm sorry about what happened, Smudger.'

'Don't mention it.'

'And thanks for not giving them my—'

Smudger swivelled angrily in his chair.

'I said don't mention it!'

'But I was only going to say.'

'Well don't!'

Huntly didn't understand. What was up with Smudger? What was wrong? He had only been going to thank him for not giving his name to the authorities. Or Huntly would have been arrested too. He knew that. He was grateful to Smudger. He just wanted to say thanks. What was so wrong about that? What had happened to him at the detention centre? What had gone on there?

'Are you OK, Smudge?' Huntly asked. 'What did they do? How did you survive? Was it true – the rumours about the aversion therapy?'

'Look, I don't want to talk about it! Just drop it.'

Huntly suddenly felt very uneasy. He felt that Smudger *had* changed, deep down inside, in a fundamental way. Something had happened to him, the fight in him had gone. The friend he had known was gone too. Some vital part of him, the defiance, the rebellion, the sense of injustice, they seemed to have been extinguished. They had died in him, like the fading embers of a fire, finally burnt out, consigned to darkness.

'Any news of Mrs Bubby at all, Smudger? Did you hear anything while you were in the . . .'

Nothing. Nothing. None of the old anger, the old fire.

'Sorry, I wouldn't know.'

'I cycled past her shop, on the way here. It's all closed up now. The homeless man's still there – remember him? I don't think he'll ever leave that doorway . . .' His voice faltered. What was the use? 'Smudger, look, I—'

'I've got a lot of school work to catch up on here. Reading and so on. Don't want to fall behind. I ought to get on with it maybe.'

It was a way out. Huntly got to his feet. It was too upsetting to stay. This wasn't the Smudger he had known. It was like talking to an empty shell. There was nothing left for them to say to each other.

And yet he couldn't just go. Not turn his back on his friend. So he struggled to find things to talk about a while longer. He even tried to bring the conversation round to the underground resistance which was building up throughout the nation. But as soon as he even hinted at it, Smudger became agitated and changed the subject.

He didn't even want to talk about the struggle any more.

Finally Huntly could bear it no longer.

They had broken his spirit.

Huntly mumbled some excuse about having to finish his own homework and stood to go.

'I'll see you again then, Smudger,' he said. 'See you Monday, at school.'

'Yes,' Smudger answered, in the dull monotone which now seemed to be his way of answering everything. 'Yes, probably. Well, cheerio.'

Then he did another very odd thing. He put his hand out, as if to say goodbye, to shake Huntly by the hand.

Huntly felt awkward and embarrassed, but he reached out in return.

'See you then,' he said. 'On Monday.'

Then he realized that Smudger's hand wasn't empty. There was a small, folded-up square of paper in it. He pressed it wordlessly into the palm of Huntly's hand. His level gaze told Huntly not to say anything, just to take the note and go.

So he did.

He left the house without a backward look and cycled down the road. He felt like looking back on several occasions, to see if maybe Smudger was watching him from an upper window, but he forced himself not to.

Instead of going home, he cycled to the playing fields. He sat on one of the empty swings, checked that he was not being observed, unfolded the square of paper, and read what Smudger had written.

Suspect my house is now bugged, the message read. *They bug the houses of anyone sent for re-education. Can't risk saying anything. Meet me at the railway tunnel tomorrow – three o'clock.*

Huntly sat there, swinging backwards and forwards on the little kids' swing. So many emotions were in him all at once that he didn't know which one to feel above the rest. Joy, maybe, a sense of exhilaration, of triumph even.

Smudger *had* survived. They hadn't broken his resistance or crushed his spirit. The fight and the revolution were still in him. The struggle wasn't finished yet, not by a long way.

Huntly could hardly wait for tomorrow's meeting. But before it, maybe he ought to have a word with Mr Blades, just to let him know that Smudger was out and that the fight was still there in him. And if they were going to strike back at the Good For You Party, the time to do it was now.

He wheeled his bike to the street, then rode off—

—to find a good window cleaner.

Back Soon

The depot of National Window Cleaners was closed and locked. A sign upon the gate read *Back Soon*. In Huntly's experience, Back Soon signs could mean anything from 'Back Soon' to 'You'll be lucky if you ever see me again. If you're going to wait, get a tent.'

So he decided not to linger.

As he took a short cut home, however, he saw the familiar figure of Mr Blades, halfway up a ladder, washing murky windows at the rear of a building, and trying to peer inside. Huntly stopped and looked up.

'Mr Blades!' he hissed.

Blades nearly dropped his bucket and fell down after it.

'Huntly!' he said. 'Wait there.'

He came down the ladder so that they could talk without being overheard.

'It's Smudger, he's out.'

'Is he?'

'You said you had a plan, for when the moment was right. Maybe with Smudger free again it is now.'

'Yes. Maybe it is. Bring him to the depot tomorrow. I'll outline what we have to do.'

'OK. And by the way – whose windows are you cleaning?'

'These windows, Huntly my boy, belong to the Surveillance and Security Bureau. And while they keep an eye on everyone else, I keep my eye on them. See you tomorrow then.'

'Oh, Mr Blades – any news of Mrs Bubby?'

Mr Blades grew thoughtful. He had taken quite a liking to Mrs Bubby. Obviously for a man of his age and dimensions, a thing like, well, romance, was quite out of the question – or was it? Either way, he wouldn't have Mrs Bubby thinking that he had abandoned her.

'She's being held in secure accommodation,' Blades said. 'And I believe she is playing what is known as *possum*.'

'Playing possum, Mr Blades?'

'The possum is an animal which sleeps a lot. And the expression "playing possum" means pretending to be dozy when you're not. It's too dangerous for me to visit her in person. But I shall try to get a message through, via one of my window-cleaning representatives. In fact, I think I see the very man for the job.'

Huntly turned to look in the direction of a rustling noise. It was coming from a nearby dustbin. The rustling was caused by somebody rummaging through it. It was the homeless man, the former Chocolate Man, Charles Moffat.

'Afternoon, Charles,' Blades called.

The homeless man waved an empty milk carton in greeting.

'Good afternoon,' he replied. 'Great treasures may be found in unexpected places,' he said. He waved at Huntly with a stale bread roll in his other hand. 'Hello, young man' he said. 'How are you keeping?'

Blades beckoned him over.

'Something up?' he asked.

'Yes, Charles,' Blades nodded. 'I might have a little job for you.'

'Oh, right.'

And it was only then that it occurred to Huntly that maybe there was more to Charles Moffat than there seemed. Maybe he too still had the spirit and the fire to fight back. Maybe he wasn't totally crushed yet.

Maybe he too was a bit of a rebel.

Huntly met Smudger in the old railway tunnel the following afternoon, as they had agreed. He was making his way slowly along in the half darkness, when suddenly a figure leaped from the shadows and grabbed him around the neck in an armlock.

'What's your game, citizen? What are you up to in here? Bootlegger, are you?'

A wave of relief followed on the wave of surprise.

'Smudger!'

'Ha! Got you that time, eh?'

'Haven't lost your sense of humour then – or at least what passes for one.'

'How are you, Huntly?'

'Never mind how I am, how are you? What was the re-education like?'

But Smudger didn't want to talk about it. That was all

in the past. It was the present that concerned him now. The present, and what the future might be.

Then Huntly remembered something which they had hidden in the tunnel wall, behind the loose bricks, a long, long time ago.

'Smudger, do you fancy some chocolate?'

'Do I! Why? Have you got any?'

'I know where there is some.'

'Where?'

'Right here. Where we left it, remember?'

Smudger followed Huntly's gaze towards the loose brick in the wall.

'I thought we were saving that – for the future?'

'Maybe the future's here now, Smudge.'

'Yeah. Maybe it is.'

They removed the loose brick and took out the chocolate they had hidden. It was still dry and fresh, wrapped up in a plastic bag.

'So what's happening?' Smudger said, as they ate.

'Plenty,' Huntly told him. 'And fast. I saw Mr Blades. We need to meet him this afternoon. He's got something in mind. And look, Smudger, there's someone else. Something you've got to know—'

But before he could finish, there was the sound of footsteps coming from the far end of the tunnel. Smudger looked up.

'What's that? Who's that, Huntly? Are we rumbled?'

A figure in a Young Pioneer's uniform walked tentatively towards them.

'Hello . . . hello?'

It was the voice of Frankie Crawley.

Huntly turned to Smudger.

'It's Frankie, Smudger. He wanted to see you. There's something he wanted to explain.'

Frankie edged forwards, visibly apprehensive, afraid, not sure as to how Smudger might react.

'Smudger—'

Smudger's reaction could have gone either way – anger or forgiveness. But for all Frankie's betrayal, at least he had had the courage to come here, alone, to face what might turn out to be some very unpleasant music.

'Smudger, I'm sorry about what happened, about what I did. I am, truly. You see, the thing is—'

'I know, Frankie,' Smudger said. 'I met your brother while I was inside.'

'You did? Is he all right? We've not heard from him in months. Only what the Party tells us. And how can you believe them?'

'He's OK. As well as can be expected. He's surviving.'

'I'm sorry, Smudger. I really am.'

'It's OK,' Smudger said. 'Maybe you did what you had to. Maybe if it had been someone in my family that they'd taken, maybe I'd have done the same.'

'Thanks, Smudger. Thanks.'

But although Smudger was prepared to forgive Frankie Crawley, he wasn't ready to let him off the hook completely, not without him first making some kind of amends.

Because Frankie was an insider, an established, reliable informant. Somebody on the inside could be useful to them – a double agent.

'The only thing is, Frankie,' Smudger said, 'there's a lot of stuff going on now. And you could help, if you wanted to, get information for us, put the authorities off the scent. We could use someone on the inside.'

Frankie looked worried. 'It's not that I don't want to help, Smudger, I do. But – what if I – if we were to get caught? I mean—'

Smudger looked at the chocolate in his hand. He wondered when Frankie had last tasted any. Maybe if a few squares of chocolate were to jog his memory, he might remember why a few risks were worth taking.

'Tell me, Frankie,' he said. 'When did you last have any chocolate?'

'Chocolate?'

'Yes, chocolate. This stuff.'

'I don't know now. I can't remember. A long time ago.'

'Well here, take a little – refresh your memory.'

Frankie wavered.

'I don't know if I should really, I mean, it's against the law. Although, I don't suppose a little bit would do any harm – just a taste.'

'Yes, that's it, Frankie. Just a taste.'

Frankie had a good long taste.

'Mmm,' he said. 'Mmm. Any more?'

Just a Poor Old Lady (Maybe)

Visitors were not, generally speaking, allowed into the secure unit of the Good For You Seniors' home, on the grounds that for the most part the inmates were not worth visiting. Or were beyond visiting. Or, even if you had visited them, they wouldn't have recognized you anyway.

Mrs Bubby sat in a rocking chair, with several feet of multicoloured knitting surrounding her, looking like an outbreak of something contagious.

She wondered sometimes if she had overdone her pretence at being a witless wonder. Maybe she had overplayed her hand. Maybe she had been too convincing and they'd never let her out again. If only somebody came to visit or sent word to her. Or had all her friends forgotten her existence?

Knit one, purl one. Click, click, click. She did a bit more knitting.

Two nurses came along. One was a new staff member, recently moved from another home. She saw Mrs Bubby clicking away on her needles.

'Isn't that what's-her-name? Who used to have the sweet shop? The bootlegger?'

'Yes. She went downhill from the day she was arrested,'

the second nurse said. 'I don't think she even knows where she is now.'

They approached the elderly lady with the endless, multicoloured knitting. She looked as if she might be knitting a rainbow, but hadn't quite worked out yet how to hang it up in the sky.

'That's nice, love,' the more senior of the nurses said. 'What's that you're knitting? A nice scarf is it? To keep you warm in the winter?'

The knitted wool was more than enough to keep several people warm in the winter. In fact you could probably have used it as a beach towel.

Mrs Bubby peered at the two nurses over the top of her reading (and knitting) glasses.

'Of course it's not a scarf,' she said indignantly. 'It's a liquorice allsort!'

The nurses smiled tolerantly, the way people do when they pat puppies on their heads or tickle cats under their chins. They left Mrs Bubby – the poor old soul – to her knitting.

Tap, tap, tap.

Mrs Bubby looked up. There was a face at the window, and the hand belonging to the face was tapping on the glass and beckoning her over.

She knew that face. But it was much cleaner than when she had last come across it. It was a face she had often seen, fast asleep in a doorway. It was him, the homeless man. Since when had he been a window cleaner?

He beckoned her over and gestured for her to open the window, quickly, while the coast was clear.

Mrs Bubby hurried from her chair to do so before the nurses returned. They would have been surprised to see the speed at which she moved. She crossed the floor in seconds and opened the window catch.

'Mr Blades sent me,' Charles Moffat whispered.

It was on the tip of Mrs Bubby's tongue to say, 'What took him so long?' but she didn't want to sound ungrateful.

'Has he got a message?'

'Yes.' He nodded. 'Something big's going to happen. This coming Saturday.' He reached into his overall pocket and took out a bunch of keys. He passed them through the window.

'Skeleton keys. Should help you get out. They ought to fit the locks.'

'OK. Got them. I'm with you!' Mrs Bubby quickly hid the keys in the pocket of her dress. 'When'll I know that the time is right?'

'Stay tuned to the TV. Saturday. Midday news – just before the—'

But he could say no more. Footsteps were approaching. The two nurses were coming back. Mrs Bubby shut the window and secured the catch. The homeless man took a scraper from his bucket, smeared some water over the window, and then began to remove the grime. He whistled as he did so, happy in his work.

The nurses looked and saw only a window cleaner, and paid him no attention. They were surprised to see Mrs Bubby out of her rocking chair, however.

'You all right, dear?' one of the nurses asked. 'Something the matter? Do you need the toilet?'

Mrs Bubby didn't need the toilet. But she was tired of being asked that question. Why was it that when you were young and once you got old, the only thing people seemed to want to ask you was, 'Do you need the toilet?'

'I'm all right,' Mrs Bubby said. 'I just dropped my wool.'

She held her ball of wool up like a trophy. The nurses helped her back into her rocker, and gave the chair a little push, to set her rocking again. Then they walked on.

'Sweet old lady, really,' one said to the other.

Mrs Bubby wiped a bead of sweat from her face. Thank heaven they hadn't found the keys, or heard them rattling in her pocket.

She took up her knitting, and resumed where she had left off.

Click, click. Knit, knit. Rock, rock. (Jingle, jingle.)

Mrs Bubby stuffed a ball off wool into her pocket. That should stop the keys from jangling.

Click, click. Knit, knit. Rock, rock.

Not long now. Not long at all. This Saturday, was it? Something big? Just what she had been waiting for.

The Plan

Huntly and Smudger found Blades at the appointed time, ensconced in the 'operations' room of the window-cleaning depot.

Blades greeted Smudger like a long-lost son (or, more accurately, considering their age differences, like a long-lost grandson). He then led the boys into a back room where they met up with Charles Moffat, the homeless ex-Chocolate Man.

He didn't look so homeless now. Mr Blades must have given him a change of clothes, a square meal (not to mention a square or two of chocolate) and have lent him a razor. He looked and sounded like a different person.

'OK, boys, sit down,' Blades said. 'While I get the plans.'

He took some printouts from a drawer and spread them out on the table-top for all to see.

'That's the Good For You Party Headquarters, isn't it?' Smudger said.

Blades nodded.

'Yes, Smudger. It is. We hacked into their systems. I can't vouch for its present accuracy one hundred per cent. But it's all we have. Now let me outline the scheme I have in mind. It's my belief that if we pick a face-to-face confrontation with the Good For You Party, we're bound to lose. We don't have the weapons or the manpower. Our only hope is to mobilize all the sympathetic elements of the population. We want all the people out there to take to the streets. It's a strategy called passive resistance.'

'Passive resistance?' Smudger said. 'What's that?'

Huntly answered the question.

'Well,' he said, 'you know when you get a small kid who doesn't want to do something, and so he sits down on the pavement and holds his breath till his face turns blue?'

'Yeah?'

'That's a sort of passive resistance.'

'So we've got to hold our breath till our faces turn blue, have we, Huntly? And that way we'll win the revolution?'

Huntly grinned.

'Not quite,' he admitted. 'Perhaps we'd better let Mr Blades explain.

'Well,' Blades said, 'the Party can't run the country without the cooperation of the people. And if the people stop giving it, well—'

'They have to go.'

'Exactly. And their bad laws go with them. Only people won't take to the streets unless they're confident of success, that others will do the same, and that there won't be any reprisals. Individuals can be picked off. But great crowds of thousands of people, in every city in the land, not even an army of Troopers can do much about that.

So we have to get a message out to the whole nation. To get them all to take to the streets – together!'

It sounded fine, Smudger thought. In *theory*. But in practice? Just how did you turn a dream like that into a reality?

'But how do we get a message out to the whole nation, Mr Blades? We don't have access to any TV or radio stations.'

Blades smoothed the plans out over the table.

'No, Smudger,' he agreed. '*We* don't. But the Party does. And their daily propaganda bulletins are broadcast from a terrorist-secure studio, right here in the middle of their headquarters!'

He jabbed at the plans with a stubby finger, pointing to a room highlighted in yellow.

A frown crossed Huntly's face.

'Hang on though, Mr Blades. What does "terrorist-secure" mean exactly?'

Blades glanced up.

'It means, Huntly, that whoever controls the studio can't be taken off air. Not for a good fifteen to twenty minutes. The door is steel-plated. You need an explosive charge to get through it. Also, the transmission can't be jammed easily. There'd be just enough time.'

'But wait,' Smudger said. 'Aren't you forgetting something? You said the studio was terrorist-secure, right? Well, if it's *that* secure we won't even be able to get in there.'

Blades smiled.

'True, Smudger. A terrorist wouldn't get anywhere near

the building. But a window cleaner, that's a different matter.'

'A window cleaner?'

'Exactly. Now the plan works like this. Each Saturday at noon the Shiny For You Cleaning Company arrives at Party headquarters to do the windows. They come in an ordinary white van, like the one I use. There are two cleaners. One about my build, one taller, like Charles. One of the men always brings his sons with him. Both Young Pioneers. They help with the work. OK?'

'So far,' Smudger said. 'Go on.'

'Now, for additional security, the window cleaners are accompanied by two Troopers. One woman. One man.'

'So where do we come in, Mr Blades?'

'This coming Saturday another van will arrive fifteen minutes earlier. Not early enough to raise suspicion. But early enough to create a window of opportunity. It will have the Shiny For You logo on the side. And guess who the window cleaners will be?

'You and Mr Moffat!'

'Exactly. And guess who will play the parts of the two Young Pioneers?'

Smudger and Huntly shared an excited glance.

'Us?'

'If you'll do it?'

They didn't need to be asked twice.

'You try and stop us. Of course we will.'

'Good. That was what I thought you'd say.'

'Mr Blades,' Huntly said, 'the real window cleaners – is there no way we could just cancel them? Stop them from coming? So we wouldn't be under pressure of time, worrying that they're right behind us?'

'Not possible, I'm afraid.' Already considered but rejected. We've no choice on this one.'

'OK. So what do we do?'

'We arrive at the checkpoint and we say we've come to do the windows and that we're running a little early this week. Once they've let us through the barrier, we have approximately fifteen minutes to access the studio before the real window cleaners arrive. We secure the studio. Then we go on air. Everyone will be watching their televisions as the Good For You lottery draw takes place straight after the news. So we go on air, with Charles's help—'

The homeless man nodded modestly. He was familiar with the inside of a television studio, and although he was usually in front of a camera rather than behind it, he had a pretty good idea of how the technology worked.

Blades continued. 'Then once on air we appeal to the nation to take to the streets. If they respond, it's all over and the Good For You Party is finished.'

'And if they don't respond?' Smudger said.

But in truth, he knew the answer to that question already.

'We're finished,' Blades said. Then he smiled. 'But we'll have tried. And if we don't try, we're finished anyway. So what do we have to lose? Well boys? What do you say?'

But Blades already knew the answer to that question as surely as Smudger had known the answer to his.

'We'll do it, Mr Blades. Of course we will. Won't we, Huntly?'

'Of course.'

'Any questions?'

'Just a couple,' Huntly said. 'You said that there were two troopers accompanying the window cleaners in the van, a man and a woman. How do we get round that?'

'We'll need uniforms, and the right people to wear them,' Blades said. 'Any ideas of who could help us with that? And obviously you two will need Young Pioneers uniforms as well.'

'Frankie should be able to get us those,' Smudger said. 'As for the Troopers' uniforms, Huntly and I might be able to get hold of them. And the people to wear them too. It's just a matter of persuasion.'

Blades was impressed.

'You know where to get two Troopers' uniforms, Smudger?' he said.

'Well, everyone needs their laundry done, don't they, Mr Blades?'

'Yes,' Blades nodded, wondering just what Smudger had in mind, 'I suppose they do. But how do you propose to get them out of the laundry?'

But Smudger could be every bit as mysterious as Mr Blades when he wanted to be. He just tapped his nose and said, 'Ways and means. Ways and means, you know.'

So they left it at that, and went their different ways, to get things ready for the following Saturday.

Seven days to go. Seven long, yet also somehow

rapidly disappearing days. Sometimes the time went by like a tortoise, sometimes like a hare. Seven days and the clocks were running. And Saturday would soon be there.

Uniforms

There was still the problem of the two Troopers' uniforms and who exactly was going to wear them. Huntly and Smudger knew who to ask. But they felt that to ask without actually first being in possession of the necessary uniforms would somehow be less persuasive.

It was Sunday afternoon. Sunday had once been a day of rest, but business went on more or less as usual in the delivery bay of the Clean For You Laundry ('Every Shirt Spotless'), the official launderer to all government departments.

Huntly and Smudger loitered around by the rear gates, where they could have a clear view of the loading bay. The laundry depot was on the same Fallowfields Trading Estate where they had once bought black-market chocolate from the man in the van, all that time ago.

A Clean For You Laundry van drove out past them, its engine rasping as the driver changed gear. It trundled off down the road, bouncing over a pothole.

'See anything yet?' Huntly asked.

Smudger shook his head.

'Let's have a game,' he said.

He pulled a frisbee out from inside his coat, and he and

Huntly began a desultory game on a piece of wasteland adjacent to the laundry yard.

As they played, they kept a close eye on the comings and goings in the loading bay. Their patience was rewarded when a laundryman came out, carrying a batch of freshly laundered Troopers' uniforms. Protective plastic bags were over the uniforms, and each dangled from a wire hanger.

Behind the laundryman was his assistant, a youth of not much more than sixteen, and still in his first flower of spots. He was also struggling with a load of uniforms. They walked along the ramp and clambered into the back of an open laundry van.

'OK, Jason,' the laundryman told his assistant. 'Men's uniforms go on the left here, and women's uniforms on the right. I hope you don't find that too difficult. Because we seem to have been having a bit of trouble with our lefts and rights, don't we, Jason?'

Jason stood sullenly with his hands full of uniforms. He did as he was told, and the two laundrymen disappeared back into the depot. The instant they did, a frisbee came flying over the barrier, two boys close behind it.

'Oh, do be more careful, Huntly. You threw it too hard.'

'Not my fault. You should have caught it.'

'We'll have to nip into the laundry now to get it back.'

'So we will.'

'Oh, no, Huntly. That frisbee you threw has gone right through the open doors and into the back of that laundry van. I can hardly believe it.'

'Neither can I.'

'You're a terrible shot.'

'I am, it's true. We'd better nip into that van and get it back, before anyone sees us.'

Into the van. Smudger grabbed the frisbee. Huntly sized up a uniform, one that should fit his mum. He took it. Smudger grabbed a man's uniform. One that ought to fit his father.

They spaced the other uniforms out along their rails, to make it look as though nothing was missing. Then they rolled the stolen uniforms up under their arms and ran, as fast as they could go.

They made it out of the depot yard, just as the laundryman and his assistant returned with another batch of freshly laundered uniforms.

'Men's on the left, Jason. Women's on the right.'

'I know,' Jason said wearily. 'I know.'

Neither of them noticed the two boys with the frisbee and the mysterious bundles stuffed up their sweatshirts, both running like the clappers up the road.

If getting hold of the uniforms was a fairly simple matter, persuasion was not so easy.

Huntly knew that his mother was, in general, sympathetic towards the bootleggers. She had never voted for the Good For You Party in her life. But to translate a general feeling of sympathy into active and illegal rebellion was another thing. Though it was not her own safety she feared for. It was his.

'Mum,' Huntly said to her, that evening after dinner. 'Are you doing anything next Saturday morning?'

'No,' she said. 'I'm not on call next weekend. Why?'

'If I said we had a chance to change everything, but that we needed your help to do it –what would you say?'

Huntly left the table. He took the uniform, now wrapped up in a carrier bag, from the cupboard where he had hidden it, and placed it upon the table. He nodded for her to open it. She did. Her face grew solemn, and sad.

'Huntly, we can't do this. You know what happened to Smudger, don't you? To Mrs Bubby? To Frankie's brother? To Dave Cheng—'

'It's a real chance, Mum. Maybe our only one. It's all planned and organized. But we need two other people, to be Troopers. Smudger's going to ask his dad – we need you to be the other. We can't do it without you. Please, Mum.'

Carol hated to disappoint him. And yet she couldn't do this. He was too young to understand, to fully appreciate the risks.

'Huntly, it's not me I'm afraid for. It's you. Us. If we were caught, we'd be separated. We might not see each other again. And we've only got each other. There's just us.'

Huntly hesitated. His mouth felt dry. He didn't often speak of his father. But that didn't mean he didn't think about him. He thought about him every day. Of when he was alive, of half-remembered gestures, mannerisms, tricks of speech. Things like that stayed with you all your life. Probably even until you were an old, old man. You never forgot. You never ever really forgot about somebody you had loved, and had lost.

'Mum, if Dad was here, still with us – what would he have done? What would he have said?'

Carol looked across the table at her son. She blinked the mist away from her eyes and then reached to take his hand.

'Your dad? He'd have said – that he couldn't have wished for a better or a braver son.'

'So you'll do it then?'

She smiled. She squeezed his hand.

'Yes. I'll do it.'

She picked up the uniform and looked at the insignia on it.

'I see I'm a lieutenant,' she said.

'Nothing but the best for you, Mum.'

'I could have been a colonel?'

'I thought that might have been going just a bit too far.'

Ron Moore was bashing baking trays around, which was not a good sign. When the baking trays and bread tins started flying, it meant that Ron had come to the end of a long, hard day, and possibly to the end of his tether.

In fact Smudger couldn't have picked a much worse moment. But he had left it so late now that he was unlikely to get a better one.

He had put off asking all week, wondering just what to say. But now it was Thursday night. He couldn't postpone it any longer. Quite often in life a bad time to ask is the only time there is, and you just have to take your chances.

'Dad—'

'What!'

An improperly greased bread tin with the residue of a burnt loaf in it winged across the bakery and landed with a clatter in the sink.

'Careful, Dad. You almost had my ear off.'

'Well don't stand in the way then, Smudger. You've been a baker's son all your life. You ought to know better by now than to stand between me and the sink.'

'Sorry, Dad.'

A baking tray followed the recently airborne baking tin and crashed on to the drainer.

'What did you want?'

'Dad—'

'Yeah?'

'You doing anything on Saturday?'

Ron was now scraping a baking tray with a palette knife.

'Saturday? Yes, Smudger. I'll tell you what I'm doing on Saturday. I'm up about four-thirty in the morning, and then I'm baking a couple of hundred loaves, and then I'm clearing up after myself. Apart from that, not much.'

'Yeah, I know you're doing the baking, Dad. I meant after.'

'Well, I won't be watching Good For You United, I can tell you that. The team that never wins a match. If they're an example of healthy living, how come they never win a game?'

'I wondered if you fancied making something?'

Ron looked at Smudger suspiciously.

'Like what?'

'A bit of history.'

'What?'

Ron stopped banging trays and pans about and watched as Smudger handed him a crumpled carrier bag.

'Look in there.'

Ron opened the bag and peered at the brown khaki of the instantly recognizable Trooper's uniform. His eyes widened. He looked from the bag to Smudger.

'What's this?' He pulled the jacket out. 'A Trooper's uniform? Oh, no. I don't know what you've got in mind, Smudger, but if it involves impersonating Troopers the answer's no, no and no!'

'But, Dad—'

'I said no, Smudger. I mean, I can't believe it! Have you gone completely nuts! You're only just out of the Re-education Camp. Didn't you learn anything in there?'

'I learned how to clean toilets with a toothbrush, Dad.'

'I'm not talking about that. I mean, didn't you even learn how to stay out of trouble? Was it that good inside that you want to go straight back in again?'

'No, Dad, of course not—'

'Well, it's where you're heading, Smudger, carrying on like this. I mean, where did you get this uniform from? Well?'

'I, er, I borrowed it, Dad.'

'Well, you just go and unborrow it, before someone misses it and comes looking.'

Smudger stood crestfallen. He could see that his father

meant it, that nothing would change his mind. Ron handed him the uniform jacket.

'Well?'

There was nothing for it.

'All right, Dad. All right.'

'You get rid of it, Smudger. Now!'

'OK.'

Smudger put the jacket back into the bag and turned despondently towards the door. Without his dad's cooperation, the whole plan was in jeopardy.

Smudger paused, his hand on the door handle.

'You know what I remember, Dad,' he said. 'About the old days. I remember what it was like sometimes, back when sugar was legal. All the cakes you used to make, and the cookies, the brownies, the icing you used to do. All your medals and trophies.'

The thunder which had gathered around his father seemed to vanish. A look of reminiscence appeared on Ron's face, a warm look in his eyes.

'The trophies – yeah – silver medal, you know, Smudger, from the Institute of Bakers. Three years running. And one year . . .' his voice dropped to a whisper.

'One year, the gold, Dad,' Smudger said, remembering the moment with pride. 'They were great cakes, Dad,' he said. 'Remember the wedding ones you used to do, with the little sugar couple on top?'

A look of concern returned to Ron's face.

'Yeah, well, all the same, we can't risk it, Smudger. There's Kylie, your mum, all of us – there's too much at stake. So I'm sorry, but no. And that's final. So do me a favour, son, and just don't ask me again.'

Smudger nodded. There was no point in arguing. He knew that his father wouldn't change his mind. He was a stubborn man. It was all over before it had begun; they had been defeated before they had even tried.

'I won't, Dad.' He opened the door. He hesitated. 'You know what I remember most of all though, from when I was small – the sugar mice you used to make. The pink ones, with the little tails. They were good those.'

Ron stood, seeming to stare back into the past, lost in a memory of another time.

'Yeah.' He nodded. 'The sugar mice. I used to make them for you, didn't I?' Then he added sadly, 'Don't suppose I'll ever make any more now, for anyone, unless – wait a minute there, Smudger. What size is that uniform?'

'I don't know really. I just took a guess.'

Ron took the jacket from the bag and looked inside at the label.

'Forty-two inch chest.'

'What size do you take, Dad?'

'Forty-four inches.' Ron thrust the uniform back into the bag and returned it to Smudger. 'You'd better change it then, hadn't you, for the next one up.'

It took Smudger a little while to understand what his father was saying.

'You mean – you'll do it, Dad? You'll really do it?'

'Course I'll do it,' Ron Moore said. 'I'm not going to live in a world without sugar for the rest of my life. If my customers want wedding cakes with little sugar couples on top and if their kids want pink sugar mice – then they'll get them.'

'Right, Dad. Only I don't think I can risk going back for another uniform to be honest.'

'Oh, all right. I'll have to squeeze into it. I just hope I don't pop any buttons, that's all.'

He went off with the uniform to try it on.

So everything was set now, Smudger thought. He had had his doubts about Frankie Crawley, but he had come across with two Young Pioneers' uniforms – one for Smudger and one for Huntly – as he had promised.

It was just a matter of waiting for Saturday.

It finally arrived. The wait had been tense and interminable. In the yard of National Window Cleaners, Mr Blades and Charles Moffat prepared to set off on the first leg of the journey which would eventually lead them to the Good For You Party headquarters, and then, to who knew what?

Success and liberty, or failure and years of imprisonment.

Charles Moffat adjusted his cap and looked at his reflection in the window of the van. He looked like a genuine window cleaner to his own eyes. But how did he appear to others?

Blades secured the ladders on to the roof rack of the van.

'Well, Charles?' he asked. 'Done anything quite like this before?'

'No, it was always acting with me,' Charles Moffat

ruefully admitted. 'I don't know if I'm so good at reality. Acting's more of an escape from that kind of thing.'

'Well,' Blades said, with a smile, 'now's your chance to find out. Ready?'

'Ready as I'll ever be.'

Blades started up the van. Several of the rebels had gathered in the yard, to see them off. But it was a brisk and business-like farewell. Time was important now; there was none to spare for sentimental goodbyes.

Next stop, the doctor's surgery. A woman and a boy were waiting near the doorway. From her uniform, the woman was evidently a Trooper – a lieutenant. The boy was clearly a member of the Young Pioneers. The name tag on the inside of his uniform said that he was Frankie Crawley. But that wasn't who was inside the uniform itself. That was Richard 'Huntly' Hunter.

The van drew up

'Carol, Huntly.' Mr Blades nodded. 'Everything fine?'

They nodded. Words weren't needed now. Now was the time for action.

The van drove on. One more pick-up, then it would be on to the Party headquarters itself, into the very lair of the dragon.

Kylie Moore sat in the kitchen painting a flower with her paint set. That is to say, she wasn't painting a picture of a flower, she was actually painting a flower itself, and was in the process of turning a vividly yellow daffodil into a red one.

As she dipped her paintbrush into the jam jar of water,

the inner door opened. Her mum looked up at the sight which now presented itself – Ron Moore in a Trooper's uniform, looking every inch the military man, and a pretty tough, heartless and ruthless military man too.

Trisha nearly dropped her cup of tea.

'Oh my goodness!' she said. 'Look at this! There's a little Hitler lurking away inside everyone, isn't there? All you need is the moustache, Ron, and you'd be well away.'

'I'll be well away in a minute anyhow,' Ron said. 'And no need to be cheeky. Ready, Smudger?'

Smudger put on his Young Pioneers cap and settled it at a rakish angle. Trisha decided that the angle was too rakish and straightened it out for him.

'It's not just looking like a Pioneer,' she said. 'It's acting like one too.'

'OK, Mum.'

A van pulled up outside in the street. Its horn blew three short blasts – a prearranged signal.

'They're here, love,' Ron Moore said. 'Better go.'

He kissed Trisha and then Kylie.

'Nice flower,' he said.

'Good luck,' Trisha told him. She took Smudger in her arms and held him tight a moment. He squirmed, seeming reluctant, but he didn't really mind.

'Good luck to you both. See you soon.'

'I hope so, love. Remember, put the telly on. Twelve o'clock. You'll know then if we've succeeded or – anyway – you'll know.'

Then they were gone, out of the door, along the path, into the waiting van.

Kylie looked up at her mother.

'Where's Smudger gone, Mum?' she said. 'Is he going places?'

'He's gone with Dad, Kylie.'

'Why's he dressed up?'

'They have to be smart, love.'

'What are they going to do?'

Trisha didn't answer immediately. Then she said, 'They're going to be brave, Kylie. They're going to be brave.'

Wonder and mystification filled Kylie's eyes, followed by a kind of determination, a steely resolve all her own, a surprising – or maybe not so surprising – strength in one so young.

'Then if they're going to be brave, Mum, I'm going to be brave too.'

'Yes, love,' Trisha said. 'I know you are.'

She thought of the danger which lay ahead of them all now, and softly added, 'We may have to be.'

But she wouldn't have had it otherwise, not for anything in the world.

Kylie took up another daffodil, and put it down on the newspaper.

'I'm going to paint this one green,' she said.

And Action . . .

The checkpoint was manned by an armed guard, who avoided the bad weather by sheltering in a small hut, adjacent to the barrier. The weather was fine today, so he was standing outside when the van drew up with the badge on the side reading 'Shiny For You Window Cleaning Services.'

The guard peered at the driver. It wasn't the usual bloke – was it? Or maybe it was. Hard to tell with window cleaners. Caps pulled down over their heads. All looked the same. A bucket, a boiler suit, a ladder, a scraper, a shammy for polishing the windows, a cheery hello, a quick goodbye, a see-you-next-week, and that was it. Not so much individuals, more a species.

'Morning.'

'Morning.'

The guard looked at the van and its occupants. There was something different here, mind. He just couldn't put his finger on it for the moment. Then he saw the time on the clock in his office. Yes. That was it. It was only quarter to.

'Bit early this Saturday, aren't you?'

'Had a cancellation,' the van driver said – the portly chap, in the blue overalls.

The guard gestured for the driver to wind the window further down. He took a good look into the van. All seemed in order. Window cleaner, window cleaner's mate. His two kids, the Young Pioneers. And in the back, two Troopers, man and a woman, riding shotgun, as it were, keeping everything nice and safe. What he didn't see, as he peered into the van, was the driver's mate lean out of the passenger window, a penknife in his hand, and run the blade over the telephone wires, attached to the pole outside. It was all done in a matter of seconds.

'Hurry it along there, if you would,' the woman Trooper said.

The guard saw the insignia on her uniform, realized that it outranked his own, and he gave her a salute.

'Yes, ma'am. Just lift the barrier.'

He went to his office and punched the red button. The barrier slowly moved upwards.

'You know where to go?' he called out to the driver.

'Should do,' he replied. 'Been here often enough.'

The van inched forwards as the barrier raised.

'And Trooper—'

It was the woman lieutenant, calling to him through the open window of the van.

'Yes, ma'am?'

'Smarten that uniform up.'

His hand went to his tie. He straightened the knot and adjusted his collar. By the time he looked up, the van had gone from sight, off around the central building of the Party headquarters complex.

A horn sounded. There was another vehicle at the

barrier now, a long, sleek limousine; its paintwork gleaming with polish. A military chauffeur was at the wheel, and in the back of the car the guard recognized the top man himself.

'Morning, sir!' He clicked his heels together and saluted the Inspector.

'Good morning.'

The guard pressed the button to lift the barrier. It rose silently. The car purred past him and drove on towards the car park, in the same direction as that just taken by the window-cleaning van.

They were at the car park.

Blades put on the handbrake and turned off the engine.

The complex of buildings looked suddenly perplexing. A map was a map, a plan was a plan. To relate those things to the realities of concrete around you was not so easy.

'There,' Blades said. 'That building. And quickly now. There's not much time.'

They got out of the van. Blades and Charles Moffat began to take the ladders down from the roof. Huntly and Smudger helped. Carol and Ron – as befitted the dignity of Troopers – did nothing but stand arrogantly around and supervise.

Then disaster came. The big, sleek limousine swooshed around the corner and pulled up in the same parking area, no more than a dozen spaces away, in a spot marked *Reserved* in yellow asphalt.

Smudger was the first to see the Inspector. He tilted his

Young Pioneers hat down over his eyes and averted his face.

The chauffeur stopped the car and hurried out to open the door for the Inspector.

'Shall I wait, sir?'

'If you would. I shan't be more than a few moments. I just need to pick up some documents.'

'As you wish, sir.'

The Inspector glanced towards the nearby van and at the workmen unloading the ladders.

'What's this?'

'Window cleaners, sir. Here every Saturday.'

'Ah yes. Right. Well, wait here. I won't be long.'

The Inspector walked on into the main headquarters building. He nodded curtly to a guard at the entrance, who held the door open for him, saluted, and then let the door swing shut.

'OK,' said Blades. 'Come on.'

'Shouldn't we wait until he comes out?' Charles Moffat asked.

'We can't afford to,' Blades said. 'We don't have the time. Every second counts now. Every delay is a danger. We have to get inside. Come on.'

Blades and Moffat took the ladders. The two Young Pioneers followed them with the buckets, cloths and scrapers, the two Troopers brought up the rear. They walked quickly over to the entrance.

'Windows,' Blades said to the guard on the door.

'Windows? I thought you only did the outside.'

'They want us to do the inside first today.'

The door guard hesitated, then he saw the two Troopers accompanying the workman. It all looked official enough. He let them by.

'See you do a good job,' he told them.

'The only sort there is,' Blades answered.

And they were in.

'OK,' Blades said, once the doors had closed behind them and they were in the entrance lobby. 'Let's find the studio.'

Carol looked up. A board in the hall gave directions to all the various departments and divisions, and told which floor they were on.

'First floor,' she said. 'Corridor B.'

'Come on,' Blades said. 'We'll take the back stairs.'

He pushed open a door which read *Emergency Exit*. It gave out on to a flight of concrete stairs. They hurried up to the next floor.

In his office, the Inspector took the documents he needed from his safe. He relocked the safe, closed the office door behind him and walked along the corridor to get the lift back down to the ground floor.

He saw the window cleaners again.

One of them, a Young Pioneer, was energetically polishing a lower window. The Inspector had a feeling that there was something familiar about him, but dismissed the thought. He pressed the button and waited for the lift. He looked along to the other part of the corridor. One of the window cleaners was up a ladder, rubbing a window with a cloth.

'Hey, you!'

Charles Moffat tensed. A wave of fear filled him. He tried not to let it show.

'Me, sir?'

'Yes, you! You missed a spot – top right-hand corner.'

Charles looked up at the window.

'Oh, so I did, sir. Thanks for pointing it out. I'll fix that straight away.'

The Inspector scowled. It was the same everywhere. If you wanted a good job done, you either had to do it yourself, or always be supervising someone else's incompetence.

The lift arrived. He got into it and pressed the button for the ground floor. As soon as the lift door closed, the window cleaner got down from his ladder, the Young Pioneer stopped polishing his window, and four other people appeared from behind the doors for the emergency stairs where they had been hiding.

'OK,' Blades said. 'Studio. Let's go.'

But then Smudger chanced to look out of the window, and it was a good thing that he did. He had a clear view of the entrance gate. And there he saw something that made his blood turn to ice.

'Mr Blades! *Look!*'

A window-cleaning van had just pulled up by the barrier and was waiting to come in.

'Look! It's the real window cleaners. They're here! They're early!'

'What?! But that's impossible. They don't usually get here until a few minutes after twelve!'

But far from impossible, it was very possible. It was more than possible. It was happening, right there.

'What do we do?'

They stared down from the window, watching with a strange fascination, as before their eyes, their carefully constructed plans began to unravel.

The Inspector's car had pulled up at the exit barrier now, waiting to get out just as the real window cleaners waited to get in. But an argument was raging between the driver of the window-cleaning van and the barrier guard.

'What do you mean, you're the window cleaners? I just let the window cleaners in a few minutes ago.'

The electric window slid down in the rear door of the chauffeur-driven car. The Inspector looked out.

'What's going on here, Trooper?'

'These people, sir. They claim to be the window cleaners. But I just let the window cleaners in.'

The Inspector felt suddenly cold. Pieces of a jigsaw fell into place. Cogs and wheels clicked together. The machinery of memory engaged, revolved, recollected.

That boy. In the Young Pioneers uniform. It was Moore. Smudger Moore. And that man, up the ladder. It was that down-and-out. He was always in the doorway, near to that shop, the one they'd raided, the one belonging to the old woman!

The Inspector turned and looked towards the main building. What were they doing there? What were they after? First floor? Of course. It could only be one thing.

The studio. They wanted to get access to the studio. He turned to the barrier guard.

'Phone! Ring security. Now.'

The barrier guard snatched up the phone. He put it to his ear and went to dial, but—

'No use, sir. Dead. It's been cut.'

The Inspector rummaged in his pockets.

'Where the hell's my mobile.'

He hurriedly looked for it in his briefcase.

Precious, invaluable seconds were running away.

'You go,' Carol said. 'You get to the studio. Ron and I will cause a distraction.'

'But, Mum, what if you—'

'Never mind about me, Huntly. Let's do what we came here to do. Go! The studio. Now!'

'Your mother's right,' Blades said. 'It's now, or never.'

'Then it's now! Don't get caught, Mum.'

'Don't worry about us. Just get into that studio!'

They ran. Huntly, Smudger, Charles Moffat, and even Mr Blades, who from his early days had been designed more for comfort than for speed.

Behind them, Ron and Carol looked around for some means of delaying the pursuit.

'Well, Carol? Any bright ideas?'

Carol looked up. Above her head was a fire alarm, fixed to the ceiling.

'Yes,' she said. 'You have to fight fire with fire. Let's get some paper.'

*

They came to the end of the corridor. Just around the corner was the entrance to the secure television studio, and probably an armed guard.

'Stop here,' Blades said. 'Get your breath. Then follow me.'

Blades smoothed his overalls, straightened his cap, took a firm grip of his shammy leather and window-cleaning bucket, and stepped around the corner.

A bored Trooper sat by a desk.

'Yes?'

'Windows,' Blades said.

'Windows? What windows? In the studio?'

'They asked us to do the glass,' Blades said. 'In the control booth.'

'Oh, right,' the guard said. 'And it takes four of you, does it, to do that?'

'Can't leave the lads to wander round on their own. They come with us every week. You ask the—'

'Yeah, yeah. I know. I've seen them. In you go then. But hurry it up. He'll be here to read the news in five minutes.'

'We won't be long.'

The guard nodded for them to go in. But as they opened the door, the telephone rang on his desk.

'Just hold on a minute,' he said. 'Till I answer this.'

They walked quietly in and let the door close behind them. The door was heavy, but precision set. It was like the door to a bank vault – thick, reinforced steel, with heavy bolts which protruded from the top and bottom and sides, anchoring it, when closed, to wall, floor and ceiling.

It closed with a gentle swoosh.

'Made it!'

They were in. Blades pushed the door to, then spun the wheel which closed the bolts. Silence. Just the faint drone of the air conditioning.

'OK. Let's get on air.'

Outside the guard was talking into the phone. He knew the Inspector's voice instantly.

'Window cleaner, sir? And two kids? Yes, sir. Just a moment ago—'

He turned around to where the window cleaners were waiting.

But they weren't waiting any more. They had gone. And the door to the studio was locked behind them.

'Too late, sir. They're already in.'

He heard the Inspector swear down the phone. Then the call went dead.

No need for that, the guard thought. Hardly my fault.

But he already knew that the Inspector might not see it that way.

Ron and Carol had gathered sufficient paper to cause a blaze. They put it into a metal waste bin and looked around for matches.

'What about you, Ron? Don't you have a lighter? I thought you smoked.'

'I packed it in, remember. Doctor's orders. You advised me to stop.'

'Oh yes, so I did,' Carol said, wishing, just at that

moment, that Ron had left giving up smoking until another day.

'Still got the lighter though but . . .' Ron took it from his pocket and flicked the wheel. There was a spark but no flame. 'Like I thought. Dried out.'

'Wait . . .'

Carol pulled open some cupboards. She found what she was looking for – an aerosol of solvent, used for cleaning computer screens.

'This'll do it.'

She sprayed the paper in the waste bin with the aerosol liquid.

'OK. Try that.'

Ron held the lighter at arm's length and flicked it.

'Do not try this at home,' he muttered. 'Unless under the supervision of a responsible adult,' he flicked the lighter again, 'who, if he really was responsible, wouldn't be doing this anyway.'

He flicked the lighter a third time. This time the spark jumped across to the paper. It ignited instantly and grey smoke poured up from the waste bin. Ron and Carol wafted the smoke up towards the fire detector. The smoke activated the alarm, a siren went off with a loud wail, and then a mechanical voice came over the building's public address system.

'*Fire detected. Please evacuate the building. Evacuate the building in an orderly manner. Fire detected.*'

Office doors opened, people streamed along the corridors. It may have been a Saturday, but Party headquarters maintained a full complement of staff, virtually around the clock.

The office workers headed for the exits and then the assembly points outside.

'Is it for real? Or a drill?'

'So where's the fire?'

'What started it?'

They streamed from the main doors, just as the Inspector, flanked by several Troopers, arrived from the barrier.

'Stand aside!' the Inspector commanded. 'Out of the way. We need to get inside.'

'Sorry, sir,' the door guard said, barring his way, 'I can't let you in there. Fire.'

'It's not a fire, you buffoon!' the Inspector snarled. 'It's a sham! They've set it off deliberately. Out of my way!'

He and the Troopers forced their way in, elbowing past the people trying to get out, swimming in against the tide. The Inspector spotted Ron and Carol, standing in their Troopers uniforms, shepherding the office workers out.

'Move right along now, please. Move right along.'

'Leave in an orderly manner now, please. No need to panic.'

The Inspector raised his arm and pointed.

'Those two!' he barked. 'Stop them!'

A contingent of the Troopers went after them. But Ron and Carol didn't stay to argue. They turned and ran back into the building, hoping to lose themselves somewhere, in the maze of now deserted offices and corridors.

'The rest of you,' the Inspector ordered, 'come with me.'

He ran on up the emergency stairs, up to the first floor, then sprinted down the corridor towards the studio. The guard stood there, apprehensive, shame-faced.

'Well?'

'They're in there, sir, like I said.'

'Damn it! They're going to broadcast!'

'Break the transmission relay, sir?'

'You can't. It's fail-safe. It's automatically connected through for every news bulletin. The system's supposed to be terrorist-secure – once you're inside. It just wasn't secure enough to stop them getting in though, was it? With an idiot standing guard!'

The guard said nothing. There was nothing he could say. The Inspector turned to one of the Troopers.

'We need to get in there.'

'But the door's armour-protected, sir. Steel-plated. It's inches thick.'

'I know that! Then we'll need something to get though it. Some explosive!'

'Explosive, sir, but in a confined area—'

'We just have to risk it. Explosive, corrosive, whatever it takes! Get it! At the double!'

'Yes, sir. Three minutes, sir.'

The Trooper ran back along the corridor, on the double – the treble even.

'And somebody,' the Inspector shouted, 'turn that damn fire alarm off!'

On Air

The studio alarm rang loudly.

'What's that?' Smudger said. 'Fire?'

'I don't think so,' Blades said. 'Just your parents, providing a much needed distraction.'

Blades went to the studio alarm, grabbed hold of the ringer and bent it away from the bell, so that it could no longer strike. The studio fell silent.

The alarm looked slightly comical now, the clapper pecking away at a bell it could no longer reach. The alarms from the other parts of the building could barely be heard, for the studio was well sound-proofed. And soon they too fell silent.

Blades took off his boiler suit. Underneath it he was wearing a suit and tie. He had felt that it maybe wouldn't be so impressive for him to address the nation in a mucky old boiler suit. His appearance might undermine the viewer's confidence in what he was saying.

He sat at the news desk and reached into his inside pocket. He had not brought a prepared speech, only a few notes, to jog his memory. He knew fairly accurately what he wanted to say, and he had waited a long time to say it.

Charles Moffat had taken charge of the control booth.

He looked at the mass of buttons and dials, faders and sliders, sound controls and mixers in front of him. As he had said, he was more familiar as an actor with the other side of the camera. But it couldn't be that difficult.

'Testing, testing. One, two, testing.'

Charles Moffat spoke into the studio link.

'Huntly, can you move the boom over a little? The sound's a bit fuzzy.'

Huntly did as requested. Charles Moffat gave him a thumbs up.

'Smudger,' he said, 'can you focus in a bit tighter with the camera? This has to be an intimate moment. I know he's speaking to the whole nation, but we want everyone watching to feel that he's addressing them personally.'

'OK,' Smudger said, speaking into his headset.

He brought the camera in closer.

'How's that?'

'Perfect. OK. Continuity should come in from Television Centre very shortly, then we're on air. Sixty seconds, Mr Blades.'

'Is there any water?' Blades asked, his mouth suddenly dry. It felt as though a desert had settled in the back of his throat.

'Huntly?'

Huntly got him some water from the cooler.

'Good luck, Mr Blades. How long do you reckon we've got?'

'Take them another ten to fifteen minutes to get us off air – or to break through the door – whichever happens first.'

'Thirty seconds. Quiet please.'

They waited. There were faint noises from outside. Drilling maybe. The Troopers, trying to break through the steel door. Packing it with explosive, maybe. Still time though. Still in with a chance.

'Twenty seconds.'

Smudger prayed. He wasn't given much to religion, but today he prayed. He didn't put his hands together, he just prayed in his mind. He prayed for freedom, for justice, for luck to be on their side.

'Fifteen – continuity coming . . .'

Charles turned up the volume on the television screen before him, which was carrying the national station.

'And now, before the lottery draw,' the presenter said, 'it's over once again to the Good For You Party studios, for our usual bulletin, as read by Arthur Moy.'

'And cue!'

Blades took a breath, he smiled at the camera, and he began to speak.

Arthur Moy, the Good For You Party official newsreader was locked outside the studio. He was standing next to the Inspector, a clipboard in his hand. He had the peeved and piqued look of the frustrated artist.

'I should be in there!' he complained. 'Reading the news is my job! I should be doing this.'

The Inspector turned his cold grey eyes in the newsreader's direction and uttered a simple, 'Shut up!'

Arthur Moy did so, and slunk away to a corner, in the

hope that he might be needed soon. He was, after all (or so he told himself), a national institution.

But then again, of course, as the Inspector would have readily pointed out to him, so was the sewage works.

The Inspector watched impatiently as the Troopers worked on the steel door. The electric drill which one of them was using suddenly erupted in a cascade of sparks and spluttered into silence.

'Burnt out, sir,' the Trooper said, his voice anxious and apologetic.

'Never mind,' the Inspector said. He looked at his watch. 'Where the hell is that man with the explosive!'

A Trooper came running towards them. Over his shoulder was slung a small munitions box, with a skull and crossbones and the words DANGER, EXPLOSIVE stencilled on the side.

He shrugged the box from his shoulder and put it down on to the floor.

'Got it, sir.'

'Pack the door!' the Inspector ordered.

They did as he said. As they worked the Inspector dialled a number on his mobile phone.

'Well?' he said. 'Are you trying to jam this broadcast or aren't you?' He listened to the reply and then barked, 'Then try harder, damn it!'

He ended the call. One of the Troopers looked up at him from where he knelt by the door.

'Begging your pardon, sir, but could you turn your phone off?'

'What?'

'The radio waves, sir. It could detonate the explosive.'

'Ah, yes, of course.'

The Inspector turned off his phone. Arthur Moy reached for his own phone and hurriedly did the same. He didn't want to be blown to smithereens. Not at his age. Not with a promising career ahead of him, and the chance of a job as anchorman on the evening news programme in the offing.

It would have been too great a loss for the nation.

The Troopers worked swiftly and efficiently, packing the door with explosive. Enough to blow the door, but not enough to injure anyone or to damage the structure of the building.

'I want them, and I want them alive!' the Inspector had ordered. 'I want to ask our friend Blades a few questions. And I'll go on asking them until I get some answers!'

Above the door of the studio was a video monitor. It carried the picture which would now be beaming its way into millions and millions of homes and rooms and shops and cafes across the land.

For a second, there seemed to be some problem with the sound. But then the voice of Mr Blades was heard, distinct, confident, clear. And more than anything, sincere, with a note of sincerity and honesty which hadn't been heard on public broadcasting for a long time.

'I'm afraid Arthur Moy won't be with us to read the news today.' Mr Blades addressed the camera.

More's the pity, Arthur Moy thought.

'This is John Blades, standing in for him. Not an

announcer. Not a professional retailer of half-truths and lies—'

Arthur Moy felt himself blush for some unaccountable reason.

'—not a Good For You Party member, in fact nobody special at all. Just an ordinary fallible person, with faults and weaknesses, and maybe with a little bit of – a sweet tooth.'

The words were like lightning. In rooms everywhere, people who had only been half watching, half listening to their television sets suddenly became alert and paid attention.

Sweet tooth? Had he had the nerve to say 'sweet tooth'? In public? On TV? You didn't say things like that. Not any more. It was understood. You went around saying things like that, you could get yourself into trouble, big trouble.

In the living room of Smudger's house, Kylie Moore turned to her mother.

'Mum, he said "sweet tooth"!' To her it was as shocking as if the man on the screen had said 'Pooh!' or 'Bogey!'

You just didn't say things like that. You might think them, but you didn't say them. Not out loud. Not on the telly.

'Shh, Kylie,' Trisha Moore said. 'Let's hear what he has to say.'

'Is this anything to do with where Smudger's gone, Mum? And him and Dad being brave?'

'Maybe, Kylie. Now, let's listen.'

*

In the recreation lounge of the secure seniors' home, one of the elderly residents took up his walking stick and prodded the woman next to him with it to draw her attention to the TV screen. Her arms were full of knitting. Whatever she was making it was very long and colourful. In fact it looked as if she were knitting a python.

'Did you hear what he just said!' the man demanded.

'Don't prod me with that flipping stick!' Mrs Bubby told him.

'He said "sweet tooth"!' the man told her.

'I heard. Though maybe "sweet dentures" might be better in some cases,' she said, rather cuttingly, for the man with the stick had neglected to put in his false teeth that morning and he was all gums. 'I'd also like to hear the rest,' Mrs Bubby asserted. 'So please don't interrupt.'

They both turned back to watch the screen.

'Yes, a sweet tooth,' Blades was saying. 'If you can remember when that wasn't such a bad thing.'

'I remember, I remember,' voices murmured. 'I remember those days. Good days too, they were.'

'Shhh!' Mrs Bubby said, as Mr Blades talked on.

'Those days when a little spoonful of sugar was still allowed to help the medicine go down. Those happier, more liberal times, when we weren't ashamed to let a little sweetness into our lives. Those days before the Good For You Party came to power.'

You could have heard a pin drop, anywhere in the land. It seemed that the very traffic had stopped in the streets; the aeroplanes hung in the sky. Silence. Waiting.

Expectation. A great hush as the nation seemed to hold its collective breath.

'What's wrong with things being good for you, you might ask,' Blades continued. 'Nothing at all. But isn't pleasure good for you too? Isn't enjoyment good for you? Tolerance? Celebration? Happiness? Joy? Aren't all these things good for you?

'In fact, aren't these the best things? The things which compensate for the unhappiness, the sometimes unavoidable misery and pain of life? Aren't these the very things which make life worth living? But where have these things been recently? Where have these things been since the Good For You Party came to rule, to dominate and, dare I say, destroy our lives?'

People gasped now. They looked around fearfully. What had he said? This was dangerous talk. Would someone be at the door soon? To drag them away from their TV sets? Just for even listening to such ideas?

Yet you couldn't switch off. Not yet. Let the man finish, after all.

'One word,' Blades continued. 'One word which we haven't heard spoken out loud in a long time. One word, which used to be a particular favourite of mine – and maybe a favourite of yours too. I'm sure some of you are way ahead of me, and you know what the word is already. It is, of course, the simple but delicious word – *chocolate*.'

Chocolate? Had he really said – chocolate! On the TV? Chocolate?

'Even the word,' Blades said, 'has a delicious taste to it, so I've always thought. A delicious word to describe a delicious thing. Chocolate. Once the food of kings, the food of the ancient Aztec royalty, and then the food of everyone. As it could be again soon. Very soon. It all depends on *you*.'

On *me*? Little *me*? But I'm just one person sitting here in front of my TV. What can I do? Just one person. I can't do anything. I'm not a soldier. I've no arms, no training. I wouldn't last five minutes. I don't even know how to fight. I've got a job and responsibilities and bills to pay and work to go to and errands to run. I've got people depending on me. What can somebody like me do? I can't do anything.

Can I?

'Because power belongs not to any government,' Blades went on. 'But to the people. To you. To me. To all of us. It isn't *their* country – it's *ours*!'

Yes, that was true. There was something in that. That was right.

'And they can imprison me. They can imprison you—'

Me? Oh, well, I don't know now. I'm not so sure. You getting imprisoned is one thing. You fighting on my behalf, well, maybe. But me getting locked up . . .

'But they can't imprison us all. Not if we act together in unity. Not if we all take to the streets, if we storm the Party headquarters and Trooper stations, the warehouses, the public buildings, Parliament itself. They can't imprison all of us. They can't imprison a whole nation. All it takes is our unity, and a little dash – of courage. And chocolate will be ours again.'

A dash, did he say? Just a dash? Only a dash of courage? I might have that. I don't have a lot. But a dash – I might be able to run to that. I think I could maybe manage just a little dash of courage. If everyone else could manage one too. And when you add all those millions of dashes together, that's a lot of courage. That's a great big long line, enough to encircle the world.

'So I ask you, all of you, everyone, all those who love life, liberty and chocolate and who want to see an end to this tyranny – to take to the streets, and to do it now. Thank you. And good luck to you all. This is John Blades, asking for your help. Do it, my friends. Act now. For freedom, for justice and for chocolate! Good luck to you. Good luck to all of us. And good b . . .'

The screens flickered and died. He was gone. The picture was lost. In the houses, the living rooms, the shops, the shopping centres, in the recreation lounges of the old folk's homes, everywhere, people turned and looked at each other. There was a hesitation, a waiting, a question. *Do we, shall we, dare we? Who's to go first? I will, if you will. Maybe you will, if I will. But who's to break the silence, the spell?*

Who had the courage to make the first move?

The lady with the wool stood up. Her great snake of knitting fell to the floor. She reached into her pocket and brandished a set of keys.

'Well then, you seniors,' Mrs Bubby said. 'You heard him! And I've got the keys to get us out of here! So are you with me! We may be old, but what if we are. The less we have to lose, I say. The less there is to be afraid of! Maybe the youngsters need a lead. Someone to show them how to stand up and be counted. So come on you seniors! Show them you can still do it. Show them you haven't lived in vain. Show them there's still a bit of fight left in the old dogs yet.'

Mrs Bubby stopped and looked around. Her words hadn't had the effect she hoped for. She was met with blank looks, incomprehension, nervous twitches, apprehension and fear.

'Not as young as I used to be—'

'Might get into trouble—'

'Miss the lottery draw on the telly—'

'It's basket weaving later on—'

'Miss my cup of tea—'

'Might be cold outside – haven't got my cardie – might get a chill—'

But then a voice rang firm and clear. The old man with the walking stick got shakily to his feet. He may have forgotten his teeth that day, but he hadn't forgotten his courage.

'I'm with her!' he said. 'I'm with her with the knitting! I want a bit of chocolate before I die. And I'm going to get it.'

Other people got to their feet.

'Yeah, and me.'

'Hang on a bit – me too.'

'Just get my Zimmer frame . . .'

'Doesn't look *that* cold out, actually.'

'Chocolate? Did he say there was chocolate? Count me in then. I was very fond of chocolate at one time—'

Mrs Bubby led the way from the recreation room and along to the main doors. Two heavily built nurses barred the way, their arms folded, their forearms thick as rolling pins. There were only two of them, but they were tough.

'Out of the way,' Mrs Bubby said. 'I need to unlock that door.'

The nurses didn't budge at first. But the seniors grew closer. And suddenly they weren't just a bunch of frail old people any more. They suddenly looked dangerous. Their walking sticks no longer looked like things to lean on, they seemed more like weapons, like clubs, which could crack your skull open.

The nurses retreated to the safety of their office.

'We never let you out, that's all,' one of them said. 'It's nothing to do with us.'

They shut the office door and locked themselves inside.

Mrs Bubby and the seniors streamed out into the fresh air. It was crisp and clean and smelt of flowers.

'Freedom,' Mrs Bubby said.

She took a deep breath of it, then led the seniors on into town. From a distance there came the chanting of other groups, of individuals coming together, of people meeting and marching and swelling into a great crowd, a great tide of life which no tyranny could ever stop, which swept aside all obstacles in their way.

'*We want chocolate,*' the voices chanted. '*We want chocolate.*'

Mrs Bubby smiled. It was late in life to be a rebel, she reflected. She was near the end, and yet here she was, beginning all over again. She felt like a girl again, young once more.

She quickened her pace and led the group in the direction of the chanting voices. It sounded as though they were all headed for the town centre, for Party headquarters itself.

'*We want chocolate. We want chocolate.*'

Mrs Bubby picked up the refrain.

'Come on, you seniors,' she urged them. 'Join in!'

'*We want chocolate, we want chocolate.*'

On they went, towards the centre of town. People were everywhere, young and old. The streets were thronged. The Chocolate Troopers in their patrol vans watched bemused, not knowing what to do. They radioed headquarters, asked for advice, for orders on how to react. But orders didn't come.

Chocolate and Freedom

The Young Pioneers were doing drill in the park. Two of the Pioneers were in their ordinary clothes, as their uniforms had mysteriously disappeared from their lockers round at the hut. What made this occurrence even stranger was that Frankie Crawley had been in there at the time, and he hadn't noticed a thing. It must have happened while his back was turned.

The Pioneers heard the distant chanting and stopped to listen.

'We want chocolate, we want chocolate!'

Frankie smiled. It had worked. They had done it. Huntly and Smudger and the others. They had succeeded in mobilizing the nation. If this was repeated in every town and city throughout the land, then the government was already finished. And his brother Derek was as good as free again.

'What *is* that?' Myrtle Perkins asked. 'What *is* going on?'

'That, Myrtle,' Frankie said, 'is the sound of revolution.'

He turned and sauntered away across the park.

'Frankie!' she called. 'Frankie Crawley! Where do you think you're going?'

Frankie turned and smiled.

'I'm going to join them, Myrtle,' he said. 'Coming?'

Myrtle stared at him as though he had gone completely mad. 'Certainly not! I'm a loyal member of the Good For You Party.'

'Then good for you, Myrtle,' Frankie said, and he walked on his way. He started to whistle. He hadn't whistled for ages. He'd almost forgotten how to do it.

'Frankie Crawley,' Myrtle screeched. 'You come back here! Or I'll report you!'

Frankie walked on. He wasn't worried. Not any more.

He didn't really see that there was anyone for Myrtle to report him to.

The explosion blew the door apart, just as Blades came to the end of his speech. He heard the dull thud, as did Smudger and Huntly, and Charles Moffat in the studio control booth.

Blades went on talking, in a calm, level voice, appealing for all those watching to take to the streets. That was all that could be done. He was like a gambler who had staked everything he owned on the turn of a final card.

And then the game would be over.

The Troopers burst into the studio, led by the Inspector. He yanked the camera cable from its socket. The monitors went blank, fizzling out.

'Well, Blades—'

He saw Smudger behind the camera.

'And you!' He turned to the Troopers. 'Take them. And the one in the control booth. Don't feel you have to be especially gentle about it.'

The barrel of a Shriek Gun pressed into Smudger's ribs. He stepped down from behind the camera.

'Over there. In the corner.'

Smudger wondered what had happened to his dad, and to Huntly's mum. They had caused a distraction, but had they been able to get away?

'And you!'

The earphones were torn from Huntly's head. He was pushed across the studio to the corner where Smudger was standing.

'Hands on your head!'

They did as they were told. But standing like that left you feeling vulnerable, unprotected.

Charles Moffat was taken from the control booth and pushed to the corner. The Inspector took hold of Blades's collar and yanked him to his feet.

'Now let's go,' he ordered. 'Interrogation block.'

A Trooper prodded his Shriek Gun into Blades's neck. 'Move it!'

They did as they were told. They left the studio and passed the mangled metal of what had been the door. The blast had shattered some nearby windows. A dishevelled looking Arthur Moy glared at Blades.

'Not even in the Broadcasters' Union,' he muttered.

But not being in the union was the least of Blades's worries. He too was wondering what had become of Ron and Carol. Maybe they had managed to escape. He hoped that they weren't already in the interrogation block, awaiting a little 'interview' with the Inspector.

The Troopers marched them down the back stairs. The

lifts were still inoperative after the fire alarm. They came outside and marched across the yard towards a window-less building of grey concrete – the interrogation block.

'You'll be going to prison for a long, long time, Blades,' the Inspector was saying. 'You'll be in there so long you'll forget what sunlight looks like – you'll forget what your own face looks like.' He looked at Smudger, 'As for you, we'll have to be a little more forceful with the aversion therapy this time, I think—'

That was when they heard it, the chant of a crowd, like the buzz of a faraway swarm of bees, getting nearer, and ready to sting.

'*We want chocolate, we want chocolate!*'

The Inspector stopped. The Troopers waited. He listened.

'What the hell is that?'

'*We want chocolate, we want chocolate!*'

Blades and Huntly and Smudger and Charles Moffat looked at each other and smiled. It had worked. They had succeeded, just as they had hoped. The nation had taken to the streets.

'*We want chocolate, we want chocolate!*'

A great tide of people swarmed past Party headquarters and on towards the town square. A Trooper stared at them, his mouth hanging open, as if he was trying to catch flies.

'Did you see that, sir? There must be hundreds, thousands of them!'

'Never mind that,' the Inspector said. 'I said never mind that, Trooper – where do you think you're going?'

But the Trooper wasn't listening. He had turned to Mr Blades.

'What you said earlier. On the telly. About chocolate for all. Was that intended to include ex-Troopers?'

'It was intended, my friend,' Blades said with a smile, 'to include everyone. Naturally.'

'Right then. Well in that case . . .'

And the Trooper removed his cap, hung it on the top of the railings, and headed off towards the barrier. The Inspector stared at him disbelievingly, his face distorted with cold fury.

'Trooper! Where do you think you're going!'

'I'm off to join them, sir, oh, I beg your pardon, I don't have to call you sir any more now, do I? Because I've just resigned. I've left the Troopers. And you know why? For the very simple reason that I fancy a nice bit of chocolate. Ta, ta!'

The Trooper walked off to join the crowds streaming by out in the street.

'Stop him!' the Inspector shouted to the remaining Troopers. 'Arrest him! What are you waiting for?!'

The Troopers stood bemused. They didn't want to disobey their superior, and yet—

Blades resolved the dilemma for them.

'Inspector,' he said, 'how many cells do you have? How many people can you lock away? I think you'll have to lock up half the country. Look at them. You're outnumbered. I'm afraid you're in the minority now. It's chocolate and freedom that people want, not to be told how to live.'

The Inspector stared at the crowd. What Blades had said was patently true, and it was futile to pretend otherwise.

Blades turned to Smudger and Huntly.

'Well, boys, I think we're free to go now – isn't that right, Inspector?'

He didn't say a word. He just stood there, the faint colour that he had draining from him, until even his lips seemed ghastly white.

'We'll take that to mean yes,' Blades said. 'Coming, Charles?'

Charles Moffat followed them as they walked to freedom. Things seemed to be looking up, he thought. If chocolate was about to make a comeback, then maybe he could make one too. He might get his old job back. They'd be needing a Chocolate Man, for the commercials.

The remaining Troopers stood ill-at-ease, waiting for the Inspector to issue an order of some kind. But what command could he give? What was there to say now, when it was plain that all his power had gone.

Blades stopped and turned back. He directed his remarks to the most senior Trooper, indicating the Inspector.

'You could always arrest him,' he suggested. 'And put him in a cell, pending a change of government. I'm sure there'll be one or two charges to answer. But I leave it up to you.'

The senior Trooper looked at the Inspector. Funny, now that he thought about it, he had never really liked him. He'd always found him a bit brutal and overbearing, a bit too cold and calculating, the kind of man who, well – had no sweetness in him.

'This way, sir,' he said to the Inspector. 'If you'd come along with me now.'

The Inspector looked for a moment as though he might try to run for it. But he didn't. He shrugged, almost as if to say, *'Some you win, some you lose, but my time will come round again.'*

The Troopers led him away towards the interrogation block. They found a cell for him, deep in the basement. And they closed the door, nice and tight.

'Mum!'

'Dad!'

Huntly and Smudger ran. Ron and Carol were out in the street, trying to explain to an angry mob that no they weren't really Troopers at all, they were rebels, and that these were stolen uniforms, that they'd been in on the whole thing, that Mr Blades on the TV was a personal friend.

But the mob didn't believe a word of it until they saw Blades himself, then they swooped on him, like he was the wanderer returned.

'It's him!'

'Him from the telly!'

'It's John Blades!'

'He saved us all.'

'Blades for Prime Minister,' I say.

'Blades for PM!'

'We want Blades, we want Blades!'

And they wanted him so badly, they took him away, and he went willingly enough, after a minor display of reluctance, just for form's sake. But there was one thing that Blades insisted on before he would go. He was adamant that his friends should go with him.

For we all have our faults. And Mr Blades had his, he was only human, after all. But he was never a man to turn his back on danger.

Nor was he ever a man to turn his back on his friends.

So they went with the crowd, all of them. They were lifted high on to people's shoulders and paraded through the streets until they came to the centre of the town and the town hall itself. Mr Blades was set down on the top of the steps and the cry went up for 'Speech! Speech! Speech!'

Mr Blades looked down at the crowd, he was flanked by Smudger and Huntly and Ron and Carol and Charles Moffat, the homeless man.

He raised his arms for silence. Yet when it came, he couldn't speak. The words wouldn't come. He was struck by a sudden sadness which tore at his heart. One of their number was missing. Without her they would be incomplete.

Then they saw her, crossing the square, leading a crowd of senior citizens, waving a great multicoloured flag of some kind (which she might well have knitted herself) and leading a chant at the top of her voice.

'What do we want!'

'Chocolate bars!'

'When do we want them?'

'Now!'

She stopped the troop of pensioners in the middle of the square, suddenly realizing that all eyes were upon her.

'Mrs Bubby!'

The crowd took up her name, not really knowing who she was, but any friend of Blades's was a friend of theirs.

'It's Mrs Bubby!'

'Mrs Bubby!'

'Oh – so it is.'

'Over here, my dear. Over here.'

So Mrs Bubby went to join them, and she took her rightful place on the steps. There had never been a reunion like it, with people laughing when they should have been crying, and crying for no real reason at all.

Finally Mr Blades managed to get a few words out to the waiting crowd.

'Thank you, my friends,' he said. 'Thank you all! For responding so bravely and courageously. For taking to the streets, for showing such solidarity. Things will change now. Things have already changed. So welcome, welcome to the revolution!'

The cheer that went up from the crowd practically took the town-hall roof off. The pigeons fled in fright, and it took several weeks and a lot of breadcrumbs before they could be coaxed back again.

It was all over soon after that. The Good For You Party resigned from power and was obliged to call a general election. The Abolition of Chocolate, Sugar and Ancillary Substances Act was repealed under emergency powers. Chocolate was made legal again, but the gesture came too late to save the Good For You Party. They were voted out of office and, by a massive majority, the Chocolate and Freedom Party, with Mr Blades at the helm as Prime Minister was voted in. He appointed Mrs Bubby as a special adviser (soft drinks and confectionery).

Huntly and Smudger would also have been given advisory positions, but unfortunately they were unable to take up such offers, as they had to go to school.

Chocolate went back into production almost immediately. The factories were reopened. There was no need for the bootleggers and eateasies any more. The bootleggers returned to their old occupations, some of them with much sadness, for being a bootlegger had proved to be the most exciting time of their lives.

Ron Moore's first act on receiving his first new batch of sugar was to make some pink sugar mice. He gave one to his daughter Kylie, who had never seen such a thing before, let alone tasted one.

It is fondly remembered by her mother, Trisha, that on tasting the sugar mouse, Kylie squealed with delight.

The Inspector was held in custody, and for a time it was felt that serious charges might be laid against him. But the problem was that none of those he had victimized during his reign of terror felt disposed to testify against him. They were all too pleased to have chocolate again to bother about revenge.

But they got their own back just the same, though perhaps in a more subtle way.

They kept sending chocolate into his cell, along with

his meals. At first, the Inspector refused even to taste it. After a few weeks, however, it was noticed that tiny nibbles had been taken from the chocolate bars, almost as if one of the little pink sugar mice had been gnawing at them.

Then bigger bites were taken.

Then the chocolate bars didn't come back at all.

Then requests came for bigger chocolate bars, and more of them.

And they knew then that the Inspector was a reformed man and it was safe to let him out into society again.

On the day of electoral victory, Mr Blades invited all his friends and supporters to join him at Number 10 Downing Street (his new home now that he was Prime Minister) and he addressed the nation via the TV cameras outside.

Everyone was there – Huntly and his mother, Smudger and his family, even Frankie Crawley, with his brother, Derek. And Charles Moffat was there. He even brought his agent. They were all dressed in their best. And of course, Mrs Bubby was standing next to Mr Blades. She was dressed in a little Italian number, which she had bought with her bootleg money, a while ago.

Mr Blades's speech can still be viewed from TV archives. This is what he said:

'Ladies and gentlemen. Boys and girls. Today, with this election result, we achieved a wonderful thing. We are all of us free again. Free from oppression, from misguided ideologies. Free from those who, in meaning well, did untold harm. Free to journey on to the future. So let us go forward, not in a spirit of revenge, but of forgiveness and reconciliation. And let us especially remember those who kept hope alive, when its flame was all but extinguished, in those dark days of oppression. What, we may wonder, do heroes look like? Well, let me tell you some of their names. Names which will live forever. Names which have been officially designated as Heroes of the Revolution. Names like Mrs Doreen Bubby, Mr Huntly Hunter, Mr Charles Moffat, and of course Mr Smudger Moore. Please. Come up now and say a few words.'

So Smudger did, nudged forwards by the others, who didn't want to speak, or who did, but were too shy.

Smudger approached the microphone and spoke as clearly as he could.

'Thank you, Prime Minister Blades,' he said. 'Thank you everyone. I'll keep it short, and as we've none of us had too much sugar lately, I'll try to keep it sweet as well. There's a lot of chocolate waiting to be eaten, a lot of chocolate waiting to be made. There's a lot of repairing to do, and wrongs to be put right. And to be honest, although nothing's better than freedom, there's maybe a part of me that's a little bit sad that I can't be a boot-legger any more. But I won't keep anyone from building the bright new future, I'll just propose a toast. A toast to freedom. And to justice. And to chocolate for us all!'

The crowd went wild. Chocolates were thrown out by the handful for everyone to share. They fell so plentifully, it was almost like rain, like a sweet, delicious hailstorm coming down from the sky.

'Chocolate for all!' they shouted, and their voices

echoed through the streets. 'Freedom and justice, and chocolate for all! Forever!'

The chocolates fell like a blizzard of snow, and the church bells rang out, and for a moment everyone was completely happy.

Because that is the effect that chocolate has on people. It makes life a whole lot better.

Acknowledgements and Afterword

Much of the research material used to compile this narrative was taken from the official archives of the Chocolate Society. It is reproduced by kind permission of 'Smudger' Moore, 'Huntly' Hunter and the estates of the deceased Mrs D. Bubby and Mr J. Blades.

The author is also directly indebted to Mr 'Smudger' Moore and Mr 'Huntly' Hunter for use of material as recorded in their autobiographies, *The Great Chocolate War* and *Surviving the Chocolate Police*. (Available in all good bookshops or over the Internet.)

Further acknowledgement is due to Denise Mallow, the author of *My Father, Tobias Mallow, and his Unsung Part in the Revolution (Plus a Selection of His Best Chocolate Recipes)*.

Thanks are also due to Mr Charles Moffat for permission to use source material from his book, *Chocolate, Revolution and Tales of a Shop Doorway*.

(Mr Moffat, as most readers will know, went on to become a great national favourite for his portrayal of The Sugar Man in the popular children's series of that name.)

The author is additionally grateful to Mr Moore and to Mr Hunter for the many hours of leisure they gave up in order to recollect their first-hand experiences of this period in our national history. It was an honour to spend time with them.

Mr 'Smudger' Moore now works in the family bakery. His father has retired, but Smudger keeps up the family tradition of excellent wedding cakes and superlative pink sugar mice.

Mr 'Huntly' Hunter followed in his mother's footsteps and became a general practitioner.

Mr David Cheng was given treatment to overcome the brainwashing he endured while in custody. He quickly responded and was soon able to eat three or four chocolate bars at a sitting without difficulty. His lunch box with the secret panel in it is now on display at the Chocolate Society Museum in London. (Viewings by appointment.)

Mr Frankie Crawley is now a leading light in the local council traffic-warden department and is renowned for the smartness of his uniform. He also holds the record for the number of parking tickets issued to motorists in one day.

Myrtle Perkins is now Mrs Frankie Crawley, but she chooses to be called by her own name. Indeed, she much prefers her husband Frankie to be known as Mr Myrtle Perkins. Myrtle works for the income-tax office.

The Chocolate Inspector now runs a sweet shop in Basingstoke. He married a very nice woman called Barbara, and they have two children. They do let the children have sweets, but not too many. As it is easy to overdo these things.

Mrs Doreen Bubby and Mr John Blades enjoyed five

happy years together before Mrs Bubby was sadly taken from him. He followed her shortly afterwards. It was said he died of a broken heart, and that not even chocolate could console him for his loss. Their memories will always be in our hearts.

This book is dedicated to all the brave men and women of the revolution.

The following words are engraved on the tombstone of Mrs D. Bubby and Mr J. Blades, their destinies united in death as they were in life.

Take a piece of chocolate
And think of me.
And remember
How sweet it was.
Freedom and justice
And chocolate for all.

There is no more to be said.

Or if there is, only chocolate can truly say it.